# REUNIONS

# &

# REBELLIONS

*Family Heritage Book 3*

By: Andrew M. Ferrell

Published by:
Cloaked Press, LLC
P.O. Box 341
Suring, WI 54174
https://www.cloakedpress.com

Cover Designed by Fantasy & Coffee
http://www.fantasyandcoffee.com/SPDesign

ISBN: 978-1-952796-04-3 (Paperback)

# Table of Contents

Prologue – Colleen's Summer.................................................................1

Chapter 1 ...............................................................................................17

Chapter 2 ...............................................................................................23

Chapter 3 ...............................................................................................27

Chapter 4 ...............................................................................................33

Chapter 5 ...............................................................................................41

Chapter 6 ...............................................................................................45

Chapter 7 ...............................................................................................49

Chapter 8 ...............................................................................................53

Chapter 9 ...............................................................................................57

Chapter 10 .............................................................................................69

Chapter 11 .............................................................................................73

Chapter 12 .............................................................................................77

Chapter 13 .............................................................................................85

Chapter 14 .............................................................................................89

Chapter 15 .............................................................................................95

Chapter 16 .............................................................................................99

Chapter 17 ...........................................................................................105

Chapter 18 ...........................................................................................107

Chapter 19 ...........................................................................................113

Chapter 20 ...........................................................................................117

Chapter 21 ...........................................................................................121

Chapter 22 ...........................................................................................125

Chapter 23 ...........................................................................................133

Chapter 24 ...........................................................................................141

Chapter 25 ...........................................................................................147

Chapter 26 ...........................................................................................151

Chapter 27 ...........................................................................................157

Chapter 28.................................................................................................165

Chapter 29.................................................................................................173

Epilogue....................................................................................................179

# Prologue – Colleen's Summer

David Nicholson felt the oppressive tension in the car. It hadn't changed in the two days since his family left for the East Coast. He didn't even need the bond to feel the daggers his daughter constantly shot him. He glanced at her in the rear view mirror. At least the block on her powers continued to hold. Her anger constantly tested its strength, threatening to unleash her gifts.

"I knew leaving like we did was going to be hard on all of us," David said to his family for the tenth time. "But when the boss says go, you go or you find another job. This will be a great opportunity for all of us to start fresh. Trust me. This will all work out for the best."

"I don't want to start fresh. I want my friends and my school. And Mike," Colleen complained from the back seat of the car as she had every time her father tried to talk to her.

David sighed. *'Why does she have to be so stubborn? At least it will serve her well when her gifts are unblocked.'* David composed his tone before responding. "Honey, you said yourself, he was different when he woke up. That this was going to be a good thing for you two." David impressed upon the bond to influence her to accept the rationale.

"Maybe you're right, Daddy," Colleen replied after a moment. She blinked away a few tears and tucked a loose strand of her blonde hair behind her ear. The act brought back the memory of her night at Tony's Restaurant with Mike. *'I still miss him.'* She stared out of the window for the next hundred miles until they stopped for dinner at a little diner.

After everyone received their order, Colleen excused herself to the bathroom. She pulled out her cellphone. The screen indicated no service available. She groaned in frustration. "Why won't this stupid thing work?" Colleen squeezed the phone in her hand as her anger rose. She dropped it when she felt it burning her hand. She looked from the phone on the floor to her hand, but no mark was visible. *'Maybe the battery went bad,'* she thought to herself. She washed and dried her hands before picking it up. The phone felt cool to the touch. *'Weird.'* She rejoined her family for dinner and the next leg of their road trip.

\* \* \*

As soon as the moving truck finished unloading their stuff, Colleen got to work setting up her room. Before she'd even made her bed she had her desk assembled

1

and computer hooked up. The WiFi had been installed before they arrived because of her father's job.

She tapped her foot, impatiently waiting for the machine to boot up and connect. "Come on," she muttered. Once in she logged into her email and scanned through the various messages until she saw the name she was looking for.

She skimmed Mike's email, looking for something to corroborate the events in her mind. He wrote how he missed her and couldn't find a way to get in touch with her, so the email was a last resort. *'He's acting like nothing's wrong. But he broke it off, didn't he?'*

She jumped up and ran to her father's office door. She could hear him shuffling boxes around and muttering to himself. She knocked before poking her head in. A box floated in the air while her father turned towards her. His eyes went wide as the box crashed to the floor.

"Sweetheart, Do you need help with something?" He asked as he came to the door.

"I, uh… Was that box floating?" Colleen asked.

"No. Of course not."

"I swear it was floating," Colleen stated emphatically.

"You surprised me and I dropped it. That's all," David replied as he reached into her mind to solidify the scenario. He felt the resistance to his manipulations through the bond formed by the Elders when she was but a year or so old. It's what negated her powers, making it possible for him to change her memories, or at least mask accidental exposure. "Now. Did you need help with something?"

"Mike emailed me. Can I use your phone to call him? Mine's not working yet."

David wrapped his arms his daughter. "Honey, you can't call Mike. He's in the past now." He pushed images of them breaking up into her mind. When her eyes refocused, he continued, "Go tell your mother to take a break. Let's get something to eat."

\* \* \*

David held his breath as he pushed open the door to his daughter's bedroom in their new home. The email from Mike was causing problems with the compulsion he had put on his daughter not to contact Mike. Thankfully, he had all outgoing email screened so he had successfully blocked several attempts to reply. Now he needed to get rid of the original email to end its influence.

Colleen slept soundly on her bed, her laptop still open on her desk. He had hoped this would be the case. He tiptoed across the room and gently clicked her email program. As it loaded he watched his daughter sleep, her slow even breathing calming his racing heart. *'I will do whatever it takes to protect you, sweetheart,"* he vowed silently.

Once the email opened he was able to quickly purge Mike's message from the machine. Closing the program he started back across the room. As his hand touched the doorknob he heard a sound behind him.

"Dad," Colleen said groggily, "What are you doing in my room?"

"Shh, sweetheart," David replied, putting on his best concerned parent face. "I was just checking on you. Sometimes I forget you aren't a little kid anymore."

"Goodnight, Daddy."

"Goodnight, honey." David watched as Colleen's head dropped back onto her pillow, back asleep before the reply was even out of his mouth. He quickly exited the room before she woke back up.

Sighing, David softly closed the door to his daughter's bedroom and proceeded to his office. She had been once again asking questions about Mike and wanting to contact him. He had decided he was going to have to take more drastic measures. First was removing the email from her computer to stop interference with the compulsion. Next would be to solidify the separation with Mike in her mind and try to nudge her towards making friends and getting out of the house. Using his connections he had already gotten her a hostess job at a local restaurant. He also arranged for a car for her to drive. *'Hopefully these distractions will get Colleen past all this,'* he thought as he closed the door to his office behind him. *'Then I can move on to trying to get a decision from the Council.'*

* * *

"Daddy. For me?" Colleen squealed the next day when the little coupe arrived.

"I thought you might need something to get around in for work, and friends. As well as school in the fall. You're responsible for gas, insurance, and oil changes." David smiled. *'This should help occupy her.'*

"Work?" Colleen asked. "I don't have a job. I don't think my allowance will cover all of it." She began to worry the pretty blue car would be taken away.

"Someone I'm working with knows the manager at a restaurant in town. His daughter worked there during the summers as well as after school and on weekends. She's starting college already this summer so they have an opening. You'll be able to make some spending money and meet new people. More than a few your age work there in the kitchen, or as servers."

She hugged him tight. "Oh, thank you, Daddy. I love it. Can I take it for a ride?"

"Just make sure you have the house address programmed in your new phone's GPS." David chuckled at the puzzled look on her face. "It's in the console. *'Complete with no way for her to contact or reach out to Mike Keller. At least the Council's hackers are good for something.'* He waved as she drove away. The weight on his shoulders pressed down heavier when he returned to his office.

* * *

3

For awhile, the new car distracted Colleen from her desire to talk to Mike. The job and friends she began to make helped. David watched his daughter blossom back into the confident young woman she had been. Several times he felt the bond holding her powers at bay waver and he worried it may snap.

A few weeks later, as David sipped his second scotch and wrapped up a business report, there came a timid knock on his door. He casually closed the folder he had open on his desk and waved his glass onto the side bar table. "Come in," he said, knowing his daughter was once again on the other side of the door. She had been troubled the last couple of days. The distractions weren't working as well as they had initially. Her feelings for Mike began overriding the compulsion used to make her think they had parted amicably but were not on speaking terms anymore. He knew things were going to come to a head eventually, but hoped he could hold her off a bit longer. He heard rumors about a new development in the case of Michael Keller. Satisfactory results could get him a hearing on his situation much faster.

"Daddy," Colleen started as soon as she was in the door. Every time she tried to focus on her last conversation with Mike, she felt like something was wrong. Then, while rereading her journal, which even her mother didn't know she still kept, her feelings for Mike kept coming back so strongly she knew there was more to the story than her father and she had discussed. "Tell me again why Mike said I cannot call him at his Aunt and Uncle's? I don't understand what went wrong. Thinking about it makes my heart and my head hurt." She stood by his desk, tears threatening in her eyes. David stood and held his arms out to his only child. She collapsed into them, crying softly into his shoulder.

Seeing her so confused and heartbroken snapped something inside. David felt his fierce loyalty to the Council begin to crumble. He knew he had to find a way to unbind her himself. He also knew he didn't have the raw strength. 'Something has to be done. And soon.' He resolved to make some quiet inquiries with those he felt he could trust. He would also have to guard his actions and thoughts with all the ability he could muster. What he was considering would be deemed treason and he would most likely lose his life if the Council found out before he was prepared. For now, he sighed inwardly, he had to hold tight the leash he had on his daughter and make sure she could function until he could tell her what was going on.

He patted her back and let her cry. When she was close to stopping, he planted the thought she had come to him and they had a talk about Mike. About how he had woken up from his accident a very angry individual, and since they were heading to opposite coasts he had given up on the two of them. David knew this twist on the memory would hurt Colleen more than the other, but he needed her to stop thinking about Michael Keller until he could tell her the whole truth.

Through the bond and her weakened emotional state, he saw her reading a small bound book. *'A journal. That's why this isn't working. I can't remove it, her connection is too strong. But maybe I can swap out the pages while she's at work tomorrow.'*

Wiping her eyes and sniffling a little, Colleen gave her father a real hug and made an attempt to smile. "Thank you, Daddy. You always know what to say to make me feel better. I will let you get back to work. Mom wants to know if you are coming down for dinner or should she hold something for you."

"Tell your mother I will be down in a minute," David said softly, glancing at the folders on his desk. A plan already forming in his head. He'd enlist someone to modify the offending pages from her journal, but in the meantime he'd arrange a contingency. A certain member of the Blood had been caught making discreet inquiries of his own, after promising the Council he would not meddle in their affairs. Perhaps an ally could be obtained. A smile formed on David's face as his daughter left the room. Shuffling the folders containing Council business into a pile, he deposited them into the safe built into his desk and went to join his family for dinner.

* * *

The replacement journal pages worked and David felt calmer. Now he had firmer control of his daughter. There had been no more requests to seek out Mike in the week since the changes to her journal. Now, he waited. His inquiries had been fruitful and tonight he meets the person who can shield him from the Council. *'Hopefully,'* David thought grimly as he waited in the shadowy alley. When the door in front of him opened, he stepped through into the abandoned building.

"The Moon lights the darkness of the ages," David Nicholson intoned into the darkened warehouse he was standing in. This meeting was to net him the ally he desperately needed if he was to break free of the Council and free his daughter from their manipulations.

"And the stars are eyes from the past," came a slightly European accented voice from the shadows. "I know who you are but for the sake of security we will utter no names." Lord Marcus Salencious stepped into the weak light and smiled, revealing the fangs he normally kept hidden. He did this more out of confirmation of his identity than to frighten the man he was meeting, but David backed up a step and gasped involuntarily. "Do not worry, I have already eaten this evening. Besides, you aren't really my type." He chuckled at the discomfort evident on his companion's face.

David stepped forward and let out the breath he had been holding. "If you are here then I trust you know what it is I seek." There was a nod from the pale vampire across from him. "I seek the knowledge to free my daughter, as well as myself, from the rule of the Council. I have grown tired of their manipulation and just want to live the rest of my life in peace and quiet. Can you help me in this?"

"I can," spoke Marcus, "but the only way I can directly free you is not a path you would like. I doubt highly you wish to stalk the night for the rest of eternity, and I can tell it is not a path you wish for your daughter."

"So there is no other options then?" David began to panic a little. He had pushed as hard as he dared, worried at every turn he would be found out and punished. Every time he faltered, the image of Colleen's anguished face would flash in his mind and he would take one more risk, one more gamble. It had taken a surprisingly short time to find himself in this warehouse with someone he had been led to believe would help him. "Is this some cruel joke? I was told you could help me."

"I can," repeated Marcus. "You humans jump to conclusions almost as fast as I could walk to you and kill you if I had wanted to. It is hard to believe sometimes we were ever the same species." Marcus paused briefly before continuing, "Forgive me, after being alive this long, one learns to be more cautious than this. I find myself acting hastily of late. I can help you, but not in the way you think. Tell me about James Michael Keller."

"Mike?" David questioned. "He was a boy in my daughter's class. They went to prom together. Why do you want to know about him?" David worried if the vampire worked for the Council, sent to flush out who was making inquiries.

"I know there is more to the story," Marcus said, to which David paled almost as much as the vampire. "I know your Council set you to watch him from the moment he was born, you a newly christened father yourself. I know that when your task was done, they shipped your family off somewhere else where you, or more pointedly, your daughter, could not harm their plans for the boy. I also know he is something of a marvel. No human in a thousand years has seen me unless I wished it, yet he glimpsed me repeatedly before your Council and I had our little chat. The eddies of power about him swirl like a typhoon. Do not worry though. I do not blame you for keeping back the best parts of the story. A man in your position must be careful."

Only slightly reassured, David said, "I worry about my family. I have had a good life but my daughter deserves to know who she is and what happened. She deserves to make her own choices. I keep seeing her face." David broke down, sobbing quietly while Marcus looked on. The human's reaction touched something inside the ancient member of the Blood, sparking a memory of a daughter he left behind a millennium ago.

"I will keep a watch on your family, David," Marcus said, watching the human brighten. "But I need you to do something for me. I need information. I need to know what is going on with this Mike as soon as it occurs. In return you will be under the protection of my kind. Even your Council will shake to retaliate against you if they even find out your purpose."

"That's all?" David asked, to which the vampire nodded. Realizing he wasn't going to have to give his daughter to this monster, civilized as he appeared, was a great relief to him. "I do not know anything other than the Council has been trying to bring his bloodline into the fold for generations. They failed once before, killing Mike's father and grandfather in the process, but it is his uncle who is part of the bloodline. They planned to contact him when he got to his uncle's this summer, he would be contacted and they would attempt to bring him over to their side. I think it's a fool's errand."

"So the Uncle is the gifted one?" Marcus asked, having been a step behind. He had not looked too deeply into the boy's family, he was more concerned with keeping up the appearance of backing off as the Council requested. Besides, he had a realm of his own to rule, one a bit unruly of late.

"Yeah. Johnson, James I think," David answered after a moment's pause. "They live out north of Seattle somewhere. Washington. I met the man a few times over the years. He stopped visiting after his father and Mike's father died. He had some sort of run in with the Council himself and from what I heard he felt better to distance himself from his nephew. I think they were all waiting to see if he would develop any gifts of his own."

Chuckling to himself, Marcus replied, "Oh, from what I have gathered he has more than enough gifts to deal with. I think your Council is in for a surprise with this one. I will be in touch." He then disappeared so quickly, David thought he must have used the power himself. Knowing it had to be the vampire's innate speed, David headed home. His spirit felt buoyed by the news he would be protected, but it still did not quite solve the dilemma of his daughter's block.

* * *

David waited in another alley two weeks later. This time not for a vampire, but for one of his own kind. "This better not be another deadend," he muttered to himself. *"Not like the last two. Disposing of them before they could out me to the Council was dangerous. But necessary."* He briefly considered the families impacted, knowing he'd do it again if it got him closer to freeing his daughter.

A shuffle of footsteps was all the warning David received before a metal bat swung out of the shadows. He dodged, taking the blow to his shoulder instead of his head. He lashed out and heard a thud as a figure collided with the brick wall nearby. The metal bat clanged on the pavement and rolled towards him.

David bent to pick up the bat, wincing at the pain in his shoulder. He stood in front of his attacker and waited. After a few minutes the man began to stir. David pressed the end of the bat against the man's throat. "We had a deal. Why am I being attacked?"

The younger man tried to back away but found his retreat blocked by the brick wall. "I don't know what you're talking about. I was told to be here and mess up whoever showed."

"Anything else?" David questioned. He pressed the bat into the man's throat harder for emphasis.

The young man squirmed. "I was supposed to make sure that whoever was here knew to back off about some guy named Keller, and playing with blood gets you bagged. I swear I don't know what it means."

"Who sent you?" David raised the bat.

"I don't know. It was a note left in a locker. I was texted from a blocked number to check it. Two hundred bucks with a warning not to try to skip on the delivery."

"If I were you I'd use the money to buy a bus ticket out of town. Tonight." David turned, the bat over his shoulder. He was already digging in his pocket for his phone before the thug scampered away into the night.

"There's no need to call," Marcus said, suddenly standing next to David. "Your bodyguard alerted me as soon as he saw you leave the house at such a late hour."

"And he couldn't have saved me the bruised shoulder," David replied, lowering the bat to his side.

"If you hadn't ended the threat so quickly, he would have stepped in. He was ordered to observe and report, only intervene if it looked like more than you could handle. Since you had it under control, he called me. Also, as he was ordered. Did you learn anything of use?"

"Only that someone is aware of what I'm doing and wants it stopped," David replied.

"Does this mean difficulties for our agreement? I've heard rumors among my own regarding Keller."

David shook his head. "It's concerning, but nothing to stop me. If it was someone with real authority, it wouldn't be some back alley thug. I'd be hauled before the full Council. Perhaps I've touched upon something behind the Council's back."

"Very well. Should you need anything." Marcus began to move away into the shadows.

"I'll call," David said to the darkness. He picked up the bat and headed for home. The only possible trouble stemmed from the warning to be on the lookout for Derek Gohr. The Council wanted him for questioning regarding some sort of 'indiscretions'. *Which is Council code for deep shit trouble. I wouldn't want to be him or anyone related to him right now.*

\* \* \*

The next day, David was reviewing files in his office when his cellphone rang. He glanced at the caller ID and his heart started racing. *Leonard Mauston calling me after last night? Maybe someone does know what I've been up to.'*

"David," Leonard's voice came over the line as soon as it was connected. "Pack a bag for you and your daughter. Your wife can come if she wishes. Your presence will be required at the Council meeting tonight and there is no time for a plane. I am sending someone to pick you up. Pack light, but you might be here a few days."

"Yes, sir," David replied as the line went dead. He immediately dialed Marcus Salencious. It took three rings before the regent's voice came over the line. "I'm being summoned. Is it time? Do I join your service openly?"

Pausing but a moment, Lord Salencious responded, "No, David, I do not think we will have to take those steps. It seems events have outpaced even your Council today. A young man from one of the middle families decided to take on your Michael Keller. From what I have learned, he has attacked innocents and some sort of trial is going to be held once he is in custody. Perhaps this has escalated the decision on your daughter because it appears they want to have young Mr. Keller in attendance at the meeting. For now, I would be cautious. Remember, within the chamber, I can do nothing to help you. If you manage to come out relatively unscathed, I will be there to assist you, if needed. You can count on it."

"Thank you," David replied, breathing a small sigh of relief. He knew the Blood Regent was well connected and if there was cause for worry, their plans would have been put into motion immediately. "In that case I need to pack a bag and get my family ready. They are sending someone to teleport my family to the Council tonight. Thank you again."

"Anytime, friend," Marcus said before killing the connection. He glanced at one of his lieutenants. "Find out what is going on, but discreetly." The underling nodded and departed with a speed born of his nature. Marcus then returned to the other business of his realm he was involved in before David's brief call. Whatever was going on, it had all his contacts in an uproar. *'Yes,'* he thought to himself, *'this Keller boy is really shaking things up.'*

* * *

"Mr. Mauston, the Nicholson's have arrived. Should I take them to the Council meeting?" asked the man Leonard had sent to retrieve the Nicholson's tonight.

"No, show them in here please," Leonard spoke as he took a sip of the aged brandy he had poured. *'Events have taken a very different turn than our plans,'* he mused to himself. Taking a seat in his favorite chair, he tried to put a smile on his face when the family was shown in. His associate took his leave with a bow of his head, his task completed. "David, I am so glad you were able to make the trip on such short notice. Please, everyone sit down and I will endeavor to explain and answer the many questions you must have."

Colleen and her mother, who never had any idea of their patriarch's abilities or connections, stared in wide eyed wonder at finding themselves transported

9

instantly, bags and all. David, for his part, had convinced them to be quiet for now, and he would tell them the story later. It appeared the time for coming clean was upon him. Instead of apprehensive, David only felt relief at finally being able to lay this burden aside. He only hoped it wouldn't cause him to lay aside his life as well.

"I will start, if that is alright, David," Leonard said, his voice warming slightly as he motioned again for the family to sit. "David has been in my employ since he was younger than you Colleen. He has been my eyes and ears, keeping tabs on the Keller family, specifically young Mike."

"What do you mean employ?" Mrs. Nicholson spoke up, looking from Leonard to her husband. "I thought you worked at the steel mill and what on earth do the Keller's have to do with anything? Let's start with how the hell we got here and where here is?"

"Please Carrie, calm down," David said, placing a hand on his wife's shoulder, he had remained standing behind the couch his wife and daughter collapsed onto. With a nod from Leonard, David addressed his family. "It was my cover. I've worked for Mr. Mauston since I was in my teens and my talents were noticed." With a thought, David called over the glass decanter of iced water and two glasses from the table in the corner. Without physically touching the items, he poured two glasses of water and put them in front of his family. Colleen's eyes looked like they were about to pop out of her head. Her mother went quiet and shook her head, unsure she was seeing what she really saw. "We're in the Mauston home, outside Seattle, Washington, and as for how we got here. Well, it's's a talent I don't have, but others do. Some can even take other people with them when they teleport."

Now it was Carrie's turn for her eyes to be bugging out of her skull, she kept shaking her head. David had been very careful to not use his gifts in any way noticeable to his family or others who might expose him. His wife's memory had been modified so she wouldn't remember the trouble Colleen had caused when she was first born either. This was completely new to her, as far as she recalled. There was something akin to recognition in Colleen's eyes as David continued speaking, "As for the Keller's. Sally's father was talented as well as her brother. It was thought Michael could potentially follow in their footsteps since their family tends to run every generation. Since we were going to have a child about the same time as the Keller's, we were chosen to befriend them."

"So it was all a lie?" Carrie demanded, "All those years, all of our years was a lie? It was all some sort of job?"

"Honey, no," David started, "Not really. My duties before being assigned to the Keller's were limited. I was free to do what I wanted in my personal life. So we met and married. Our love is real. Just my job wasn't. And yes, at first, befriending the Keller's was a job as well, but I came to like them. It was real. Your friendship with Sally, and Colleen's with Mike was all real. And besides, until towards the end of the school year, it wasn't sure what was going to happen.

I thought my assignment was a dead end. However, when things started happening at school for Mike, I knew, and then contingencies were put in action."

"So, we had to move? I had to leave Mike behind?" Colleen spoke for the first time since arriving. "I don't begin to know what's going on, but I know Mike would have stayed in contact. What really happened, Daddy?" Colleen had risen to her feet and was staring down her father. Her anger at being manipulated had brought a flush to her cheeks. As she stood there, clenching her fist, something snapped and she fell to the couch as memories rushed through her mind. She saw everything, from when she was a baby and her powers were bound, to all the times her father had nudged her memories. She got angrier and the couch started smoking around her. Before it burst into open flames, she saw the images of her father's face when he was modifying her memories, saw the pain and torture reflected there at what he felt he had to do to protect her. Her anger softened and she sat up, looking around her with newly awakened eyes. The look in her father's eyes as he looked from her to the couch confirmed what she had seen as real.

"Well, David," Leonard spoke into the ensuing silence. "It appears your daughter has broken her binding all on her own. It was bound to happen someday, but I am glad you are here when it happened. I would gladly teach her, but as I am no longer a member of the Council, it is for Clifford to decide who will be her teacher. I daresay, he will want to take her on himself, it has been awhile since he had a student."

"No longer a member?" David began, but was silenced by a raised hand from Leonard. Colleen's demeanor had perked up at the mention of a binding and the Council as well, her memories were still filling in, but she remembered enough to know what was going on.

"I have resigned and turned over my seat to my son, Damien," Leonard continued, "Young Michael Keller has really changed things around here tonight. He has taken the abilities of two people who tried to harm him and overthrow the Council, thereby eliminating threats to himself and our world. You may remember my friend, Samuel." At a nod from David, he continued. "He and his son, Derek, were attempting a hostile takeover, and apparently key in their plans was controlling Michael. He proved more than their manipulations accounted for. I suspect he has been awarded the Gohr estate. Samuel and Derek will be turned over to another family to watch and care for. Michael opened my eyes to how petty and bitter some of us have become. It is a new era in our world, David, and I think it is our children who will be telling us how it will go." He looked meaningfully over at Colleen.

"Now, I think we should get this business settled so you can all get some rest. I will take us to the Council chambers and your daughter's teacher can be assigned. You will be given a place to stay with the family who will handle it." Leonard stood up and the Nicholson's all joined hands quickly, having been instructed by his associate when they were brought from their home earlier. As Leonard placed a hand on his employee's shoulder, David gave a grim nod and the family felt the world shift around them for the second time of the night.

They arrived within the small semi-circle of the torch lit room. It was archaic, but something of a tradition, though the torches were augmented with power to never burn out. Leonard smiled to see his son talking excitedly with the younger Doornick and a few of the other members of the council. He appeared to be taking to his duties with gusto. All conversation stopped when the quartet appeared in their midst however.

"Leonard," the elder Doornick said when he saw his old friend, "I thought you had gone into retirement tonight, but I see you have brought guests with you. It has been a long time, David. Your family looks well. I hope everything is alright."

"Cliff," Leonard said while David bowed his head in acknowledgment of the highest ranked member of the Council. "David's daughter has broken her binding on her own. Not many things have been explained, and she will need a teacher. I would gladly accept the responsibility, but in light of my retirement, I know the decision lies with the Council."

"I can see it in your eyes there is more," Clifford said from his seat as he looked over the four. "I have ample room in my home and have not taken on an apprentice since my own son. Since it looks like I will be semi retiring as well, perhaps it is time for me to teach once again. I would welcome your advice and assistance. If the assessments of Miss Nicholson here when she was a baby are true, it might take more than one teacher."

"There, settled easily enough," Leonard said. "I will retire and leave them in your care then, Clifford. I will have their things brought over immediately." Leonard left the only slightly scared Nicholson family in the care of the Council.

* * *

"I can't do this," Colleen yelled for what could have been the hundredth time. A brief break for lunch and then Mr. Doornick had her back practicing to move and arrange objects. It seemed every time Colleen got frustrated, something caught fire or exploded. The household staff all cringed in the corner with buckets of water and fire extinguishers, preparing for her next outburst.

"I think you've had enough for now," Mr. Doornick spoke softly, trying not to give the young woman more cause for frustration. Her raw talent seemed to outstrip even what Michael Keller possessed initially, before adding the power of both father and son Gohr to his own. An event the old man never expected to see in his life. "Why don't you relax and do whatever it is you teenagers like to do. The staff will get anything you require and if we do not have it, it can be sent for. We will pick up again tomorrow.

"I want to see Mike," Colleen demanded, her stamping foot sending up sparks which thankfully didn't catch the carpet on fire. "Why can't I call him or see him? Why am I going to be a prisoner here?"

Clifford van Doornick the Second looked at the scorch mark appearing under the girl's foot and sighed, "Because of precisely what is going on right now. You are burning a hole in an antique rug. Would you like to get excited and set him on fire? Or blow up the car you were in? You need to learn control and patience." *'And,'* he added to himself, *'You will have to deal with the fact he has started seeing a local girl and may not want to rekindle old flames.'* The irony was not lost on the old man.

"Fine," Colleen said petulantly. "Can I go talk to my dad now?" With a nod from her new teacher, Colleen bolted from the room, heading down the hall for the rooms her family had taken up residence in. Some of their things were being brought from their house and it appeared in flashes as the workers teleported back and forth. She recognized the signs now. She had all of her memories. Colleen couldn't believe all of this was real. She had dreamed about it sometimes, but thought it mere flights of fancy. Now she was a part of it, and soon would be able to do whatever she wanted. Then no one would keep her from Mike ever again.

She found her father reading in an overstuffed leather chair. He looked up when she came in the room, "Hello sweetheart, how's it going? Learn anything this afternoon." He looked hopeful. He had sat in on the morning training session, but didn't want to be a distraction. Therefore, he had skipped the afternoon. He had been kept informed, and was worried it wasn't going well.

"This is so hard," she said exasperated, plopping down in a chair across from her father. "Mr. Doornick is nice, but I can't seem to control it and when I get frustrated, things catch fire. Or worse, explode. Will this ever get easier, Daddy?" She looked to her father hopefully. She had forgiven him immediately for what happened, especially in the wake of what she had seen. A child with those abilities would have even less control than she did as a young adult. And her control now was lacking.

He leaned forward and patted her knee, "It will dear. Just give it time. And try to remember, those around you have been dealing with this most of their lives. And your talent, once refined, will be greater than several of them combined." He glowed from the knowledge. His family would have status and importance because of his daughter's power.

"Do you think I could call Mike and see how he's doing?" she asked suddenly. Her father had been expecting this as it wasn't the first time it was asked today. "I've been trying. I really have. I want to talk to him. Tell him I'm sorry about everything."

"Honey, I'm sure he won't hold it against you," David told his daughter. "I don't want you to be hurt. He may not be ready to handle all the changes in his life as it is. Add into the mix your reappearance, with gifts of your own.

Concentrate on your studies and when the time is right, I will go with you. This is only your first week."

"Fine," Colleen gave in grudgingly, deciding she would learn to control her talents and get to Mike as soon as possible. "I'm going for a walk." She got up and stomped out of the room in search of the gardens she had heard about.

* * *

Clifford van Doornick the Third was wandering the gardens behind his family's home, lost in thought. He feared the added responsibilities his father was handing over since he had taken on the Nicholson girl as a student. He worried he wouldn't be taken seriously acting in his father's name because it was no secret he was not as powerful as his father. Cliff stood staring off into nowhere, thinking about the changes wrought so quickly in the world he had grown up in. The crunch of gravel behind him pulled him from his thoughts.

"Sorry," Colleen said quickly when she rounded the corner and saw Cliff in this part of the gardens. She had seen him earlier in the day at her morning class and knew he was the son of her teacher. He had a geeky look about him which reminded her of Mike. For a moment she froze, caught in a memory of watching Mike their freshman year, when they started to go their separate ways. The look on Cliff's face could have been a near mirror of Mike's. Colleen started to reappraise her initial assessment of her teacher's son.

"Don't mind me," Cliff said softly. "I was just thinking and it's nice out today. There's plenty of room out here for both of us." Cliff was always nervous around pretty girls, and Colleen was certainly beautiful. Damien and Derek had always been the ones good with the opposite sex.

"Your name is Clifford right?" Colleen asked nervously, taking a step forward. She had remembered and learned enough to know he was gifted, and though she had talents of her own, she was still nervous around those with more experience. "No offense, but your dad's a real slave driver." She giggled slightly.

"Yes he is," Cliff responded, laughing. "He was the same with me. Said he was going to teach me to use what talents I had if it was the last thing he did." Cliff relaxed somewhat. *Maybe this won't be so bad after all,* he thought to himself. "Well, I think you need the peace and quiet more than I do. I'll leave you to it." He started for the path, where he would have to pass within inches of Colleen.

"Wait," Colleen said, grabbing his arm above the elbow as he started to squeeze between the hedges past her. Both of them were knocked breathless by an electric jolt when their skin made contact. They stared at each other for a moment. "What just happened?" Colleen said after she caught her breath.

"I don't know for sure," Cliff responded thoughtfully. "Perhaps my gift reacted to yours? Our gifts act on instinct sometimes, so maybe you telling me to wait caused something more to manifest?" He wasn't sure if it was what had happened, but it was the only thing which made sense.

"I don't know," Colleen said, in the aftermath of the shock, she had seen herself kissing Mike, but then the face changed to Cliff's. "Will you stay and maybe help me practice? Please?"

"Um," Cliff froze, he wasn't sure what to do now. She wanted to spend time with him. He almost wished his father had not taken her as a student, so she would be Damien's problem, almost. Cliff started to like the touch of her skin, as she still held his arm. "Sure, I guess. There is a bench around the corner there, and we have the gravel to try moving around. Hopefully we won't burn any of my mother's precious flowers."

Colleen flashed one of her best smiles and half dragged the reluctant and shocked Cliff over to the bench. They sat facing each other for the next couple hours until one of the house servants was sent to find them for supper. During their time, Colleen managed to not burn down the garden hedges, and even demonstrated a measure of control. Cliff's quiet demeanor, which she misread as confidence instead of utter nervousness, seemed to help calm her nerves. It also helped he reminded her of Mike, but in a good way. He settled her mind for the more disciplined work of manipulating her talents.

When they stood up and smoothed out the pile of gravel she had been working with on the garden path, Colleen turned and quickly gave Cliff a hug. "Thank you so much for helping me, Cliff," she smiled at the way his face went pale before blushing bright red. "Will you help me again tomorrow?" Cliff nodded and led the way to the house.

# Chapter 1

The work day drew to a close, leaving Mike of two minds. Today was his last day working for his uncle. *"At least until next summer, maybe."* After the events with the Gohrs and the Council, Uncle Jim had offered to hire a temp since Mike really didn't need the money. Mike politely refused. He ran his fingers through his stringy dark brown hair as he remembered their conversation the morning after he visited his mother and sister:

"Morning Mike," Uncle Jim said over his cup of coffee when Mike entered the kitchen in the morning. "Aren't you a little overdressed for the relaxing days you have ahead of you now that you're, independently wealthy?" Uncle Jim knew from the dollar amounts on the statement sheets, unless Mike mismanaged his money, he shouldn't need to work the rest of his life. He was proud of his nephew, but was also prepared for a little stumbling as the teenager came to grips with his windfall.

Mike glanced at his uncle, thinking about the money he had 'inherited' from his encounter with the Gohr family. Their unsuccessful bid to control him and take over the Council had dropped a not insubstantial amount of resources into his lap. "What do you mean?" Mike asked, pouring a bowl of cereal and grabbing an apple from the basket on the counter. "We have work today, don't we? I made a commitment and I plan to see it through, Uncle." Mike watched with amusement his uncle's eyebrows try to climb towards his receding, short cropped hair before the older man recovered.

"Glad to hear it," Uncle Jim responded, pausing to sip from his coffee mug. "I told your Aunt the money wouldn't go to your head but she said I better be prepared for you to take a bit of time off to enjoy it. Personally I think it was more out of a desire to see you stay home so she can fuss over you like she wanted to when you arrived. Oh, Morning dear." Uncle Jim ducked behind his newspaper as Aunt Jenny came around the corner from the hall to the kitchen.

The house was built with a bedroom and bathroom on each side, separated with the living, dining, and kitchen areas in the middle. The laundry room was down the hall from the master bedroom the adults shared. It left Mike with nearly an apartment of his own on the other end of the house.

"Morning, you two," Aunt Jenny said. She paused, noticing Mike dressed for work. She placed her hands on her hips and sighed. "So, I guess I'm still going to get left here all alone again. How did it go with your mom and sister? Did you and Laurie have a nice time yesterday?" Typical of Aunt Jenny, always wondering about her nephew's social life. It was especially true where it concerned her Goddaughter, Laurie.

"Went great," Mike replied after swallowing his mouthful of cereal. "She's totally fine with everything. At least, she's accepting it. I could tell she was worried about another incident similar to the church happening again, but I doubt it's an issue. As for mom and Connie, I think they are ok with my decision to stay. Mom really loved the car I brought her, which reminds me. Aunt Jenny, there is a really nice BMW at the house. If you want, I can take you to it any time you like. I am not going to need to drive all those cars."

"How sweet of you dear, maybe another day," Aunt Jenny started. "If you still want to get rid of it in a week or so, I will come take a look at it with you. I don't really understand how they go and turn over a whole estate to you, but it is yours. You should enjoy it before you give it all away." She reached over and ruffled his brown hair with a twinkle in her green eyes.

"But I want to," Mike began, stopping when his uncle raised a hand. "Alright Aunt Jenny, but when you change your mind, it will be waiting for you. I don't need all this stuff and have no idea what to do with it anyway. Oh, Uncle Jim, I have your necklace for you." Mike pulled it from his pocket and tossed it to his Uncle, who caught it deftly.

The pendant was one of two left to their family; a talisman against others who have similar talents, as well as an aid to those who are coming into their gifts. The making of them was considered a lost art by their family. Mike had placed a ward and given Laurie the one passed from his grandfather to him. Uncle Jim had given his to Mike for the confrontation with Derek Gohr two days before.

"Did you find a replacement for Laurie yesterday?" Uncle Jim asked, holding the pendant in his hand and staring at the swirling pattern a moment before he reached to put it on. While he had not agreed with Mike revealing the pendant to Laurie as he had, it had been necessary since she had already been targeted once. However, when Mike started talking, he paused in the motion of looping it over his head.

"No," Mike replied, grinning. "She decided she didn't want anything different as it meant more to her being a family heirloom than a generic piece of jewelry from a store. I think I'll be alright without it." Mike put as much confidence into his voice as he could. He knew his uncle was going to worry over Mike giving up the protection the necklace offered; but he couldn't stand the idea of leaving his Uncle defenseless if anyone decided to test the threat Mike had made.

The night he stripped Derek and his father of their power, and ultimately their wealth and standing with the Council; Mike had issued a threat, 'If anyone came after his friends or family, he would see to it they were punished.' There had been a fair amount of outrage at first, but the head of the Council, Mr. Van Doornick, had put a stop to it and put his support behind Mike's request.

Uncle Jim stood and placed it on the table in front of his nephew, "I have no need for it. You keep it, then you and Laurie have the set." He grinned at the look on Mike's face. "Alright, if you are going to work, I guess we better finish up. Maybe I will let you drive your big SUV instead of taking my pickup today." After their brief conversation, the trio finished their morning routine mostly in silence. Mike slipped the pendant around his neck and tucked it into his shirt as he and his uncle were going out the front door. Mike had to talk to Laurie about it so she didn't wonder where the second one came from when she inevitably saw it.

Shaking his head to clear his reminiscing, Mike closed the file cabinet he had been working in and looked around. He finished the stack of files in record time and went in search of his uncle. Mike found him gathered with everyone else around the desk he would no longer be occupying. Kathy, the woman he had been filling in for this summer had brought her baby into the building. Mike had retreated to the filing room so as to be out of the way. Babies are cute, but he wasn't terribly interested in them.

"Hey Mike," Uncle Jim said when he saw his nephew reappear. He noticed how Mike had been the last week as his tenure was coming to a close. He figured the mild depression his nephew must be feeling would quickly be overtaken by the excitement of a new school year. It had only been a little difficult getting Mike into the advanced classes at the high school in town. "If you are done with those files, you can knock off early if you want. Tell your Aunt I will be home the usual time."

Mike nodded and gathered up the box containing the few items he had brought in to decorate the desk. The empty copier paper box contained a couple pictures of him and Laurie, and a few knick knacks he had collected, along with a desk calendar with funny cartoons on it. His favorite picture was on top where he could see it. It was from a Fourth of July celebration their friend Anne had hosted. Mike had discreetly arranged a little fireworks show with his new wealth everyone loved, even though they didn't know who set it up. At the end of the show, Laurie had leaned over and whispered softly, "I loved it." It was the exact moment their friend Deb had snapped a picture of the two of them. Deb had become a photography fanatic the last week of June and drove everyone crazy snapping pictures all the time. Several of the pictures turned out pretty good though.

Mike headed down the hallway of the office complex and glanced around to make sure he was alone. It become an easy trick to learn where the cameras had a blind spot and he quickly teleported himself to his room at his Aunt and Uncle's. He dropped the box on his bed and heard his Aunt start down the hallway. "Hey Aunt Jenny, Uncle Jim says he will be home usual time. He cut me loose early since it was my last day."

"How wonderful dear," Aunt Jenny said when she reached his doorway. "You and Laurie going out tonight? Or staying in? I can come up with a casserole for dinner if you two feel like staying in." From the way she hovered, it was clear

Aunt Jenny was hoping to see her nephew and goddaughter this evening, at least for a few hours.

Mike considered the look on his aunt's face before responding. "Why don't we have Uncle Jim meet us at the Italian place we all like?" Mike suggested. He had come to enjoy his multiple weekly dates with Laurie, but felt he had neglected his relatives a little the last couple weeks since he was spending every evening Laurie wasn't working with her. When she did work, he was spending most of his free time with Damien and Cliff. He needed to learn how the Council works. The three friends were working together to push an agenda for the Council to do more humanitarian and charity work with their wealth and talents. Most members seemed on board, but a few of the families had grumbled about it. Changing thousand year old attitudes was not going to happen in one summer. Damien and Cliff were more optimistic than Mike had felt lately.

"Sounds lovely, Mike, I'll go call him at the office," Aunt Jenny said as she started to turn around and head for the other end of the house. "If I ride there with you and Laurie, I can ride back with Jim so you two can have time alone." She giggled to herself as she went to call her husband.

Mike arranged the pictures and other items on his dresser, which had considerably more clothes in it than he had started the summer with. He had eventually brought most of his stuff from home. There was also a weekend about a month ago where he had spent more on clothes than he ever remembered in his life, at least at one time. Laurie had organized the other girls; Anne, Deb, and Liz, into a shopping trip since Mike could afford a new wardrobe. Damien was forced to attend because Liz and he had become an item since their meeting at the bowling alley when Mike was still getting to know his powers. Chad, who Mike had become good friends with, was Deb's long term boyfriend. The other two guys had stood by and laughed as Mike was forced to try on the multiple outfits the girls had selected for him. He smiled recalling how he had turned the tables by telling Liz and Deb he would pay for whatever they picked out for Damien and Chad. Mike grabbed his cell phone out of his pocket and pressed Laurie's speed dial button.

"Hey Mike," Laurie said as soon as the line connected. She put her phone on speaker and went back to brushing her long blonde hair. She had almost settled on what she was going to wear for the night when she saw Mike, and needed to get her hair sorted. "How was your last day of work? How does it feel to be officially unemployed?" She giggled. She knew he didn't have to work, but she admired how he had fulfilled his commitment to his uncle for the summer. The two of them had become very close and she was looking forward to their senior year together since Mike was staying. While they were exclusive, they had not really discussed much in the way of plans. Laurie was trying to be supportive of Mike's hesitance on relationships. His last relationship, which started a couple months before the end of the previous school year, had left scars in its aftermath he had not fully dealt with yet.

"Hey darling," Mike replied, her voice bringing a wide smile to his face. It had become easy for him to picture her anytime he wanted to see her, and the glow in her green eyes always brightened his day. "It went well. Kathy brought in her baby so everyone was oohing and ahhing over it this afternoon. Uncle Jim let me cut out a little early since we were all done. I figured we could have dinner with him and Aunt Jenny tonight before we meet the gang at the dance club if it's alright with you." Mike was sure he was ready to really commit to Laurie. They had an unspoken agreement, but Mike still held back a little. His last experience was with Colleen, who had been his crush since they were childhood friends. He never did receive any word from her all summer, though he had tried multiple times to track her down. It was like she had disappeared. Even with his considerable new resources he had not managed to find her or her family.

"Sure," Laurie responded, smiling. "How are you picking me up?" She thought about the times Mike had appeared, no car, and whisked her off for lunch or an afternoon movie at the mall. It had been scary the first few times, but she became accustomed to it, and still got a thrill thinking about how they could disappear and reappear anywhere they wanted. She had been a little worried at first when Mike revealed what he could do, because her first experience turned out to have been when Derek had tried to hurt her while she was singing at church one morning. Mike had used his gifts to save her, she learned later. In her mind, his bravery had sealed her heart to him from the beginning.

"I will have Aunt Jenny with me, so we will drive over and get you in a little while," Mike grinned. He was thinking the same things Laurie was, but he had successfully mastered not listening to her thoughts so it wasn't because of his gifts. They had learned they were very much in synch over the last few weeks. This close connection was what made Mike's plans for the evening easier to prepare himself for. "We are waiting for Uncle Jim to finish work, so it might be a couple hours before we pick you up."

"Ok, if I must wait to see you," Laurie mock pouted, which turned to a squeal of delight as Mike appeared in her room. He leaned over and gave her a kiss before vanishing. Laurie touched her blonde hair where Mike had held when he kissed her. He had done this often as well over the last couple weeks.

"See you in a little bit," Mike laughed before they hung up. He enjoyed the games they had. Mike had shown up when Laurie was on break at work and disappeared as quickly as he appeared. He knew it left her momentarily breathless because it set his pulse racing as well. Other than being exclusive, they had not yet discussed serious feelings. Things progressed at a slow pace, which seemed to be fine with both of them. Neither figured there was much rush. As his relationship with Laurie had developed, Mike found his memories of Colleen hurting less and less. He took it as a sign he was finally over his first love. Maybe.

# Chapter 2

"Colleen, you're doing really well," Cliff said as he watched his new friend go through the practice exercises his father had set for her. Cliff and Colleen had become close during her time at his family's home, but it was definitely platonic at least as far as Colleen was concerned. There had been one incident when they had procured a bottle of wine from the cellar to celebrate Colleen's graduation from one of the trials. It didn't go further than kissing, but both of them were too embarrassed to look at each other for three days, much less talk.

"Does that mean I can stop?" Colleen said, a little breathlessly. Cliff was always encouraging her and it made her feel good to have him in her corner. She still had awkward moments when the night they kissed intruded on her thoughts. She would focus on her memories of Mike and push the image of Cliff from her mind. Along the way, the images of Cliff started winning more and more often.

"I think we can call it for this afternoon," Mr. Van Doornick said. "I think we can give it a rest this weekend, as well. I'm very proud of you. Next week I think we'll start really working on teleporting, which is what I know you want most of all." He grinned at the two young people. He was pleased to see his son getting along with the girl, but worried about him getting hurt because Colleen was still very much in love with Michael Keller. Thankfully he hadn't been brought up the last few weeks, even as her control was improving greatly. The older man took this as a sign she was perhaps moving on. It was for the best if what he had heard about Mike's relationship was to be believed.

As he retreated to his private study, the elder Clifford thought about the whirlwind of events Michael Keller had brought into his calm world. So far the secret Colleen was at his home and training in the use of her gifts, which potentially could match Mike's own, had been kept from Mike. Clifford worried over it as he poured himself a strong whiskey from a small bar he kept stocked. It had been nothing to convince his smitten son to keep the news from his new friend as there was nothing more the younger Cliff had wanted than for Colleen to keep paying attention to him. Clifford smiled and took a sip as he walked over to his favorite reading chair. "Perhaps it will all work out in the end," he said to the room in general.

\* \* \*

"So what do you want to do tonight?" Cliff asked Colleen as they left the room set aside for her lessons. "There are a couple new movies on pay per view. I can have the kitchen send us up drinks and snacks."

"I really wish I could get out of here for a night," Colleen said, loosening the ponytail her long blonde hair was in. "But your father and mine say I can't until I pass the last trial." She put on her best pouting face and batted her blue eyes at Cliff. She watched him start to shift his feet a little as nervousness took over. She knew what she was doing to him and part of her knew it wasn't fair, but she really was about to go crazy cooped up in the pretty prison this mansion had become.

"Well," Cliff started, pondering if this was a good idea or not. "I do know a club in town we could go to. If we can convince everyone we were up here watching TV, we might be able to sneak out for an hour or two."

"Really?" Colleen nearly squealed in joy. "That would be so awesome Cliff." She hugged her friend which made the young man turn beet red as the blood rushed to his face.

"Let, uh, let me see," Cliff stuttered, before stopping and taking a breath. "Let me see what I can work out with the kitchen staff. If we get snacks going and queue up a couple movies, we might be able to convince everyone to think we were here. It might work. And working with you, I think I can manage to teleport us both."

"If you think we can manage it, that would be great," Colleen said. "You are the best." They had discussed Cliff's limitations, but Colleen had not shown any disdain and certainly didn't look down on him for being less powerful. She found his strength in being the weaker of his friends without being bitter as a very endearing quality in a confidant. She also knew the spot he was in because he had to see Mike, but wasn't allowed to talk about Colleen being there. Based on the few things she had been able to needle out of Cliff, she knew Mike was seeing another girl. After nearly burning a hole in the first practice room they used, she had started to deal with it a little better. Part of her figured she would show up, she and Mike would be able to rekindle their romance. In her mind, there was no way Mike could really be serious about another girl.

* * *

"Ok," Cliff said to Colleen as he shut the door behind himself to the rec room they had commandeered for their movie watching hoax. The kitchen staff had brought up a giant bowl of popcorn and the mini fridge was stocked with sodas, there were also chips and a small plate of sandwiches spread on a table to the side. "I think we're set. No one should have cause to come into this room. My father and yours are actually going over to the Mauston house for the evening, and your mother is with mine talking about a book they're both reading. As long as the movies are playing we should be able to sneak out for a couple hours, but no more. If we get caught,"

"I know Cliffy," Colleen smiled her best smile. "A couple hours will be perfect. I must get out of these four walls for a bit." She reached over and turned on the movie channel, where an action adventure flick was beginning. The noise should give the illusion the two teenagers were still in the room. "So, where exactly are we going?" Colleen hoped it was the dance club she had heard mentioned a few times.

"It is a little club in town for teenagers. They don't serve any alcohol and if you are old enough to drink, you cannot get in. It's perfect for us," Cliff said without thinking. He really wanted to impress Colleen and hoped one day she might give up this notion of getting back to Mike. Cliff wouldn't dream of holding it against Mike. He knew his friend had been trying very hard to move on. Life would be harder if Colleen were to come back into Mike's life as a romantic interest. When he realized what he had suggested, he remembered the phone call from Damien earlier in the evening. The club was where the rest of them were supposed to meet later. Hopefully he and Colleen would be in and out before the rest of them arrived. It was still pretty early.

"That sounds wonderful," Colleen squealed. She had dressed better than for a night watching movies in hopes this would be what Cliff suggested. She had heard him talking to his friend Damien earlier in the day and wondered about the outing Cliff had turned down. It was apparent to her Cliff was becoming interested, but at this time, her heart still belonged to Mike. Soon she would be able to get in touch with him and everything would be settled. "So, how are we getting there?"

"Well, hold my hand and I will get us near enough so we can walk up without looking suspicious," Cliff replied, "Remember, we are not supposed to expose our gifts to the general public. Most would not understand and the hassle is not worth it at all. It is why we keep things like this a secret."

"I understand," Colleen reassured him as she took his hand gently. She felt him tremble and thought, 'He really is a sweet guy. If he would loosen up a little he might be able to find a girl for himself.' After a moment, the two of them vanished from the room in Cliff's house and reappeared in an alley behind a large building right next to a large garbage bin. Smiling, Cliff led Colleen around the corner towards the doors to the club. He never let go of her hand and Colleen found she didn't seem to mind.

# Chapter 3

"I really don't know how you can stand to drive this monster," Jenny exclaimed as she and her nephew were pulling out of the driveway in his SUV to go pick up Laurie for dinner. She smiled at how well her little match making endeavor had worked out. She couldn't get over what a cute couple her nephew and Laurie made. "I love the little coup you gave me. I don't know what I would do with a vehicle this size."

"I am glad you like it, Aunt Jenny," Mike replied. It had taken almost a month to convince his Aunt he really had no interest in the other cars he had inherited with the Gohr estate. His financial advisor, Raymond "Ray" Burke, had transferred the title to his Aunt immediately upon her saying yes. It warmed Mike's heart to have performed this gesture for his Aunt. "I guess I'm like Uncle Jim a little with his truck. I like to be sitting up higher and the extra room this thing provides is nice when you are as tall as we are."

"Mmhmm," Aunt Jenny nodded her agreement. "You two and your big toys. There are times I think he loves that truck more than he loves me." She giggled a little. "Well, almost more than he loves me."

"No chance, Aunt Jenny," Mike quickly stated. "I know he would be lost without you."

"That's sweet of you to say," Jenny replied, adjusting her long brown ponytail. "I think I would be lost without him as well."

Aunt and nephew finished their ride to Laurie's house with only the radio playing. When they arrived at the Sterling house, Jenny had to spend a few minutes chatting with Laurie's mom, Missy. Jenny and Missy had been friends since they were in grade school together, which is why Jenny was Laurie's Godmother. The two older women would have reminisced the night away if Mike had not politely reminded his aunt they had dinner plans and Uncle Jim would be waiting. It took another ten minutes to separate the two old friends, but Mike finally corralled his Aunt and Laurie to his SUV. Aunt Jenny insisted on sitting in the back while Laurie rode up front with Mike. When they arrived at the restaurant, Uncle Jim was standing by the door and came jogging over to open the door for his wife.

"What took you guys so long?" he asked, closing the door behind his wife. "You look lovely, honey, but I am sure it didn't take you long to get ready. Was Laurie still trying to decide what to wear when you arrived, Mike?" Aunt Jenny punched her husband in the arm playfully. He rubbed his arm in mock pain and laughed.

"No, Uncle Jim," it was Laurie who had spoken up. The kids all called Jenny, Aunt Jenny, but lately Laurie had begun calling him Uncle Jim instead of Mr. Johnson. It was a measure of how much time she was spending with Mike and at their home with both adults, instead of just with her Godmother. "It was my mother and your wife. You can't put the two of them in the same room without it being a half hour conversation about their days as kids before I was born." Mike laughed with her until Aunt Jenny looked like she was going to give her nephew a slug to the arm for good measure.

"Shall we go in and eat?" Mike asked quickly, moving out of arm's reach. He had called ahead and let the maître d' know they would be coming. Even though it was short notice on a Friday night, this secured them a slightly secluded table and top notch service. Mike was still learning about his connections through the Council which spread much further than he would have thought possible. The owner of the restaurant had a nephew who had developed minor powers and so was given an apprenticeship with a smaller family.

"Good Evening," the maître d' said as the quartet entered. "Ah, Mr. Keller, so nice to see you again. Let me show you to your table." Mike learned quickly he would be noticed by those who were aware of the secret world he had been born into. It had surprised him on more than one occasion when a stranger out of the blue knew his name. The news of him stripping the power from two moderately gifted people had spread through their world rather quickly. Mike found it had earned him no small amount of respect, awe, or fear; depending on the individual's personal feelings about the whole thing.

"Thank you, Kevin," Mike replied quickly, thankfully the name was easy for him to remember, even if it wasn't for good memories. Kevin was his old school's star quarterback, a life lost to Mike's Darkness. It still bothered Mike his second fight with Kevin had resulted in injuries which killed his classmate. Whenever it happened, Mike remembered the attempt on his life by Kevin on Prom night. Thankfully Mike's powers had saved him, but it had come at great cost. This Kevin was a middle aged, very thin man who looked vaguely like a stick bug. The thought made Mike's forced smile more genuine. The man before him now had nothing to do with those awful memories from a short few months ago.

After they were all seated, Kevin the maître d' smiled warmly at his important guests, "I will make sure your server is with you in moments. Mr. and Mrs. Johnson, would you like me to have them bring you a wine list?" He knew Mike was too young to drink, but thought he should show special consideration to the older couple. After all, he wouldn't want to be labeled as slighting them in Mike's eyes. Doing so could cause problems for him he didn't want to think about. He enjoyed his life the way it was. Not only did Mike's reputation include how he had helped thwart the hostile takeover attempt by the Gohr's, but his temper was known to strike quickly as well.

"I am not much of a wine drinker," Jim replied casually, already glancing over the fancy menu with its half Italian half English listing of offerings. "Honey?" he glanced at his wife.

"Oh, no thank you," Jenny replied. Kevin nodded and retreated to his post at the entrance to the restaurant, where an elderly couple was walking through the doors. "So, what do you think looks good here?" Jenny asked into the silence of the man's departure. Typically when her and Jim went out, they went to the steakhouse in town because the atmosphere was less stuffy.

"Well, I am going to have the chicken parmesan," Mike said, barely glancing at his menu. "It is absolutely fantastic, Aunt Jenny."

"Isn't that what you had last time?" Laurie needled her boyfriend. "You should try something different this time. What is the use of going out if you always get the same thing?" She smiled at the look on Mike's face. He was a creature of habit, but had been slowly coming out of his shell because Laurie's enthusiasm was quite catching.

"Oh, alright," Mike mock grumbled and flipped his menu back open as a young woman not much older than he and Laurie stepped up to their table.

"Hello, my name is Colleen and I will be your server this evening," Mike nearly dropped his menu at her name, but recovered quickly. Laurie had glanced in his direction and he looked sheepish as he hid behind the menu a moment until the color drained from his face. All this happened within the notice of their server, but she had been told the couple at her table was very important and be the best server they had ever seen. She assumed the older couple were the ones her boss meant, so she addressed herself to them, "Can I interest you in an appetizer? Or a drink to get you started?"

"I think we will take the Best of Italy Sampler appetizer," Mike spoke up, surprising the waitress this time as she was expecting the older man to order. "Better make it two, I don't know about the rest of you but I am so hungry I could probably finish one myself, and I wouldn't want anyone else not to get to try the delicious food. I will have a cola to drink." Laurie quickly echoed Mike's drink order.

"I think the sampler will work," Jim spoke up next. "Add extra of these stuffed mushroom things, I don't know the Italian, but it sounds good. I will have a coffee, cream and sugar, and a water to drink please." For her part, Jenny ordered a diet cola and went back to perusing the available entrees. Their server nodded and promised to return quickly with their drinks.

"You alright?" Laurie leaned over and whispered to Mike. "I'm sorry for picking on you about ordering the same thing. Get it if that is what you're craving." She suspected Mike's uneasiness was for a different reason. However, she had learned to tread carefully around the memories of the girl before her. She knew Mike had cared about Colleen for most of his life, but had pushed the feelings deep and was sincerely trying to move on for the sake of their relationship. It had been a hard confession when he told her the entire heart wrenching story, but it had brought them much closer.

Smiling as soon as he looked into her green eyes, "I am fine now. Was caught off guard. It will get easier," he said reassuringly. For his part, telling Laurie about Colleen had dredged up painful memories he had buried. It had been good for their relationship to get it out in the open. Jim and Jenny shared a look and let the two young people sort out their own situation.

Their waitress returned a few moments later with their drinks and said their appetizer would be out in a couple minutes. When asked if they were ready to order everyone said yes. Jim and his nephew both ordered the chicken parmesan, Mike giving Laurie a look and a wink as he did so. The two women ordered a pasta dish with alfredo sauce. Mike commented it was the same thing Laurie ordered last week and quickly ducked as both women reached over to slap his shoulder from opposite sides. Though it was a reserved and upscale restaurant, Jim's booming laughter was heard in the kitchens when he watched his nephew get assaulted. He recovered a few moments later when the appetizers arrived and the four settled into the meal.

"So, what are you two's plans for the rest of the evening?" Jenny asked as the waitress cleared away the meal a little while later. Up to now it had been mostly quiet, with only occasional comments about the food.

"We are meeting the rest of the gang for dancing," Mike replied quickly, wiping his mouth with his napkin. The waitress paused a moment with the check in her hand before handing it over to Mike. He raised a hand for her to wait and quickly pulled his bank card out of his wallet and handed the check back to her without even looking at the total. He rarely worried about the cost of items anymore on the occasions he splurged for a fancy dinner.

"Sounds nice," Jim commented when the waitress had departed. "Don't stay out too late. You may not be my employee anymore, but you are still my nephew. I expect you to have Laurie home before her curfew and yourself home shortly thereafter." He chuckled at his own joke. It had become quite common for Mike to have Laurie home mere minutes before her curfew. He would then teleport himself and his SUV home with seconds to spare. So far Laurie's parents had only commented regarding a worry Mike was getting home too late. Laurie assured them Mike had been given an extended curfew. They had not been clued in to the status and abilities of their daughter's boyfriend.

"You two kids have fun," Jenny smiled as she stood up. "Where is the restroom? I have to go before we leave, Jim." Laurie quickly stood and walked with Jenny to the bathroom. While the two women were gone, the waitress reappeared with Mike's card and the slip for him to sign. He quickly added a generous tip and scrawled his signature on the bottom. The waitress wished them a good evening and hoped they would come back again soon. She then moved on to check on another table of hers. When Laurie returned ahead of Aunt Jenny, the younger couple said their goodbyes and headed for Mike's SUV.

On the way, Laurie called Deb and Mike called Damien to confirm if everyone else was coming. Damien said Cliff had declined again, citing he was going to stay in and watch a movie on TV. While disappointed, Mike had noticed Cliff becoming withdrawn except at Council meetings. Mike made a mental note to talk to Cliff the next time they were alone and make sure his friend was alright. Mike hoped Cliff wasn't feeling awkward or jealous of how close Damien and Mike had become. It had become quite clear the three of them were rapidly rising to leadership positions on the Council, especially since the third member of the Council's leadership had no heir to take over for him and only mediocre apprentices. It was obvious Mike would be taking over for him when he retired or stepped down. This meant the three young men would be the new power base for the Council. There had been grumbling and politicking over that particular scenario.

# Chapter 4

"So, Mike," Deb asked when her and Chad joined the rest of their group at the table they had secured in the corner of the club. Anne had disappeared onto the floor with a random guy she had picked out of the crowd. No one was surprised because she was the odd one out with the other three couples. "Are you glad to be done with work for the summer?" She laid her head back on the chest of her boyfriend Chad and he stroked her brown hair.

"I guess," Mike replied from behind Laurie's head. She perched herself on his lap as soon as he sat down. She also helped herself to his soda, and he knew he was going to have to go get another one shortly. She laughed at the look on his face, before he continued, "I guess I will have more time for other things before school starts up. You are lucky you are all done, Damien." He turned to his friend who appeared to not be paying attention to the rest of the group. In his defense, he was forehead to forehead with Liz, both of them whispering only loud enough to hear each other over the music. "Earth to Damien. You know you guys should come up for air once in a while."

Grinning, the third couple broke eye contact and Damien turned toward Mike, "What were you saying?" He pulled Liz close and her red hair fanned across him. He reached up and grabbed their shared soda and took a sip before handing it to Liz. The two of them had become nearly as inseparable as Mike and Laurie. The main difference being Liz was not aware of Damien's real gifts and influence. He was enjoying spending time with a love interest who didn't know about his gifts. Being normal with Liz was what appealed to him the most about her. Laurie, as Liz's friend, had been sworn to secrecy regarding Mike and Damien's abilities. Mike's improved finances had been explained as a trust fund his grandfather had opened which came available shortly after his eighteenth birthday. Other than the SUV and a little extra spending money, Mike had not really shown off his money after the clothes shopping trip. While Damien hadn't really needed Mike to spend money on him, he went along with it for the sake of his budding relationship with Liz. She had been ecstatic about dressing him in clothes she liked.

"I said, I'm jealous you won't be returning to school with us this fall," Mike repeated, smiling at his friend. He was glad Damien and Liz had hit it off, and didn't begrudge his friend keeping their secret world secret from Liz, for now. It would be less awkward if things didn't work out long term. This had been part of what Mike had considered before telling Laurie. Given how she had been targeted by Derek for her association with Mike, it had been easy to decide she should know who she was going to be getting involved with.

"Oh, well," Damien began, "Don't. I, am jealous of you guys really. I never had the whole high school experience. Now it is too late for me." When the music changed, all three girls squealed and dragged their guys onto the floor to dance to the slower song the DJ started playing.

Swaying on the dance floor, Laurie looked up into Mike's eyes, "I have to tell you something, Mike." He almost stumbled, his mind quickly racing to the worst possible scenario. Laurie felt the stumble and guessed where Mike's mind had gone. "No way no how, Mike. I am not planning on leaving you. I wanted to say, that whether you are ready to say it back or not, I think I am in love with you Michael Keller." She stared up into his eyes, biting her lip gently while she waited for his reaction.

Mike was stunned, he actually stopped moving momentarily, before the motion around him caused him to get back in step. He stared down into Laurie's twinkling green eyes and smiled. He closed the distance and kissed her softly, "I don't know if I am ready myself, but you mean everything to me, Laurie. I don't know how I would have survived this summer without you. I don't," he paused and could see understanding in Laurie's eyes, "I don't know if I am ready yet. Can you forgive me?"

Smiling reassuringly, she replied softly, "Of course, but I wanted you to know how I felt. So there was no doubt in your mind about where I stood." They danced another song or two before the couples reconvened at their table and Mike excused himself to the restroom.

As he was walking across the crowded room towards the little hallway where the restrooms were, he caught a whiff of perfume reminding him of Colleen. Mike turned quickly. He didn't see anyone and shook it off when he reached the bathrooms. As he pushed the door open, Cliff walked out. "Cliff, you made it after all," Mike said, clapping his friend on the back. "Damien is with the rest of the gang over by the back wall. I am sure you can't miss him." Mike hung his arm around Cliff's shoulders, his trip to the bathroom momentarily forgotten.

For his part, Cliff felt like a fish tossed into a frying pan, he opened and closed his mouth a couple times before responding, "Mike, Hey, I.. Yes I thought about it and decided to come by anyway, but I had to make a pit stop first. Where did you say everyone was?" Mike pointed in the direction of the table, though it couldn't be seen from where they were. "I will go check in with them now Mike, good thing I ran into you. I might have never found you guys in this crowd."

"No problem, Cliff," Mike began, turning back towards the bathroom. "Oh, by the way man, I hope everything is ok. Seems like it is getting harder and harder to drag you out of the house lately."

"Everything's fine," Cliff began, "Got so much going on at home. I've been enjoying the quiet evenings. I will see ya when you get done ok? I am going to go look for Damien." Mike nodded and walked into the bathroom, leaving Cliff standing in the hallway.

Cliff ran back onto the dance floor, looking around frantically for Colleen. They had overstayed their couple hours and it was pure luck they hadn't crossed paths with Mike and the rest of the group sooner. He finally spotted her in a corner talking to a guy he didn't recognize. Cliff felt jealousy rear its head. Colleen was talking to another guy. Even though there was nothing official between the two of them except his crush on her, it still made him angry. He raced to her side and grabbed Colleen's arm, ignoring the guy.

"We gotta go," Cliff said quickly once they had started to move away. Colleen saw the panicked and angry look on Cliff's face and suspected the anger was at the guy who had cornered her. He was unsuccessfully trying to get her to dance with him. The rest she wasn't too sure what to make of Cliff's demeanor. The pair stopped dead as the guy Colleen had been talking to grabbed her other arm and pulled her back.

"Listen buddy, she and I were talking," he was a jock type, content and assured of getting his way. He certainly didn't see Cliff as a threat. "Why don't you run along and find a girl more your class."

Puzzled at first by Colleen's stopping Cliff had let go of her arm. At the guy's words, Cliff became angry again, "I don't care if you were discussing world peace, we have to be leaving and I suggest you let her go before something bad happens to you."

Recognizing the look in Cliff's eyes, Colleen was reminded of the night Mike had fought her ex-boyfriend Kevin. Cliff looked and sounded almost like Mike did. She knew things were not going to go well for the guy trying to get in Cliff's way. "Cliff, it's alright, I'll handle this," she laid her free hand on Cliff's arm and pulled her other out of the other guy's grip, none too gently. "Look, it was nice talking, but I'm leaving with the guy I came with. I wish you luck." She started to walk away when he grabbed her arm again.

"You came here with this loser?" the guy demanded. "You should drop him and get a real boyfriend, sweetheart. A pretty little thing like you deserves a better looking," he stopped as Cliff's roundhouse punch knocked the guy against the wall, where he sank to a seated position. Again, Colleen was struck by the similarities to her night with Mike. She looked around the crowd to see who was paying attention, which didn't appear to be many as of yet. Across the floor, walking in profile was a guy who looked quite a bit like Mike. Colleen's heart skipped a beat. Cliff was leading her over to the exit door and soon they were standing outside again in the cooler night air.

"I want to go back in, Cliff," Colleen began, "I think I saw Mike." She started to head back into the club, but Cliff managed to tug her around the edge of the building and quickly brought them both back to his house, to the room they had left earlier. A movie was ending on the TV. She noticed they were back already and she pushed Cliff's arm away. She wished she had been able to master teleporting but her concentration was still not enough for anything so difficult. The objects she had been practicing on often came out in pieces on the other end of her sending it across the room. What it could do to a person was obvious, so she had not tried to teleport herself yet.

"I am sorry, Colleen," Cliff began. "A guy recognized me and we had to go. If they were to tell my father they saw me out when I was supposed to be here with you, it would have blown our chances of sneaking out again. Stay here and if anyone comes by, tell them I went to the bathroom. I need to go handle this." Soon, Cliff was gone again.

He reappeared outside the club and got himself readmitted so he could go in search of his friends. He found them quickly enough and waved as he closed the distance to them. "Hey guys, how's it going?"

"Cliffy, my man," Damien said, reaching over to clap his friend on the shoulder while still keeping one arm around Liz. "Glad you decided to join us. Mike said he thought you would have beaten him back, but we hadn't seen you yet. Did you hear a guy got knocked cold a couple minutes ago?"

"I hadn't heard what happened, but I saw a commotion." Cliff feigned shock. "They aren't going to shut the place down tonight are they? That would be a shame." A sudden closing was exactly what the company did on the rare occasions any violence broke out.

"Doesn't sound like it," Mike answered into the break in conversation as he and Laurie returned with a replenished soda. "Did you get lost, or distracted, Cliff?" Mike grinned at the late comer.

"No, I had a call from my dad," Cliff lied easily. "I stepped outside to hear him better. He wants me to check a shipment for him so I have to leave again. I told him, I at least had to come in and tell you guys so you didn't think I bailed without even saying hello."

"That's too bad," Liz spoke up from Damien's side. "Anne is around here somewhere and with you we would have been even guys to girls." There had been more than a few unsuccessful attempts to set Anne up with Cliff. Then the topic of conversation arrived.

"Hey guys, oh, Hey Cliff," Anne said breathlessly from her latest trip to the dance floor. "When did you get here? Are you sticking around? If so, you owe me a dance." Anne had seemed at least partly interested, even knowing Cliff was gifted like she, Mike and Damien were. So far her charms had not seemed to draw Cliff in.

"Sadly, I cannot Anne," Cliff said, "I have to go help my dad with something, so rain check?"

"You owe me two then," she said before grabbing him into a hug and planting a kiss on his cheek. She felt sure kissing him would get a reaction out of him. He surprised her by merely trying to wipe off her colored lip gloss instead of turning beet red like he normally did. He nodded and after saying a brief good bye he headed back outside, where he could safely teleport himself back home.

He appeared in the rec room he had left Colleen in to see her standing over by the table of food nibbling at a finger sandwich, an open soda can next to her. He headed across the room towards her, taking in again her beauty as she turned to look at him. He watched as her smile turned to a frown.

It was Colleen's turn to feel jealousy. While it was true she had not taken Cliff seriously as a romantic interest, she did feel more than a little protectiveness because he was her only friend at the moment. When she turned around and saw the colored kiss on his cheek, an old green eyed monster welled up inside. Along with her jealousy came a measure of anger and the floor under her feet started to smoke a little. "So. That's why you dumped me off here? To go get a piece of some girl you saw at the club? And you were angry I was being hit on by a random guy I had no intention of dancing with, much less leaving with. You're impossible."

Realizing the look on her face and what caused it, Cliff stopped dead. "No, it was Damien and his girlfriend I saw. I had to go back and talk to them to make sure they wouldn't say anything about seeing me out. A friend of his girlfriend's tried to get me to stay and dance with her since she was feeling like the odd one out. When I turned her down she told me next time and kissed me on the cheek. I thought I got it, but apparently, I didn't get it all."

The sincerity in his voice calmed Colleen. When combined with the realization she was getting jealous when she had no real claim on him, it was her turn to be embarrassed. She had politely rebuffed all of his tentative advances and they had settled into a platonic friendship, for the most part. She knew Cliff still nursed a crush on her, even if she didn't reciprocate. She wet her fingers and reached up to wipe it off his face and they found themselves staring into each other's eyes for a moment before a knock on the door caused them to spin away from each other.

"I wanted to say goodnight and tell you kids I was going to bed," Laurie's mother, Carrie, stuck her head in the door a moment. She had also noticed the way young Cliff had looked at Laurie and hoped perhaps it would make things easier on her daughter. She came over to her daughter and gave her a brief hug and a peck on the cheek. "Goodnight, sweetheart. You two stay out of trouble and don't stay up too late now." With a ruffle of Cliff's light brown hair, she left the room. The two teenagers stared at each other.

"Well," Cliff yawned, "I am going to head to bed as well, unless you really want to stay up and watch a movie." He looked slightly hopeful, his cheek still tingling where Laurie had touched him.

Aware of the slight spark developing between the two of them, Colleen felt conflicted. Cliff reminded her of Mike more than she cared to admit. He was also here, trying to help her and support her training, while she wasn't even able to reach out to Mike. Her confusion spun her in circles so she decided the best course of action was the one she had maintained all along. "No, that's alright Cliff, I think I'm going to get some rest too. I want to practice on my own this weekend so I'll be ready to master whatever your father throws at me. Good night, and thank you again for this evening."

Cliff watched her depart to her rooms before he grabbed a soda and went to his own. He sat up an hour sipping his soda and thinking. "She's never going to settle for you, Cliff, why do you beat yourself up over this?" he mused out loud to the empty room. "She's twice as powerful now as you will ever be, and she's been in love with the most powerful gifted in centuries since before either knew they had power. You're being stupid about this." He flopped on his bed and pulled a pillow over his head to block out the world. What he didn't know was Colleen had been about to knock on his door when she heard him talking and stopped. When he stopped talking she fled back to her rooms, more confused than she was before. Her intention to set the record straight with Cliff about her plan to rekindle her relationship with Mike was momentarily forgotten as she imagined her new friend's tortured existence.

* * *

"Well, I'm glad he at least put in an appearance," Mike said to Damien later as the girls made a final bathroom trip before they left. Chad had become partly familiar with the situation and knew Cliff was an old friend of Damien's. He had accepted him as part of the group, when Cliff showed up of course. For now he stood by, waiting for Deb to return so they could head home.

"I know," Damien agreed, "I wish I knew what all was going on, but Cliff has always been a bit withdrawn. Not sure he likes all the attention, he always did better with a small, close group of friends."

"I always felt the same way until I got here," Mike spoke softly, his mind drifting to his close friends back home. He had talked to Darrell a few times, but hadn't felt right about sharing much and dragging his friend into all the changes in his life. Darrell still insisted on coming out west if there was an option too and was sad his friend wasn't returning to school in the fall with him. Mike had almost offered to bring him out to Washington, he could certainly afford it, but thought better of it when he heard Darrell's little brothers in the background. Darrell was committed to helping his mom, and Mike didn't feel right offering to take him away from those responsibilities.

"We can crack his shell like we did yours, Mike," Chad joked. "Maybe next time the three of us will have to go to his house and drag him out of it?" Chad played a couple sports, and looked like he could handle himself in a scuffle, though Cliff was unlikely to put up much of a physical fight. The difficulty would be if Chad was exposed to the other side of his friends.

"Sounds like a hell of an idea, Chad," Damien cheered, high fiving him. The three laughed about the spectacle of them carrying Cliff out of his house when all four girls returned.

Anne, Deb, Liz, and Laurie stood staring at the three guys laughing and miming as if they were carrying something for a few seconds before they were noticed. All three straightened up at once. Chad took Deb's arm, while Liz wrapped herself around Damien. Laurie and Anne took ahold of Mike's arms and started the procession towards the doors leading to the parking lot. Anne had caught a ride to the club with Deb and Chad, but during the night it was decided Mike and Laurie would drop her off. The group of friends waved final goodbyes and got into their respective vehicles. A figure flitted away, causing Mike and Damien both to glance towards a darkened part of the lot. They shared a look to express they would talk later, and then everyone left for home.

# Chapter 5

"Mr. Kosgrove," the young man said, bowing respectively when he entered his teacher's study. "Keller and Mauston, along with the rest of their little group are heading home. The younger Doornick visited them briefly, but I wasn't able to get close enough to hear anything. It didn't look very important, not with all the 'Normals' hanging around. It was probably just typical chit chat."

"Thank you for your report, Matthew," Blake Kosgrove said without looking up from the book he was reading. "I appreciate your diligence today. I will transfer your bonus for the week to your account in the morning." With a nod, the younger man left. Blake Kosgrove, the third member of the Council's Triad and ruling elite, reached over and grabbed his drink. Draining what was left, he closed the book and placed it on the table next to him. He stood and walked over to the windows looking down upon his garden. Though it was dark, he could make out a chipmunk running around looking for an acorn to eat.

"Soon, Blake," he said to himself. "Those three think they will squeeze you out and take over with their fool humanitarian efforts. They are all well and good if we wanted to win an election, but we can simply take whoever is in office and bend them to our decisions. We don't have to play these games." He coughed violently and grabbed a handkerchief from his pocket to dab at the slight specks of blood he coughed up. He had managed to hide his failing health from everyone so far, but using his power to augment his health constantly was a downward spiral. As soon as he solidified his power at the top of the Council, he would bargain with the Blood for the immortality they could grant. The old man put the cloth back in his pocket, having eliminated the blood stains with his gift. He then strode unsteadily to his bed.

* * *

"Your boy is turning into quite the leader, Leonard," Clifford Van Doornick the Second said to his longtime friend over drinks that evening. They had been joined by David Nicholson, whose daughter Colleen was training with Clifford in the use of her own gifts, recently returned to her. A child's gifts are often bound until they are a little older, but Colleen's had been held till she was nearly an adult because of her father's assignment to watch over the Keller family.

"I have come to be much prouder of him in recent weeks than I think I ever was of him growing up," Leonard admitted sadly. "I did not give him quite enough credit because our priorities didn't match up exactly. I always saw it as weakness, but it is a strength of character I do not possess myself."

"Now now, friend," Clifford admonished, "Do not sell yourself short, Leonard. We are from a different era. It is right our children would hold different ideals sacred from us. Wouldn't you say, David?" Clifford waved to the youngest member of their group with his drink before taking a sip of it.

Swallowing hard, David replied, "It only makes sense. The world constantly changes around us and our children are going to be more adept at handling change than we will be. I am pleased to hear my little girl has mostly stopped setting your belongings on fire, Mr. Doornick."

"Call me Cliff, or at least Clifford," the older man smiled. "We're all going to be blessed with seeing our children take a leading role in the future of our little world. Colleen shows such potential. I daresay she would have rivaled Michael himself, before he added the strength of the Gohrs to his own. I have noticed looks between her and my son though. Has she continued to bring up Michael and her desire to rekindle their relationship?"

"Not recently," David responded after a moment's thought, "She seems to be focused on mastering every test you put in front of her. Having your son for a confidant seems to have helped immensely. I love my little girl more than myself, but I feel badly for anyone getting in her way once she sets her mind to a decision. I cannot begin to tell you how difficult it was those last few weeks to keep her reigned in. I thought she was going to find a way to track Mike down with or without my permission."

"She is very strong willed," Leonard chimed in, having sat in or assisted with a few of the young woman's training classes over the last month. "It will serve her well once she tempers it with wisdom and experience. The only one I feel sorry for is Michael Keller himself. I think we are all going to have to hide when they finally stand face to face again."

"Agreed," Clifford responded, heading to the bar to refill his drink. "I only hope my son has the good sense to stay out of the way when the meeting occurs. I fear his crush on Colleen is going to cause him more headache than he is prepared for. He is a good boy but was never what one would call 'comfortable' around females. Girls were always the domain of Damien and the Gohr boy."

Leonard nodded in agreement. "Charm is a talent my son has always been successful at. I was proud to see he gave more respect than he often got in return from those little gold diggers who come out of nowhere. Personally, I think your two children would make a very powerful force. I have watched them together and even if she won't admit it out loud, I think Colleen has come to rely on and appreciate young Cliff more than she realizes. He certainly has a crush on her."

"I would be inclined to agree," Clifford said, "David, Here is to hoping things work out for our children better than they have for us." He raised a glass to the slightly uncomfortable David who saluted back and took a long pull from his drink. A few minutes later, a few other powerful family leaders arrived and the old men settled into a friendly game of cards. This was a tradition with those of influence. With David being the father of the most gifted female in generations of their world, he was naturally now a part of this tradition. Though deemed merely a way to socialize, many a deal was brokered during these evenings.

\* \* \*

"You know, things would be easier if you would dispense with the secrets and tell Liz about your gifts," Mike said as soon as Damien appeared in the car next to him. He had sent out a mental call as soon as he had safely seen Laurie to her door, and true to form, Damien appeared almost as soon as Mike was back on the road. "I can tell you want to, so what's holding you back?"

"I forget how insightful you can be at times, Mike." Damien laughed as he settled back in the seat. "It's almost like you're reading my mind." They both laughed at this, remembering the first encounter they were able to have a conversation, where Damien had been reading Mike's mind. "I have thought of little else. I was almost ready to tell her tonight until I felt a surge on the way to the cars. Did you pick up anything?"

"It felt like a person teleporting," Mike replied thoughtfully, "but why they wouldn't have said hello concerns me. Maybe it was nothing, but it was awfully coincidental wasn't it?"

"I agree," Damien said, pausing. "which is part of why I haven't told Liz anything. We have more than one set of ruffled feathers right now with the changes we have been making and are proposing. I don't want to have to split my focus until we get things settled out and rolling smoother. I wouldn't want some hot head to get it in his head she's a bargaining chip. I don't envy your situation with Laurie, but I think your little display with Derek and his father has everyone on eggshells. We seem to accomplish more when you are there, rather than only Cliff and me."

"I know I haven't been in attendance as much as I would like," Mike sighed, "I had to finish my commitment to my Uncle. Now we have a couple weeks before school starts to try and wrap up as much as possible. I would like to be able to enjoy my senior year and see where things go with Laurie. She told me she loved me tonight."

"Whoa," Damien exclaimed, "Really? She said she loves you huh? Well, congratulations man. She's a great girl and she accepts what you are. Her attitude is rare. It's also obvious she isn't in it for what she can get out of it. Most girls turn into gold digging bitches when they get ahold of one with gifts like ours. You got lucky with Laurie. She is very grounded in her own ambitions. So, what did you say?"

"I told her," Mike began, remembering the conversation again, "I told her she means the world to me, and I hope she understands if I am not quite ready for what she is. I don't know how I would have survived this summer without her, Damien, but I need a little more time. She took it well, saying she wanted me to be sure of how she felt. She has been so great about my past. There are times I wonder if she doesn't deserve better, a boyfriend who isn't as messed up as I am."

"You aren't messed up, Mike," Damien interjected, "trust me, there are people with so many more issues than you. It is understandable with what you went through you would be a little gun shy about jumping totally into another relationship with both feet so quickly. Have you made any decisions about Colleen? I know you had been trying to track her down, but hadn't found anything yet."

"She hasn't reached out to me," Mike said. "It is probably best for us both if we move on. I need a little more time to piece my heart back together. Tonight, I swear I smelled Colleen's perfume in the club. It stands to reason other girls could use it too. It was so perfect I almost thought she had to be there. Probably because our waitress at dinner was named Colleen. My mind is playing tricks on me."

"Makes sense," Damien replied, thinking again how dodgy Cliff had been. Damien began to wonder if perhaps Cliff had taken Colleen out of his family's house. It would have been crazy to take her where Mike was going to be, at least right now. From what Damien had heard, Colleen hadn't burned anything too badly lately, but what would her seeing Mike out with Laurie do to her control? "I think you are making the right decision taking time until you are comfortable man. Anyway, I gotta run. Going to get some sleep, see you soon." Mike waved and Damien disappeared quickly. Mike then flashed himself and his SUV the rest of the way home and after shutting the engine, went right to bed so he wouldn't disturb his aunt and uncle.

# Chapter 6

"Look," Mike snapped, getting in the faces of two Council members the next week late on a Thursday afternoon. He had been sitting with members of the Council, either in small groups or as a full court for most of the last four days from sunup until after the sun went down most days. He had explained to Laurie what was going on, and she had been working extra anyway to save a little more money before school started and her hours would be cut. The senseless bickering, as Mike had been seeing it, had finally pushed him too far. "I don't care we have never done things this way before. This is how we should be doing things. It is the right thing to do. It doesn't hurt anyone financially more than the other, it is fair across the board. The better treatment of our employees will garner more loyalty and prevent thefts and sabotage anyway. Thus saving us more than this is going to cost us on the front end." Mike was glad he had spent those afternoons with his financial advisor, Ray Burke. He understood more of his financial numbers better than he had before. It seemed like simple logic to him, but he was dealing now with a bunch of tightfisted old men who felt it was their right to exploit their workforces.

"But it could be seen as we are growing soft," Joseph Parker repeated. "If I go to my people, and make these changes, they are going to think I am going soft. The unions will eat it up and then we will have more problems on our hands." He dealt with construction labor unions often and was familiar with the nearly hate/hate relationship in his negotiations regarding wages and benefits. What he saw in these suggestions were akin to folding into all the demands he had fought off for the last two decades. "I get it you have these great gifts and had your spot handed to you here, but I am not going to stand for a child to tell me how to handle my businesses."

"Mr. Parker," Damien stepped in as Mike had become distracted when his cellphone went off, "We are only looking at this as a way to improve society. The concessions you are being asked to make are nothing more than the rest of us are making." Mike was hanging up and Damien could tell by the look on Mike's face things were about to get ugly.

"Listen to me, Mr. Parker," Mike began, approaching the older man again. For his part, Joseph Parker did sit back when he began to realize he could be facing the famous temper of Michael Keller. "I am going to give you, and anyone else, a week to look over the financial reports Mr. Burke put together for me. You will see from the projections the initial investment will reap benefits far beyond only your businesses. It will benefit us all in the end. In the process, society as a whole will see a much needed boost. If after a week, we cannot come to a reasonable compromise to satisfy us all, we will look into other options." The older man, along with a couple other members, heard the veiled threat in Mike's speech. It had come up before the entire original Council should abdicate in favor of the next generation with fresh ideas. "For now, I have other business to attend to, with the permission of the Triad, I move we reconvene next week and take the weekend off." Mike turned to Mr. Kosgrove, the only original member of the Triad in attendance. Clifford's father had all but passed over his seat to his son, and Damien had become firmly ensconced in the seat held by his family for generations.

"I think your course of action is wise, Mr. Keller," Blake Kosgrove replied, nodding. "I think it best if we all take the weekend to think over Mr. Keller's compelling arguments and supporting data. Let's talk again on Monday evening shall we gentlemen?" There was mumbled agreement and then after shuffling of papers, everyone else disappeared, leaving Cliff, Damien, and Mike alone in the Council chambers.

"You alright there, Mike?" Cliff asked, gathering up the papers spread out before him. He had noticed these negotiations taking a toll on Mike and wondered if he was going to be able to continue. Cliff had been glad for his part to let Mike and Damien take the lead. It had become clear Damien was the more charismatic leader, because Mike's short temper got the better of him at times.

"Yeah," Mike replied, "I'll be fine. I can't believe we're still haggling over these pathetic percentage points. I have proven it time and again this will return dividends higher than before. It is clear the opposition to us is because of our age, no matter the research supporting us." The most important thing Mike had pushed for was higher contributions to charities as it would bring exposure to their businesses and help them form stronger ties to the communities they were based in. This would work to bring more revenue in from the increased exposure. Several members of the Council only saw the initial expense and shut down right away.

"A few of them are being rather cagey for no logical reason," Damien agreed. "We have to keep our heads and we will win them over. It may take longer than we thought, but we have made progress. Once those initial ones who jumped on board start seeing the return on their investment, the others will fall into line." Several Council members had embraced the young men's ideas and immediately implemented them. It was too early to have born any real fruit, but the seeds were sown at least.

Mike nodded, "I know, I'm tired of this dungeon and the endless circular logic. Why don't we have a boardroom or conference room in a high rise? With windows so we can see the world we are trying to convince them to become a part of?"

"I don't know," chimed in Cliff, looking around. "I think it is like most traditions. They've been this way for so long, no one has questioned it until us.

I'll add it to our topics of discussion next week. See where it gets us. It would be nice if we had our own offices and space to work instead of meeting in our homes or here. It might also get their minds to think about something else for a bit. It might help get them to see things our way."

"Agreed," Damien said, nodding. "Well, I'm going to go meet Liz for dinner tonight. You guys don't get into any trouble without me now." With a wave, he disappeared from the room.

"What are your plans, Cliff?" Mike asked, gathering up his own stack of papers. He had already added a file cabinet to his room at his aunt and uncle's, though he had thought about utilizing the office of the house he had gotten from the Gohr estate. "Laurie is working until at least eleven, so I really have nothing to do."

"I have to report to my father on the day's events," Cliff said resignedly. "Then I'm supposed to meet a Council member's son. He is returning from Europe where he was working on building a few investments. Going to be another boring night I'm afraid."

"Well, bring him with you to Anne's tomorrow," Mike responded. "She has a big party planned before we start school next week. If you say you aren't coming, I fear Chad, Damien, and I are supposed to come to your house and drag you there kicking and screaming." Mike laughed and Cliff joined him momentarily. Then the realization of Mike coming to his house might mean Mike would see Colleen there, or her parents, hit him like a punch in the gut.

"No," Cliff sobered from his merriment quickly. "You won't have to come after me. I think I will bring him along. He's only a year or so older than all of us, which meant he got to go after these opportunities. His father is Dawson, sits two seats down from you. Mr. Dawson was all in support of the changes we put forth, but he was always a progressive one. He took over from his father at a young age. His son Joey is the one responsible for the import/export business in Denmark you ended up getting a part of when you, well, when you earned your place on the Council."

Mike thought about the elder Dawson from their meetings. Mike recalled having his support from the beginning, but it was a quiet and firm support. Mr. Dawson wasn't one to get involved in the politicking the rest were. He made a decision and stuck with it, end of story. "Sounds great. If he's anything like his father, this Joey will be a great addition to our group. Well, I guess I will go see what my mom cooked up for dinner. I haven't been home in a week or more. See you tomorrow, Cliff." Mike waved and was gone.

Cliff paused over a document and stood there reading a few minutes when a noise startled him. He looked up to see Matthew Stenton stepping from the shadows at the edge of the room. Many members used the area as a safe place to enter the chambers so they wouldn't bump into anyone. "Oh, Hello Cliff," Matthew said brightly. "Mr. Kosgrove asked me to make sure he had all his papers. He thinks he forgot something." Matthew walked up to where Cliff was standing at the head chair. Mr. Kosgrove occupied the seat to Cliff's right, with Mike on the other side of him.

"These are all mine, I don't think I saw anything he may have left behind," Cliff replied, gathering his into the file folder he had and turning to go. "Have a good evening, Matthew." Cliff concentrated and teleported himself home, he had paused long enough to notice Matthew disappear as well, empty handed.

# Chapter 7

"**M**om, Connie," Mike called as he arrived in his old bedroom and walked out into the hall. "It's Mike, I'm home" He bounded down the stairs when poking his head into his sister's room revealed it was empty. He turned towards the living room and saw the two of them sitting on the couch, laughing at the show on the television. "Mom, Connie, I'm home." Mike called again, leaning casually in the doorway.

"Mike?" his mother turned and looked the same time his sister did. Then they were both screaming, "Mike!" and running to hug him. After a few joyous minutes of reunion, there was a beep from the kitchen and Sally Keller excused herself to go see to dinner. This left the two siblings alone.

"Geesh, brother," Connie said, stepping back. "You look like hell. I thought you were supposed to be done with work. Is Laurie running you this ragged?" She grinned at her brother, enjoying getting to tease him about his current girlfriend. Mike had brought Laurie out to meet his mother and sister once a couple weeks ago. Mike had bought his sister a cellphone and knew Laurie and Connie had started texting each other on occasion. "You would think Mom was psychic herself. She thought for sure you were coming to visit tonight, so she had a pot roast simmering in the crock pot all day. She even made you a peach pie. I don't know why she is making such a fuss over you, you are still lame, bro." Connie said with a smile. She had missed her brother and their sudden closeness after his accident had been tested with him deciding to stay in Washington for the upcoming school year.

"I know, but I have to make sure you don't look lame all by yourself, sis," Mike teased back. Now his nose was assaulted with the smell of the roast from the kitchen. His heightened senses also picked up the smell of the mostly finished peach pie, probably his most favorite. The two siblings had grown closer the last few months and had talked more often than Mike talked to his mother. "No, it has been a rough few days dealing with stubborn old men who have no idea how to get with the times is all. I thought I would pop in and see you guys tonight. Tomorrow and this weekend are going to be pretty busy. Then school starts next week for us." Connie had an extra week off due to differences in when school started.

"Sucks to be you," Connie said and stuck her tongue out at her brother. "Did you bring Laurie with you tonight?" She looked around, wondering if he was hiding her. The two girls had bonded pretty quickly and Connie had been very supportive of Laurie when she asked questions about Mike's previous relationship and how to best handle him. Connie was fairly certain if Mike knew, he had decided to let it continue.

"Come on you two, it's time to eat," Sally called her two children from the kitchen. "Mike, set the table, Connie, fix everyone something to drink."

The two Keller children both chimed an exasperated, "Yes, mom." And then with a grin to each other went to help their mother.

Over an hour later, Mike pushed away his plate from his second helping of peach pie and smiled at two of the most important people in his life. "Everything was wonderful, Mom. I will have to come home more often I think."

His mother smiled at the compliment. While unnerved at first her son could pop in at a moment's notice, it was very nice to have him home more often than conventional travel methods would allow. "You will have to give me advance notice when you get time to visit again. And, next time you'll have to bring Laurie with you. I want to make sure she's keeping you in line."

"Trust me, Mom," Mike laughed, "Laurie is doing perfectly fine in that department. I don't get to step a toe out of line. If you two start talking, I will really be unable to do anything fun with the guys." The two females laughed at him. The trio retired to the living room where they watched a made for TV movie and chatted about the upcoming school year. Before long, Mike stood and stretched, signaling it was time for him to head back to his new home.

"You make sure you visit as often as you can this year, or at least call your mother once in awhile," Sally admonished. "And you be sure to take care of your Aunt and Uncle." She hugged her son and then moved out of the way for his sister.

"Talk to you soon, bro," Connie said, giving her brother a hug. "Don't be such a stranger."

"I'll try not to," Mike replied, "And you two can still come visit or move to Washington anytime you want. I got this big house I am not even using. We wouldn't have to sell this one if we didn't want to." His mother waved him off again and he quickly departed back to his room in Washington.

Connie turned to her mother after her brother was gone, "You know mom, I think this is the first time he hasn't asked if we had heard from Colleen."

"I think so too, dear," Sally said, patting her daughter's reddish brown hair. "I am hopeful he is moving on. I don't know what happened to Colleen, but I hope she's happy with how much she messed up your brother's heart and mind. Well, I'm going to bed. See you in the morning, honey."

"Night, Mom," Connie called back as her mother headed off to her room. She quickly texted Laurie, "Hey Laurie, Mike came to visit us tonight, first time he hasn't asked about you know who. How is he doing? He was pretty closed lipped about how he is feeling." After pressing send, Connie went to get ready for bed herself. As she was tucking into bed, she got a reply, "I think he's processing, but it's going to take time. I don't care though, I'm going to wait until he's ready. Your brother is always going to be my hero. Night, Connie."

Connie had been told the story about how Mike had saved Laurie's life in an accident at the church. She wasn't sure how she could be prouder of her brother than she was for his bravery. Plugging her phone into the charger, Connie curled up and fell fast asleep.

\* \* \*

"Is that you, Mike?" Aunt Jenny said as she started down the hall at a noise from her nephew's room. "Are you hungry? I can warm up the leftovers from dinner. We weren't sure how long your meeting was going to be today." She turned the corner to his room to see Mike sorting the day's papers into the filing cabinet in his room. While she was glad he had decided to stay, she had been initially concerned about him bringing the Council business into her home. Mike had assured her any meetings would be held out of the house, he only needed a place to keep important papers.

"Hey, Aunt Jenny," Mike said, turning the key in the lock after he closed the drawer. He didn't lock it because of his Aunt and Uncle, in fact, Uncle Jim had a key. It was his way of making sure no one else could pop in and get access. By locking with the key, the cabinet was warded against intrusion. "I actually went to see mom and Connie tonight, had dinner with them. Sorry I didn't call." There had been many late nights lately and Mike had been feeling the strain.

"That's nice, how are they?" Aunt Jenny asked, standing casually in the doorway to Mike's room. "Are they still holding up ok with your decision to stay here this fall?" Aunt Jenny had been nervous about their reaction, even though she was excited about the prospect of Mike staying. She didn't want a rift with her sister in law, and this could have caused a pretty big one.

"No, everything is fine," Mike replied, smiling. He didn't have to read his Aunt's mind to know she was still a little nervous about what his mom would do about him staying in Washington with them instead of coming home. Aunt Jenny had brought it up often enough those first few weeks after he made his decision to make clear her anxiety. "Was a stressful day of meetings and it was nice to relax and catch up with them. If anything, I think Connie is more torn about the decision. She is excited to not have to be in my shadow this year, but at the same time, this whole thing has brought us closer. I guess I feel the same way, but I have to stay here. The work with the Council is important. And of course, your beautiful goddaughter," he added for his Aunt's benefit.

"That is right young man," She smiled, pleased again with her matchmaking efforts. "You will not break that girl's heart or you will answer to me." She laughed before turning to go, calling over her shoulder, "Well, if you change your mind, leftovers are in the fridge. Your uncle and I are in the living room watching TV."

"Be there in a minute," Mike called to her retreating form. He finished tidying up his room and went to join his relatives in the living room. During the commercials, Mike texted Laurie to firm up plans for the next day. Laurie was originally going to stay over at Anne's when she got off work, but the plans had changed. Mike was supposed to pick Laurie up on his way over now. The back to school bash Anne's parents were throwing for all her classmates was going to be larger than ever this year, given the healed relationship between Laurie and Anne. No one outside the small group knew exactly why, but many had noticed the healed rift and didn't feel like they had to walk on eggshells anymore. This meant many who would have skipped the party to avoid drama, were actually looking forward to going.

After a brief visit to Laurie on her break, Mike turned in for the night. As he lay in bed about to fall asleep, he thought about the changes to his life. He should be preparing to return home and face his old friends, old school, and a life without Colleen. Instead, he was wealthy, embroiled in a secret world of gifted individuals, and considering whether he could love again with Laurie. His heart had taken a beating rather rapidly after pining away for Colleen his entire young life. Could he handle turning his heart over to anyone else, even one who accepted him as completely as Laurie did? Shaking his head, Mike used his dream walking talent to put himself into a deep and dreamless sleep.

# Chapter 8

During the night, Mike awoke with a start, feeling like he was being watched. He looked around his room, his heightened senses peering into every dark corner or shadow as if looking for an intruder to be hiding in the smallest of spaces. Shaking his head when he saw nothing, he rolled over and went back to sleep. Matthew Stenton stepped from behind the door, where he had been using his talent to hide within the smallest sliver of a shadow. Surprised he was able to fool Mike, he thought about how easy it would be to end this little threat to his master once and for all. Sighing inwardly, he merely flitted back to his rooms at the Kosgrove estate.

Pacing his room for a few minutes, Matthew raged silently about the restrictions placed on him. His master, Blake Kosgrove had given him specific instructions to watch, observe and report. He was not allowed to take any direct action against Michael Keller, no matter how much he wanted to. Matthew didn't know what Mr. Kosgrove had planned for the Keller boy, his apprentice had not yet been made aware of their end game. All Matthew hoped was for it to raise him above the minor family status afforded to him by his father and his association with a member of the Triad.

Second on his mind was the return of Joey Dawson. Matthew had heard Cliff telling Mike about the successful trip to Europe his rival was returning from. Joey Dawson had been awarded the opportunity to network with mundane and gifted counterparts of the Council in several countries of the floundering European Union. Matthew felt he had been passed over when Cliff's father, the head of the Triad at the time, had picked Joey instead of Matthew to go. The Stenton's and Dawson's had never had a close association, and the rivalry between the two young men had started when they were much younger. Joey and Matthew had both spent time training with several members of the Council, but it seemed Joey would surpass his classmate at all turns. This made Matthew bitter, as he silently cursed the success of his rival.

"He is one problem I can do something about," Matthew said to himself, thinking about all the ways he wanted to bring Dawson low. "Joey is going to see what happens when you cross a Stenton." Matthew continued to pace for hours, plotting and scheming. He knew he would never be able to touch Joey's reputation or business deals directly. He would have to find a way to get his rival to trip over his own success and land in hot water. "I will get you Dawson, you wait and see."

\* \* \*

"Cliff," Colleen spoke, barely above a whisper as she knocked on her confidant's door. "Are you awake?" She knew she was tempting fate with her night time visits with Cliff, especially given his crush on her. Colleen couldn't help herself though, he was her link to Mike and the outside world. After the events Friday at the club, Cliff had never suggested they sneak out again and if anything had become even more withdrawn. She had been making progress with teleporting, and managed to move objects without them blowing up or getting destroyed, well, mostly. She still hadn't been brave enough to try it with a person and Cliff's father had strongly suggested she not. She was close, he kept saying, but one misstep could cause her, or anyone she's taking with her, to not survive.

"What is it Colleen?" Cliff asked, half expectantly, half dreading her response. He had become accustomed to her visiting him, but mostly she wanted to talk about her progress and Mike. Cliff was fearing an end to their association once she mastered teleporting and could go track down Mike. He didn't want to lose her friendship, especially when he felt so close to getting her to move past her previous relationship. Part of him argued he knew he was fooling himself, but he still held hope deeper feelings would develop. It is what made putting off Anne's advances so easy, but he couldn't tell his other friends his secret. Only Damien seemed to suspect the truth, but he was bound by the same secrecy Cliff was in regards to Colleen.

"I wanted to see if you were still awake, can I come in?" Colleen asked, hearing in his tone how he felt. She knew Cliff had been spending long days in Council meetings with Mike, which was why she kept coming to him. She needed to try and get information about Mike. Her dreams lately had been turning more and more to the night she and Cliff had drank a bottle of wine and kissed. It left her more confused than ever in the morning.

"Sure Colleen," Cliff said, having resigned himself to another evening of talking about Mike. He grabbed a couple sodas from the mini fridge and plopped down in a leather arm chair as she entered the room. Her blonde hair swirled as she turned quickly to close the door. She then turned around and her blue eyes flashed as she looked for Cliff. She quickly took a seat across from him and opened the proffered soda. "He has quite a temper doesn't he?" Cliff decided to get things in the open instead of dancing around it like he had on other nights this week.

"Oh, Mike?" Colleen asked, surprised with the directness in Cliff's question. It appeared there would be no coy questions tonight. *Perhaps I haven't been exactly fair to him. He has been such a great friend,'* she thought to herself before answering Cliff's question. "I never really noticed until after he came out of his coma. When he threw the doctor across the room it scared the hell out of me. I couldn't believe he was like that. I guess I saw it when he punched out Kevin, my ex. I didn't want to believe sweet Mike from around the block was truly violent. What did he do today?"

"He," Cliff began, having heard all about the weeks after Mike's gifts started to manifest, either from Mike himself or through Colleen. "He is very adamant about the humanitarian efforts he wants the Council to start embracing. There is more than a few in opposition. I think it is mainly because of our age, because in all other aspects, everyone is terrified he will strip their powers like he did the Gohr's. Even those who support him have a small measure of fear he will turn on them."

"I highly doubt that," Colleen spoke quickly. "One thing about Mike is how fiercely loyal he is. He reminds me of a song I heard once. It talked about: shaking your hand and looking you in the eye, means damn sure it is the truth. Or something like that, I never had a good memory for song lyrics." Colleen giggled slightly, watching Cliff for a reaction.

"I get the same impression as well," Cliff responded before taking a sip of his soda. "But not everyone knows him as well as you do, so there is a bit of understandable fear. I think we have about half the Council won over. A few are on the fence. I think there are one or two only trying to goad him and use it to discredit him for his age. Those are the ones who should be the most worried he will take matters into his own hands."

"I will admit that the changes I saw in Mike scared me a little," Colleen said softly, thinking about the day in the hospital when he woke up. Then her mind drifted back to his fight with Kevin, where he was defending her honor. The images blurred with Cliff punching out the guy in the club the other week who was trying to force her to go with him and suddenly she felt a tear roll down her face.

Cliff was at her side in moments, "Everything alright Colleen?" Cliff asked, reaching out to her. "I know Mike won't do anything crazy. This is the fear of those members of the opposition to our plans and new direction. Don't cry." Cliff was momentarily shattered. He didn't know what to do or how far he dare try to comfort his friend.

"It isn't that," Colleen smiled weakly as she wiped the tear from her cheek. She sniffled slightly, surprised herself how quickly it had come on. "I was thinking about the fight he had with Kevin, and I saw the similarities to when you defended me from that guy at the club. I have thought about it before, and it makes it clear to me I have not been very fair to you Cliff. You are my friend, and given what's happened between us, I keep rubbing Mike in your face." She looked up into the concerned grey eyes of her friend and confidant. She noticed again how pretty his eyes were and almost reached up to him before she came back to reality.

Cliff too noticed the awkwardness in their position as he leaned down towards her. To cover himself he pushed a strand of her long blonde hair behind her ear and placed his hand on her shoulder. "It is ok. I understand your feelings for Mike. I only worry about you is all. Mike is in the dark about you being here.

If he knew," Cliff began before pulling back and dropping into his own chair across from her.

Colleen for her part missed some of what he said, she had felt a tingle again when Cliff touched her hair and shoulder. Memories of Mike doing the same thing blurring with Cliff's face all over. It seemed the more time she spent apart from Mike, her memories of him were being replaced by the young man across from her. Her one friend in this new world she was reawakened to. Having caught the end of Cliff's brief speech, she quickly acted to reassure him, "Mike would never hold it against you and Damien. I am sure I can sort it out with him. He has to know I had to figure out my powers before I could go out in public. It will be alright, I promise." She stood up to go back to her rooms, knowing it was better to get out of Cliff's rooms before anything went wrong. She desperately wanted to hold onto the friendship they had, even after she had sorted things out with Mike. She was slated to return to school this fall, which would cut her training time down, unless she went the home school route.

"I hope you're right," Cliff said softly as he watched her prepare to leave. He felt like such a klutz around her and wished he could articulate his feelings better. When Mike saw her for the first time, Cliff was sure they would all be lucky to escape unscathed. Hopefully Colleen would have the effect she thinks she will on Mike.

Cliff was aware her parents were intending to send Colleen to the public school, which happened to be the one Mike was going to be attending. This was, of course, contingent on whether she mastered the last of her gifts. This left her seventy two hours. If she did, it looked like the school year for her was going to start with a bang. As Colleen waved and left the room quietly, Cliff prayed she wouldn't get the hang of it, so she would be setup with tutors and stay away from Mike a little longer. Otherwise, Cliff worried he would lose two friends.

# Chapter 9

Friday morning dawned clear and promised plenty of sun for Anne's Back to School Pool Party. Mike stretched and rolled out of bed, unable to shake the odd feeling from when he woke up in the middle of the night. As he grabbed clothes and headed down the hall to his bathroom, he heard his Aunt or Uncle rummaging in the kitchen. Uncle Jim would be returning to the office this morning without his nephew. Mike thought about it as he showered and got dressed for the day. Entering the dining room less than a half hour later, he was greeted by the familiar signs of a weekday morning in the Johnson household. Aunt Jenny was in the kitchen, making coffee and her breakfast, while Uncle Jim was reading the morning paper.

"Morning Mike," Uncle Jim called from behind his paper. "Exciting plans for your last weekend before school?" Jim was well aware of the all day party his nephew was attending, but it made for interesting morning conversation. Jim remembered his senior year fondly and hoped it would be a great one for his nephew. He hoped there would be less time spent with the Council in Mike's future, but so far it hadn't appeared to be going his way. Jim wasn't comfortable with the idea of his nephew being involved in the Council, but so far it appeared to be positive, albeit long hours. The changes Mike talked about seemed to be very uplifting for the communities and charities who would benefit.

"Nothing special," Mike replied, grinning as he grabbed a banana to cut up into his cereal. It was going to be a food filled day, but he didn't want to go on an empty stomach. "Anne's party is today. Not sure if we will be there all day into the night, or if it will turn into a trip to the dance club. Depends on how everyone gets along. Since we might be swimming, I won't have my phone right on me if you need to reach me today. I will try to check it often."

"Don't worry about that dear," Aunt Jenny said as she joined the two males at the table. She had a grapefruit and a cup of coffee in front of her and she went to work dismantling the fruit. "I am sure your Uncle and I can get along without you today. Enjoy yourself and be safe." She winked at her nephew.

"I will," Mike laughed. He and Aunt Jenny had had to have a talk about teenagers and the trouble they tend to get into at parties like this one. She was worried about her goddaughter Laurie getting hurt, but Mike assured his Aunt neither of them were ready for anything along those lines. It was slightly comical having the 'sex talk' with his Aunt, but he understood her motives. She knew enough about Mike's past to know he was still a little hesitant in his relationship with Laurie. Aunt and nephew had become close during his stay in Washington and he had felt comfortable confiding in Aunt Jenny about Laurie's feelings.

Mike thought about the evening when he had told his aunt about Laurie professing her love:

"And then she told me, while she didn't know whether I was ready or not, she wanted me to know she loves me," Mike had said, fearing reprisal from his aunt. "I don't know if I am ready for that yet Aunt Jenny. Laurie is great and I don't know what I would do without her. But, it's hard to think about placing myself at anyone else's mercy right now."

"I understand," Jenny had patted her nephew's hand. "I see the way you two look at each other, and I'm not worried. With time, it will get easier. Be honest with her if you don't see things progressing with the two of you. She will handle it better if you are up front with her all along, rather than springing a surprise on her."

"I know she means the world to me," Mike had replied. "I was caught off guard by the L word and... I don't know if I'm ready to go down that road." Aunt Jenny had smiled and hugged her nephew.

Mike shook himself out of his reminiscing and started on his breakfast. The last week with the Council had taught him he was not going to turn into a bitter old man at such a young age. He smiled as he thought about seeing Laurie today. He knew there would come a time and he was going to have to be alone with her so they could talk about the other week. He hadn't thought he was ready, but he realized now he was being foolish. Laurie was the greatest thing to happen to him this summer and he was being a fool holding onto the past. As he finished his cereal and went to the sink to wash his bowl, Mike resolved to find the right time to tell Laurie how he was feeling.

* * *

"Sounds like your ride is here, Laurie," her mother, Missy, called as she went to peek between the living room curtains. Sure enough, there was Mike climbing out of his big SUV he had acquired this summer. The first time he showed up in it, she had been surprised. It was very flashy and obviously expensive. She thought for sure his Uncle must have fixed him up with it. Then she heard about a trust fund which had apparently become available after he turned eighteen. While unexpected, Missy Sterling couldn't think of a more deserving young man. She still got tears in her eyes when she thought about the day he saved Laurie at the church when the organ pipes started to fall. She went over to answer the door before he had time to knock.

"Oh, Hello Mrs. Sterling," Mike began as the door opened, catching him with his hand raised. "Your flowers out front are looking beautiful. Is Laurie ready to go? I would hate for us to be late to Anne's party."

"Why thank you, Mike," Missy replied, smiling. She had always thought he was such a polite young man. To hear her daughter tell it, he was the same even when he wasn't under the watchful eye of adults. This calmed most of the fears she and her husband had had of Laurie dating. Him being her best friend's nephew and living up to their expectations had certainly helped matters. "Laurie should be down any minute, why don't you come in. Would you like anything to drink?"

"No thank you ma'am," Mike said, stepping into the house. Mr. Sterling was a moderately successful attorney, but Mike had always been impressed with how comfortable the Sterling house was. It was tasteful without being opulent and flashy. Then Laurie came bounding down the stairs from the second floor, her blonde hair flying behind her. She had a little backpack, likely stuffed with swimsuit, lotion, and a towel, slung across her shoulder. She immediately stepped to Mike and they shared a quick kiss. "Ready for a day of fun in the sun?" Mike asked, blushing slightly still at the display in front of Mrs. Sterling.

"You two kids have fun and enjoy yourselves," Mrs. Sterling said before Laurie could respond. She thought the way Mike got nervous about displays of affection in front of the adults very endearing. It reinforced her beliefs in Mike being a solidly good guy. Mike was the kind of guy she could count on not to hurt her daughter. She waved and turned to go into the kitchen as Laurie started dragging Mike out the front door.

"Bye mom," Laurie said, shutting the door behind her. She then turned to Mike on the front porch and kissed him more thoroughly, which he returned with less hesitancy than he had in the house. "It's cute that you get nervous in front of my mom, but I am pretty sure she has seen us enough to know we have kissed before." Laurie giggled at the blank look on Mike's face.

"I know, but I don't want to flaunt in front of her, or your dad either. I don't want to do anything which might make them put any restrictions on our time together," Mike replied, taking Laurie's bag and then her hand to lead her to the car. He opened her door and gave her a hand up into the passenger seat, before stowing her bag in the back with his. He had been considerably less formal, and had his suit, towel, and a change of clothes tossed in a plastic grocery bag in the back seat of the car.

"Oh please," Laurie giggled when Mike had climbed into the driver seat. "They adore you. Not as much as I do but they do. I doubt you could do any wrong in their mind. Haven't you figured that out by now?" After Mike got the car backed out of her drive and heading down the road, she quickly took his hand in both of hers. She was preparing for Mike to teleport them over to Anne's. Scary at first, being with him when he used his gifts now gave her a little thrill. She had been nervous at first he would end up finding another with gifts and leave her. As the weeks had gone on and he still came around every chance he could, she had started to relax. It was his persistence which prompted her to finally tell him how she had felt ever since the day of the accident at church. To find out later it had been a targeted attack and he had been so heroic to save her and Anne, only cemented she was not going to let Mike go without a fight.

"I know I know," Mike said, enjoying the feel of Laurie's hands wrapped around his. He could tell from the twitch in her fingers she was anticipating him to teleport them. He wanted the alone time with her however, so he took his time driving to Anne's the old fashioned way. "I don't want to give them any reason to mistrust me. I could tell from how your father acted at first that even with my Aunt and Uncle vouching for me, he was going to be a hard sell on letting you date. I don't want to disappoint him."

"Believe me, you haven't," Laurie smiled thinking about the talk she had with her father. At times it was hard to tell which parent she was closer with. When she had made up her mind to tell Mike how she felt, it was an easy choice to go to her father. Her mother was great for girl talk, but what she needed was to know her father supported her choice. He had only told her, 'If you are sure honey, then you tell that boy how you feel. He would be a fool to not feel the same.' Mike's reluctance to reciprocate didn't put Laurie off at all. She could tell in the way he acted how much he cared for her, even if he wasn't ready to admit to himself it was what it was.

"I'm glad to hear how much he approves," Mike squeezed Laurie's hands with his. They rode in comfortable silence for the rest of the trip to Anne's. When they arrived, there were a couple cars already there and they could hear sounds of music coming from the back of the house. After Mike put the SUV in park, Laurie started to unbuckle and reach for her door, letting go of Mike's hand. He quickly placed his hand on her knee and she looked over at him. "Laurie, I want to talk to you about something before we go in."

"What is it, Mike?" Laurie asked, her heart trembling. She could see a different light in Mike's eyes since he arrived to pick her up, but she wasn't sure what it was yet. She hoped by the way he had squeezed her hand it was going to be good news. After she had told him she was in love with him Friday night, they hadn't spoken of it.

"Laurie," Mike began, then fumbled for how to continue, "Laurie, you mean the world to me. I don't know how I would have survived this summer without you. I wanted you to know I love you too." It was a good thing Mike had not opened his door yet, or they both would have tumbled out of the car to the ground from Laurie jumping over into his lap. They kissed for a few minutes and held each other, staring into each other's eyes, until there was a tap on the window behind Mike's back.

"Hey you two, get a room," called Chad as he and Deb stood outside the driver side of Mike's SUV. They then waved and started to head towards the walkway leading into Anne's back yard. Laurie and Mike untangled themselves with red faces. They grabbed their bags and ran to join their friends. When Mike and Laurie caught up, their friends gave them big grins and laughed at their beet red faces.

As the quartet got closer to the enclosed area where the pool was, it was obvious from the splashing the early arrivals had already begun the festivities.

The two genders split off to head into their separate changing rooms. Chad turned to Mike as soon as they got away from the girls. "So how's it going man?" Laurie was like a sister to Chad, so he was aware of most surface details of her relationship with Mike. He didn't have to be told to see how she obviously felt about Mike. Chad had been skeptical at first of the new guy in town, but Mike had continued to surprise him all summer. He also would never forget their shopping trip gone awry. Deb hasn't let him get away with forgetting which clothes she picked out for him ever since.

"All's well," Mike replied. "Hey, if I haven't said it lately, thank you for helping me with Laurie and trusting me. I know you two are close and I think it's safe to tell you she and I are taking a step forward in our relationship."

"Making out in front of your friend's houses?" Chad joked from across the wall in the next changing room stall. Anne's parents had built one for each gender when they enclosed the pool. Each side had a couple stalls as well as a sink and shelving area for personal effects. "It is a big step forward from making out in her driveway or on her front porch." Chad laughed. He hadn't really wanted to know so much detail about his friends' relationship, but Laurie had to tell him and Deb about it.

"Funny," Mike laughed back. "No, I am sure she told you what she said to me Friday at the club. I have come to a realization. Yes, I do love her. I didn't think I was ready to be in love again. I am though, and I'm glad she stuck it out with me until I was ready."

"Glad to hear it man," Chad said as they both came out of the changing stalls at the same time. They quickly stored their belongings on a shelf and headed for the door to the pool area. Chad clapped his friend on the back as he pushed on the door. "Now we get to go admire our girls in their swimsuits." The two laughed as they entered the chaos of Anne's Back to School Bash.

* * *

"So, spill it," Deb said as soon as the girls were ensconced in their changing room. "What has you glowing so much?" Deb was tying her brown hair up into a ponytail so it would stay mostly out of the way when she went swimming. She knew her friend was more than smitten with Mike. Deb had to admit to herself Mike is a truly great guy. The four of them especially had been spending most of their free time together this summer. With Mike's friend Damien dating Liz; it had made the group even closer.

"He loves me," Laurie gushed immediately. "He said he has realized this past week that he does love me, he was frightened, which is understandable given what he has been through before he came to work for his uncle and I am so ecstatic I can't stand it."

"Take a breath there girly," Deb chided her friend. She was glad to hear things were working out. She had only been slightly concerned when she heard

Laurie had professed her love for Mike, and he had side stepped it. Laurie had explained in brief terms about Mike's previous relationship and how it had been very hard on him. It was understandable for a guy to be gun shy, but she had seen the way Mike looks at Laurie. There had been no doubt in Deb's mind he was in love with Laurie. "Tell me everything."

"Well, it was when we got here," Laurie began, telling Deb how Mike had stopped her from getting out of the car. "He had this serious tone when he said he had to talk to me about something, but there was that stupid grin on his face. The one he had when he suggested you and Liz pick out clothes for Chad and Damien. I swear he is up to mischief every time he gets that look on his face." Laurie paused and smiled, "Then he told me he had been thinking about it and realized, whether he thought he was ready or not, he does love me. Isn't that great?"

"I am so happy for you, Laurie," Deb replied, smiling and then hugging her friend. "It is so great you found your guy like I have my Chad." The two girls finished adjusting their suits in the mirror and winked at their reflection. "Now let's go make sure those boys are only paying attention to us today shall we?" Both girls were laughing as they exited the dressing room.

They entered the pool area and quickly located their boyfriends. Mike and Chad were carrying someone above their heads, who was squealing and protesting, towards the deep end of the pool. At first the girls weren't sure who it was, but then they were able to make out their friend Anne's voice, "Don't you even dare think about it you two, I swear I will tell," and then she hit the water with a splash. The two boys started congratulating themselves as Anne's head broke the surface of the water. It was about this time Laurie and Deb walked up behind them and shoved them both face first into the pool.

Mike and Chad both came to the surface sputtering. "What's the big idea?" Chad called to Deb and Laurie, who were helping Anne out of the water. The two dry girls grinned like Cheshire cats.

"Yeah, we were only having a bit of fun with our host," Mike said, grinning as well. When he and Chad had come out of the changing room, they noticed a very dry Anne standing over to the side talking to a member of the catering staff. The two guys had shared a look and nodded to each other before quickly running up behind Anne and picking her up into the air. They had paraded around the pool for a minute before settling on dropping her into the deep end. While they were celebrating was when the tables were turned on them.

"Well, us girls have to stick together against a bunch of bullies like you two," Anne laughed as she high fived her friends. Their laughter turned to screams as all three came tumbling into the water. After the initial splash cleared, Mike and Chad were able to see they had been joined by Damien, Cliff, Liz, and a young man that neither of them recognized. Before she could be caught and tossed into the water before she put her suit on, Liz took off at a run towards the changing room. The three guys stood laughing on the edge of the pool.

"Good job there Damien," Mike called to his other friends. "Now all three of them are going to gang up on us." Sure enough, the three girls, now in the pool, decided three against two were better odds and proceeded to try and dunk Mike and Chad under the water. Figuring he was safe to use his gift to let him hold his breath a little longer than normal, Mike decided to dive down and pull Laurie's legs out from under her. It worked until all three started after him. Their fun was interrupted by a splash as another person jumped into the water and came to Mike's defense.

Mike surfaced to see Chad with his arms around Deb, holding her back, while Anne was fighting off the new face who had arrived with Damien and Cliff. It struck Mike this must be Joey Dawson. Cliff had said he would bring him along. It didn't look like Anne was fighting too hard to get out of his arms. This left Mike with only Laurie to contend with, who was still trying desperately to dunk him by herself. Mike quickly subdued her and kissed her lips. "Got ya babe," he grinned at her.

"Not fair, we were supposed to get you guys," Laurie laughed, looking around. Cliff and Damien were still standing near the edge of the pool, neither of them had changed into swimming trunks yet. "Hey Damien. Nice to see you out Cliff. Who's the new guy?" Laurie was also watching Anne's struggles subside as her and her assailant whispered to each other.

"Meet Joey Dawson," Cliff called back, not feeling a bit of jealousy over the obvious initial attraction between Joey and Anne. *'At least she will leave me alone now,'* thought Cliff with relief. "He's an old friend of the family. He got back into town from studying abroad yesterday, so Mike had said we should bring him along to hang out with us." He then turned his attention to Joey and Anne, "Joey, this is the rest of our group. Deb and Chad are over there, closer to you is Mike and Laurie, and the royal pain you are holding is Anne." He then dodged as Anne turned and splashed water in his direction. "I'm kidding, she really is a sweet girl who would never harm a fly." This got him another wave of water sent his way. "Well, come on Damien, we gotta change before they decide we need to go for a swim too."

For his part, Damien had been silent and was pleased to see Cliff speaking up and handling introductions. "Be right back then gang. Mike, keep an eye on Joey, we wouldn't want our little Anne to corrupt him." No wave of water was forthcoming for him as Anne had gone back to conversing quietly with Joey, the two now floating next to each other in the water.

"So Joey," Mike called as Laurie snuggled up to him in the water. Her wet blonde hair was loose and floated in the water around the two of them. "How was the flight? Major jet lag?"

"Oh," Joey said when he realized Mike was trying to make conversation. For his part, when Cliff and Damien pointed Anne out, he had been surprised neither of them were dating her. In his opinion she was a gorgeous raven haired beauty. When she had turned around and he saw her piercing blue eyes, he was snared.

Breaking eye contact for a moment, he replied, "It wasn't too bad. I slept like a log yesterday when I got in and again last night. When Cliff mentioned this pool party, I figured a bit of exercise would do me good. Not to mention he said there would be lots of pretty American girls in bikinis. Europe was nice, but I missed the States."

"I bet you did," Anne smiled. "Welcome home," she called before using Joey's shoulders to pop up out of the water, where she used her small weight to dunk him under the water. Before he could surface or react, she took off through the water towards the stairs in the shallow end. She could see instantly Joey was from the secret world not everyone within hearing was privy to. This intrigued her. Since her repeated attempts to attract Cliff had gone unrequited, Anne thought she would see what she could find out from this new face. If he was an old friend of Cliff and Damien's, they wouldn't have brought him if they didn't think he would fit in.

Joey came sputtering to the surface in time to see Anne's legs kicking away from him. He laughed, having felt a spark between them. Cliff had warned him of Anne's gifts, explaining she was aware of very little in their world. He had also been warned not everyone at this party was in possession of the same knowledge. He casually drifted over closer to Mike. Deb and Chad had slipped over to a corner of the pool and were talking, Chad in the water and Deb sitting on the edge with her feet dangling over. Between the music and new arrivals making noise near the entrances, Joey thought he could make a better introduction with Mike. He extended his hand to Mike, who had one arm around Laurie, "Nice to finally meet you. My father has talked non-stop since your arrival. I am glad to put a face with the stories."

Mike grinned as he shook Joey's hand, "I don't think I will ever get over my reputation preceding me. I hope he didn't embellish anything too much. I only did what had to be done, which is all I am still doing. By the way, thank you for the work you've been doing. It's been a great benefit. You're a talented negotiator."

It was Joey's turn to grin, "Thank you sir. I do try my best. And I do not think he exaggerated at all. I can't say I'm sorry to see you know who gone. He was bad for all of us." Part of his briefing in coming today had included a warning to not mention the Gohr family by name. Laurie and Anne both were likely to react poorly, and it would not do well to get on Mike's bad side.

Laurie was not oblivious to the exchange. She had decided she would not allow Mike's other commitments to concern her, unless it affected her. She knew who Joey had to be referring to and a shiver went through her as she remembered Derek's attempt on her life earlier in the summer. Mike caught the tremble and looked at her quickly. Laurie shook her head and smiled. "Well, I'm glad you could join us today Joey. It seems you have already made quite the impression on Anne."

Joey glanced in Anne's direction before responding, "Well, Cliff and Damien said I should keep an eye out for her, since claims were already made for the other pretty girls in their circle of friends. I must say I was pleasantly surprised. Do you think I have a chance?" He leaned in conspiratorially. He knew the key to fitting in, whether he hit it off with Anne or not, was to make sure he stayed on Mike's good side. Being on Laurie's good side would help tremendously. No one in the gifted community wanted to be on Mike's bad side at this time.

"Well, if you keep throwing around words like pretty you might have a shot," Laurie laughed. "I will let you boys talk, I am going to go join the other girls for a little sun bathing before we eat." She kissed Mike briefly, "Love you." She then started swimming for the stairs at the other end of the pool.

"Love you too babe," Mike called to her, before turning his attention back to Joey. Damien and Cliff were coming back and dove in, surfacing near them. Chad was still talking to Deb, but she was being called away by Laurie, Anne, and Liz. He turned and swam over to join the other guys in the middle of the deep end of the pool.

"So, what do you guys say to a race?" Chad asked as he approached. All five of them were in fairly good shape, even if Cliff was stockier than his friends. He seemed at home in the water though so Chad thought it would be a good way to gauge the newcomer. Nothing like a little testosterone fueled competition to get the measure of a man.

"Sound's like a great idea," Damien replied. "Say, four laps, end to end. First one to slap the edge wins?" He started to tread water over towards the wall of the end they were in. The water was at least four foot deep the whole length, so it should allow for a decent race. If the guys all lined up, it would leave them with barely enough room for elbows and knees so they shouldn't bump into each other.

"We will need all of the girls to judge the race, and no shenanigans," Mike admonished as he moved to line up next to Damien.

"Thanks for taking all the fun out of it, dad," Joey said, giving Cliff a push as he lined up on Damien's other side. The four gifted knew it wouldn't be fair to cheat with Chad in the race, but it was very tempting against each other. "Ladies," Joey called to the assembled girls as they were heading out the patio door. They all turned at once and looked at him. "Would you ladies be so kind as to judge our race. We want to make sure it is fair. I think it would help us to swim faster to see all of you standing by the finish line. What do you think guys?" The guys all echoed his sentiment.

"Sure thing," Liz called out, before turning to Anne, "He's laying it on thick isn't he? Must be trying to impress someone." Anne turned red and swung her towel at Liz, who ducked it. "I meant me, I am not sure what you thought." Then she stuck her tongue out at Anne and raced to stand behind Damien. "Come on girls. The guys obviously want to show off for us."

Once everyone was in position, Laurie counted off and guys pushed away from the wall powerfully and headed for the other end. One turn in, it was clear Joey and Chad were the better swimmers. They were commanding a hefty lead with Damien, Mike and Cliff following, respectively. By the time the slower three made the final turn, Joey and Chad were coming up for air and reaching for the wall. Joey's hand closed around Anne's ankle the same time Chad grasped Deb's. Both girls yelled, declaring it a tie. Damien, Mike and Cliff slowed down when they heard the end of the race and finished at a more leisurely pace. Liz and Laurie greeted their guys with a kiss at the finish line. Cliff seemed unperturbed by his lack of congratulations, content to watch his friends receive their consolation reward. After the race the girls headed out to the patio to lie in the sun, while the guys pulled themselves up on the edge and sat watching the rest of the guests go back to swimming now that the race was over.

Unknown to all of them was the observer peeking in a window near the side of the building containing the changing rooms. Colleen had taken a chance and managed to follow Cliff when he left with Joey to meet up with Damien. She knew there was a big gathering going on and was sure Mike would be there. She had overheard Cliff telling Joey to be careful if he brought up a guy named Derek, or it might make Mike angry. This was supposed to be especially true if Laurie was in ear shot. 'Finally,' Colleen had thought, 'I have a name for who it is Mike is seeing.' She had been surprised to see Laurie was quite pretty. She had only caught the tail end of the race and saw Laurie lean down to the water to give Mike a kiss before she and the other girls went out the back door to a patio. Now was her chance to talk to Mike face to face. She could see all the guys were sitting around the end of the pool, talking about who knows what. Colleen gathered her courage. She went around towards the door which went straight into the pool area, skipping the changing rooms.

* * *

"So, impressive showing by the new guy," Liz teased Anne as the girls setup on the patio to have girl time and work on their tan. A couple others from their class were already set up on one end so the group moved to the farther end where they could talk. "He's trying really hard--maybe a little too hard. It could spell trouble."

"I think he's sweet," Anne piped up. "Nah, he just knows if he's on our bad side, then he's going to have a hell of a time hanging with the guys. What did Damien tell you, Liz? He had to have said something to you."

"Not really," Liz said thinking over the brief conversation when Damien picked her up. "He said Cliff was bringing an old friend of theirs. And he spent the last year or so studying in Europe. He wondered if you would mind, but I said more the merrier." Liz and Damien's relationship had started off quickly, but she was still put off a little by not ever going to Damien's house. He always picked her up when they went out, but she had never seen his home. He had put her off, saying he was embarrassed about his father's money and preferred to spend it on her than showing off his home. So far it had been enough, but she was curious about his life when he wasn't with her.

"Well, he seems like a nice enough guy," Laurie spoke up. "I think he's nervous, coming back to his old group of friends." Laurie had taken an instant liking to Joey. She had learned a little bit in the last month or two about the secret world Mike was a part of. It was obvious to her Mike was important because of his talents. Joey had seemed respectful, almost as if deferring to the younger man. Joey's demeanor won points with Laurie. "He also seemed to know which of us were taken and which of us were not," she continued, pointedly looking at Anne.

"I can't help it if my charms don't seem to work on those guys," Anne said, mock pouting. "It's nice someone finally recognizes the best looking of us." All the girls laughed and they began applying lotion and stretched out to relax. "I'm glad we can all start our senior year together. To good friends." Anne raised her soda she had brought out with her. The other girls grabbed their sodas or water bottles and raised them in toast with Anne. Then they all settled back on their towels.

# Chapter 10

"Quite impressive," Joey said to Chad after they watched the girls depart. "I thought I'd be able to mop the pool with you guys. I won a few competitions over in Europe, and was all state at my private school out east two years in a row. You sir, should consider swimming competitively."

Chad laughed, "I don't know. I have enough on my plate. To add anything else would be overkill. I think I'll stick with my soccer and Deb. Nice to know I have a fall back option if those don't work out. What happened to you guys?"

"You were too good for us," Damien replied, returning from the buffet bar with Cliff and cans of soda. He handed them out and then plopped down with his feet dangling in the water. "I thought for sure we would all be watching Joey show us up, but thanks for putting up a fight there Chad. He would always beat Cliff and me at everything, so it was nice to not see him come out completely on top for once."

"Don't be a sore loser, Damien," Joey teased, "I didn't come out completely on top. Anne is a fox, but you know I have a weakness for red hair, and you snatched up the redhead of the bunch it appears. Liz was watching you pretty close. Obviously she cares for you." He laughed as Damien kicked water in his direction.

"Now we just need to find Cliffy here a girl," Damien chided his friend, nudging him in the shoulder. "When are you going to let us fix you up. I'm sure the girls can find you a perfect match. Tell them what you like."

"I'm fine like I am," Cliff started, after swallowing his drink of soda. "I like things the way they are, uncomplicated." He shot Damien a look as if to say, 'Drop it.'

Mike caught the look but was confused. "Ah well, lay off him, Damien," Mike jumped in. "Cliff will find a girl who sparks his interest and then we will never get him to come hang out with us anymore." Damien noticed Cliff twitched when Mike had said sparks, but decided to leave him alone about it. Suddenly Cliff turned white and almost dropped his can of soda. Cliff stared over towards the changing room and Mike followed his friend's gaze. Mike did drop his soda as Colleen, his first love, strode through the door and started towards their little group. Luckily, but unnoticed by Mike, Damien had scooped up the can and discretely kept it from spilling with a little of his own power. He caught the look in Cliff's eyes and recognized what was going on a bare second faster than Mike.

Mike jumped up and with Cliff and Damien a half step behind headed towards Colleen, who smiled and walked in their direction. She jumped into

Mike's arms and kissed him soundly. Mike, in shock, stood frozen. Chad and Joey were on their way when Mike finally found his voice, "What… What are you doing here, Colleen?"

"Is that anyway to greet your girlfriend?" Colleen asked, assuming things would go back to normal. She noticed how Mike had not really hugged or kissed her back, but she put it off as shock at seeing her after so long.

Chad gave Mike a look at this point which spoke volumes, his fists clenched. Damien sensed impending violence from multiple sources and quickly intervened. He tapped Chad on the arm and drew him aside.

Damien whispered, "She's Mike's ex. Clearly she's tracked him down somehow. Give Mike a chance to set things right." Using a little of his gift, which he hated himself for doing, Damien convinced Chad this was the best course of action.

"What are you talking about, Colleen?" Mike sputtered, still shocked. He noticed Damien lead Chad away and speak to him. It registered what Chad must have seen and thought. This snapped Mike to reality quickly. He started to think he had hit his head and was dreaming. Then he got angry. "You up and disappear, then ignore me for three months. Now you pop up and think everything is going to be exactly like it was? Where have you been and what the hell have you been doing?" Mike took a step back away from Colleen. He had finally convinced himself to take a leap with Laurie and here was Colleen standing in front of him like nothing was wrong. While thoroughly confused, it started to anger Mike even more. He pushed away the threatening Darkness. It wasn't as easy without his necklace on, Mike noted.

"I will explain everything, can we go and talk alone?" Colleen said, putting on her best pout, hoping to soften Mike's attitude. He was looking dangerous again, like he had when he fought Kevin over her honor. "Please Mike? You know I would have called or wrote if I could. Tell him, Cliff."

This rocked Mike back on his heels and he turned to his friend, "Cliff, what is she talking about? How do you two know each other? You two better start making sense. What the hell is going on Colleen?" the last came out as a shout. Those other guests who had been swimming around rapidly found themselves a reason to be at the buffet at the far end of the pool house. No small few went out the patio door. This alerted Laurie and the other girls who quickly returned to see what was going on.

As Laurie came inside the pool house, she saw a blonde pulling on Mike's arm while he stood there looking furious. Jealousy reared its ugly head as she could hear the girl talking to Mike, "Please Mike, you know me. I only want to talk to you, explain why I couldn't write or call. Then you will see things can go back to normal now." Laurie quickly realized who the blonde girl was and started running in Mike's direction. She knew how messed up he had been over Colleen. Laurie had no intention of letting him fall back into the emotional chaos again.

"Colleen, I don't know what is going on, but you and Cliff both have a lot of explaining to do," Mike was starting, then he felt Laurie come up behind him. "Laurie, I," he started, not knowing what she had seen or heard. "I guess you should meet Colleen Nicholson. I have no idea why she is here, or why Cliff would know her, but I was trying to explain to her I have moved on. With you. Please don't be mad at me, I didn't know she was going to show up here." Mike was panicking. On the one hand, seeing Colleen was pulling up every memory he had managed to bury. On the other, here was Laurie standing face to face with Colleen, an event he had never thought would happen. He was torn and didn't know what to do or say.

"It's alright, Mike," Laurie said, much more calmly than she felt. She had never thought she would ever run into Mike's ex, but the scene had crossed her mind more than once. She had prepared herself for how she was going to act and what she was going to say. She turned Mike's face to look him in the eyes and smiled before kissing him. "I love you Michael Keller and that is that," she whispered.

"I hope that was a kiss goodbye," Colleen said in a snarl. "Mike and I have unfinished business, like the rest of our lives for one." She started to pull on Mike's arm again, but found him a solid wall. She looked into his eyes and saw the look he had when he had thrown the doctor across the room after waking up from his coma. Colleen tensed, prepared to throw whatever she could at him if he tried to do the same with her. Suddenly his eyes softened. Colleen had a brief moment of elation, perhaps Mike was coming around. Then she noticed Laurie whispering in his ear. With her improved senses, a benefit of her gifts awakening she had been told, she heard clearly what Laurie said.

"Go talk to her Mike," Laurie was repeating. "I know you two have to sort this out. Know I love you and you are always going to be my hero." With her final words Laurie squeezed Mike's arm and he turned towards her, where she promptly kissed him again. She then turned to the other girls, "Come on ladies, we have tans to finish before school starts." She led a stunned Liz, Anne, and Deb out the door to the patio to return to their chairs they had vacated so quickly.

Mike watched Laurie until the wall hid her from his sight before he turned to face Colleen. He sighed heavily and looked to see Damien was still talking to Chad over to the side away from the rest of them. "If you know Cliff, I am going to assume this has to do with a certain Council. Let's go you two. We are going to have a chat out front where no one will bother us," as Mike finished he looked pointedly at Damien, who caught the meaning and pulled Chad over by the buffet table.

# Chapter 11

"Why are you not trying to scratch that bitch's eyes out?" Anne was asking as the four of them returned to their chairs. "No way I would let her near my man." Anne took a drink as she settled back.

"Seriously," chimed in Deb with Liz nodding agreement.

"If I've learned anything about Mike it's this; once he gets that look in his eyes, an entire army will not stop him from doing what he wants. And what he wants is to get to the bottom of why she abandoned him." Laurie settled comfortably in her chair and pulled her hair out of the way. "And then he will tell me all about it, and everything will be fine." Laurie put as much confidence in her voice as she could, but inside her heart was cracking and threatening to shatter. A small part of her had feared this day would come, and Mike would take Colleen in his arms, to disappear from her life forever. Now Colleen had shown up, Laurie wasn't sure how she would go on if Mike did decide to leave her.

"Of course, hon," Liz said. "And once he gets his answers, he better send her packing back to whatever rock she crawled out from under." The other girls expressed their agreement and the four settled down to try and relax and enjoy their day together.

\* \* \*

"You two better start talking," Mike said as soon as they were outside. He carefully pushed a shield out to keep their voices from carrying, but not to seem suspicious should anyone walk towards them. Cliff and Colleen kept looking at each other. Things were clearly not going the way Colleen had hoped they would go.

"Well," Colleen started, trying and failing to clasp Mike's hand as he pulled away and crossed his arms. "I guess we better start at the beginning. My father worked for Damien's father since he was younger than us. When you were going to be born, we were moved so he could watch over you. Our meeting was arranged by the Council. So was our departure. They wanted you to come here this summer and weren't going to let me stand in the way of you being here. It's why I wasn't allowed to contact you after we left. I didn't know why at the time, only that my father was being transferred. I've been told a lot in the last couple months. Including that I have gifts like yours. Don't you see it means we belong together, Mike?"

Mike chewed over the information Colleen had laid on him. He looked to Cliff who was standing to the side. "And you knew about this Cliff? For how long?" He confronted his friend. Mike's mind was reeling from the news Colleen and him meeting had all been arranged so the Council could keep an eye on him. Mike felt even more betrayed than if Colleen had merely decided she didn't want to be with him anymore. Cliff keeping this from him hurt deeply.

"I only found out the day after you took out Derek and his father," Cliff said quickly. "Colleen has been staying at my house while my father and Damien's try to help her control her gifts. Although, for her to be here means she has finally gotten the hang of teleporting. Otherwise she should be sitting at my house." Cliff looked nervously from Mike to Colleen, unsure how to defuse the tension building in Mike's eyes. "I've struggled with not telling you, but it was thought best to make sure Colleen could control her powers before she saw you. Otherwise things tend to..." Cliff trailed off, looking at Colleen.

"Oh Cliff," she said. "Might as well tell him that things tended to explode or catch fire once my gifts were unblocked. You would be so proud of me now, Mike. I haven't set anything on fire in nearly a week." Colleen tried again to get one of Mike's hands but he stood stoic, his face impassive. "Now that I can control my gifts, we can be together again Mike." She waited patiently but Mike's expression never changed. "What are you thinking? Tell me you feel the same."

"I don't feel the same," Mike said after a few moments pause to gather himself. "I felt like my heart had been shredded when you were gone. I have spent the last three months finding out about my own family heritage, and putting myself back together. Now, I have finally moved on. Then you come walking in and tear me back up. How can I know what we had was ever real? The Council has meddled in my life since before I was born. How do I know this isn't a new plot?"

"If they knew I was here, I am sure Cliff's dad would flip," Colleen said quickly, with Cliff nodding agreement. His face had paled at the mention of his father. There would be questions, and Cliff was not looking forward to giving the answers required. "They've been pushing me to learn my gifts and to give up on you, but I never have Mike. I never gave up on getting back to you. I knew that once I could control my gifts we would be together again." Colleen got more nervous the longer Mike stared at her.

"No," Mike repeated, shaking his head. "I cannot do this. I'm with Laurie now and I cannot put myself back where I was three months ago. I am not the same person anymore, Colleen. I think you should go." Mike turned to head back into the pool area, dismantling the shield he had put up as he went.

"Mike, wait," Colleen called, trying to grab him by the shoulders. "This isn't fair. I came back to you as soon as I could. I love you, Mike."

She was shocked when Mike turned around suddenly. His eyes were intense and bored into hers, "I will always love you Colleen, which is the problem. My heart is finally starting to heal, and I refuse to let it be ripped up again. But I am 'in' love with Laurie and that is final. You should go." He then turned and disappeared back into the pool house.

"Mike," Colleen whispered one more time to his retreating back, knowing he would be able to still hear her. She then turned to Cliff, who was standing nervously nearby. He looked like he was trying to melt into the wall of the building. "Cliff, take me home please. I don't know if I could do it again. I was barely able to follow you here." Cliff nodded and took her hand, whisking them home.

They stood there, staring at each other for a few moments before Colleen collapsed into Cliff's arms and cried into his shoulder. For his part, he was conflicted. Part of him tried to comfort her and the other part was enjoying holding her in his arms a bit more than he should. He restrained himself to holding her and patting her back while she cried. The urge to try and kiss away her pain was nearly overwhelming.

After a few minutes, Colleen looked up into Cliff's face, "Why would he say that? Doesn't he know I would have called him if I could? You have to explain to him Cliff. I didn't have a choice. You have to." Colleen looked pleadingly into Cliff's eyes, tears falling down her face and her hair disheveled.

Reflexively Cliff reached up and wiped a tear from her cheek, the motion continuing into him pushing a strand of Colleen's hair behind her ear. They both froze, feeling the spark between them again. Colleen quickly pulled back and the two friends looked away. "I..." Cliff began, "I better go try and explain everything. To try, and, calm him down." He quickly vanished, leaving a confused and torn Colleen standing in the room they had used as their cover when they had snuck out to the club. As the tears starting falling again, Colleen fled to her room and locked herself away for the rest of the afternoon.

# Chapter 12

"**M**ike. Everything alright?" Damien asked when his friend came back into the pool house. Damien could see on Mike's face he wasn't but he hoped he could defuse Mike's famous temper. Damien looked to see a still slightly upset Chad was finally being talked into another race by Joey. 'I'm going to have to thank him later,' Damien thought to himself. He was having trouble overcoming Chad's desire to pound Mike into the ground because of Colleen saying and doing what she did. Thankfully the girls were staying outside for now.

"No it is not alright," Mike began, confronting his friend. "Why am I finding out like this? Colleen is not only back but one of us?" Mike dropped his voice in the last part, knowing there were too many non-gifted about. As angry and confused as he was, instinct still had him hiding his gifts from those not of their secret world. "You better have good answers, and so had Cliff when he gets back here."

"We do," Cliff said quietly, having slipped back and was standing behind Mike. "I think it best if we have this discussion somewhere a little more private, don't you think Damien?" Damien nodded and the trio headed towards the guy's changing room, careful to make sure no one was in there before Cliff spoke again. "It is true what she said Mike. Her father worked for Damien's father since he was younger than us. He exhibited minor telekinetic abilities and was picked up right away as an enforcer of sorts. Your family has always stood outside the establishment of the Council. This holding themselves apart, along with the minor interferences over the years made them wary. So when it was clear your mother was going to have a son, and knowing parenthood can often bond people. His family, including baby Colleen, were sent to befriend your parents."

"So everything about that part of my life was orchestrated by the Council?" Mike began, his temper flaring. "I should have stripped every one of them of their gifts and abolished the damned old men's club when I had the chance."

"Mike, peace a moment," Damien cut in, seeing his friend about to spiral into another rage. "We are in charge now remember? Things will be different now. And besides, your relationship with Colleen was real. Sure it was the Council who forced you two to meet, but it was you and her who formed the bond you did yourselves. It was entirely possible you wouldn't have gotten along and nothing would have happened there. Relax a moment and let us explain why things were done as they were."

At Mike's slow nod, Cliff continued, "When Colleen was a child, her gifts manifested right away, and they were wild and unpredictable. For her own safety, and the safety of those around her, her powers were bound. The night after your confrontation with the Council, she broke the barrier herself and her gifts, along with her memories, came flooding back. She has nearly burned down parts of my house several times until she could get control of them. This is part of why I have been staying in. I am trying to help her get the control she needs to be out in public. We cannot risk the exposure she could bring down on us."

"But I could have been there for her," Mike started again, seeing a little bit of wisdom in his friend's explanation. The betrayal he felt still burned hotly though. "The Council put us together, and then took her away from me. I said the meddling had to end."

"And it was going to," interrupted Damien quickly before Mike could get on a roll. "She needed to learn a measure of control. Given how emotional she is about you, everyone was worried she might set you both on fire, or worse, blow you up, if she saw you in the state she was in when she first broke the binding on her powers. I won't lie. Part of the decision was you were so happy with Laurie. We thought she might move on given more time and then it wouldn't be an issue. It's plainly obvious we were wrong and for that I am sorry Mike. Please, we only thought we were helping."

"Helping?" Mike retorted hotly. "I can see perhaps the apple didn't fall too far from the tree there, Damien. You are still meddling, exactly like your father. I had come to expect better of you too, Cliff. Keeping this from me all summer. Your hiding out from the rest of us makes sense now. I wish you guys had trusted me enough to tell me what the hell was going on so I could make my own decision."

"Mike," Cliff began, then fumbled how to continue, "We were trying to help, like Damien said. You were so happy with Laurie, and we didn't want anything to interfere. Honest, we thought she might have moved on as well because she hasn't tried to needle information out of me in over a week. I see it was her way of making me let my guard down. It must have been how she was able to follow me here. Once she had control, we had planned on getting the two of you face to face, in a private setting. Where we could all talk things out."

"Well, so much for that," Mike spat out. "I am going to go and try to salvage my relationship with Laurie. The four of us, Colleen included, are going to have a little talk very soon." Shaking his head, Mike turned and left the changing room to look for Laurie. Damien and Cliff exchanged looks before Cliff teleported home and Damien went in search of Joey and Chad. There was going to be harsh words from Chad, Damien knew.

As the trio exited, a fourth person they had not noticed stepped from a shadow he had been hiding in. Matthew smiled to himself at the information he had learned. His master would be very pleased to learn the Colleen situation could be turned to their advantage as it was already creating a rift between Mike, Damien, and Cliff.

* * *

"What's the big idea, Mike?" Chad started when he saw Mike come back into the main pool area. Joey was coming out of the water as well and it was obvious he wasn't going to be able to distract Chad any longer. "Who was that girl and why does she think she's your girlfriend? Are you two timing Laurie? Damien and Joey said there was more to the story but said I had to talk to you." It was obvious Chad was barely holding back from taking a swing at Mike. Mike suspected the reason Chad hadn't swung yet had more to do with Damien's powers than any self-control on Chad's part.

"Chad, I'll explain everything," Mike said quickly, an eye to the door leading to where the girls were sunbathing. "She's my ex from back home. Apparently she looked me up and somehow found out I was here. This is after her not talking to me for three months. I am probably more shocked than you are that she showed up here. I also sent her away and told her I'm with Laurie now. Trust me, if I had known she was going to show up I never would have let anyone else see her. I would have made sure to send her away quietly. Now, can I go talk to Laurie? I need to explain things to her. I told her today I loved her and then this happened. I'm sure she's more upset with me than you are." Chad nodded and Mike nearly ran through him to get to the door.

As Mike stepped out into the sun, four sets of female eyes locked onto him. There was confusion and no small amount of anger staring back at him. Mike almost felt like they were throwing daggers at him, by the hostility he saw in their eyes. He approached Laurie's chair and dropped to the ground next to her. He paused to look deep into her eyes, "I am sorry you had to see that. I had no idea Colleen was going to show up here. I haven't had any contact with her in three months. I swear I am telling the truth, Laurie." Mike gazed pleadingly into Laurie's eyes, hoping she wouldn't see the maelstrom of emotions swirling inside him. Mike believed what he said to Colleen, but it didn't stop the memories and emotions he had buried from bubbling back to the surface.

Laurie looked down into Mike's eyes where he was seated on the ground next to her. Her heart torn because she knew the impact Colleen had had in Mike's life. She could see the pain in his eyes but also knew the sincerity in his words. She grabbed his face and kissed him hard before speaking, "I am not giving you up so she better be prepared to lose if she tries again." The other girls seemed relieved by both Mike's speech and Laurie's reaction. "Now, as much as I like having you around, this is girl time Mike, so go back to the guys." She kissed him again, seeing the shock on his face. She giggled at having caught him off guard.

He only paused a moment before recovering, "As you wish, my lady," Mike replied seriously before his grin spoiled it. He kissed Laurie again before he got up to leave. He smiled at the other girls as he went back inside. His face didn't show the turmoil inside of him but he was pleased things weren't damaged between him and Laurie.

"See girls, nothing to worry about," Laurie said after Mike had disappeared back inside the pool house. She took a drink of her water and reached for her sunglasses before settling herself on her lawn chair. The other three murmured they were glad to see it before they too turned back to their tanning.

\* \* \*

Cliff and Damien met Mike as he came back in, both wore worried frowns until they saw Mike's smile. It dipped slightly when he saw his two friends, and a shadow flashed in his eyes. Mike quickly put his smile back in place, thinking only of the fact Laurie was not upset with him. He stopped in front of his friends, "Laurie isn't mad at me and knows I had no idea Colleen might track me down. I think the shock has no one wondering how she tracked me down, but at some point, one of the girls is going to question it. Cliff, you are going to say Colleen's father has taken a job with your father, but you had no idea of the connection between him and my past. He had brought his family with him and she must have figured out we knew each other and followed you here. That should satisfy any curiosity from the girls. If they push the issue, we will have to turn aside their questions. I don't like the idea of messing with their memories, but until I can sort out how Colleen factors into my life now, I do not want any problems. Are we understood?" The other two nodded quickly. It was times like this, when he used a certain tone of voice, they all knew Mike was the one in charge of their little group.

"Understood sir," Cliff replied instinctively, then he realized he had addressed Mike as a superior. Mike noticed it too; similar to how Joey had when he was talking with Laurie and him. "I think it better if we arrange the sit down quickly, Mike. Perhaps later tonight or first thing tomorrow? Probably best for all of us if we get this sorted out."

"We will see how late tonight runs first," Mike replied, noting the way Cliff's aura pulsed dimly. Mike had found over the last couple of months he could see a person's gifts even when they weren't actively using them anymore. It was strange at first. Then he figured out the difference. He still had never figured out what seemed so off about Cliff's powers. It was almost like they were tinted, or muted in a way. Out of respect for his friend, Mike had never asked Cliff about it. Cliff nodded in agreement with Mike's plan.

Things settled down for the guys the rest of the morning as even Chad seemed more relaxed about the revelation about how Colleen had tracked Mike down. Mike caught Chad looking at him from time to time, but there was minimal hostility. Mike knew there was mainly concern from Chad, who felt Laurie was like a sister to him.

When lunch was served, the girls all came parading back in glowing slightly from their time in the sun. The gang and the other classmates all gathered around the buffet table before breaking off back into little groups. Anne, as hostess, made rounds to each group and made conversation. Joey was dragged along and introduced around by Anne. Several of the single girls in their grade gave appraising looks Joey's way. By the time they had reached the fourth or fifth one, Anne had started to show a little possessiveness, taking Joey's hand in hers. For his part, Joey wasn't complaining. The rest of them thought it was hilarious as Anne made her way back to them, dragging him along.

"So, Anne," Laurie teased, "Are you going to let Joey eat or are you planning on monopolizing his hand all day." Anne turned red and dropped his hand immediately, then stuck her tongue out at Laurie.

"It's a good thing you are feeding Mike, because I don't think he has use of either hand," Anne tossed back, laughing. It was slightly true, Laurie had plopped herself down in Mike's lap and had been popping pieces of fruit in his mouth between kisses. For Mike's part, he had wrapped his arms around Laurie and looked to have no interest in getting any food for himself. The whole group laughed.

Mike glanced across at Chad, who had been distant the last couple hours, even after Mike's repeated reassurances everything was good with Laurie. The wariness which had crept into Chad's eyes melted entirely once the girls came inside and it was apparent Mike and Laurie were still solidly together. Deb talking to him about what Mike had said outside also seemed to help.

"So, Damien," Anne began from the chair next to Joey she had taken ownership of. The looks given any other females who walked too close made it clear Anne was staking her claim, for now. "What are you guys going to be doing while Mike is studying for exams and spending all his time in school this year?"

"My father wants me to spend time with a group of his business managers," Damien replied in a bored tone. "I think he is grooming me to take over more of the business as soon as he can convince me to get a management degree. If I do it doesn't look too much like favoritism." Damien laughed. The group had all heard the way he talked about his father. "I think I may push college off a year and go to Europe like Joey here. It seems to have done wonders for him."

"You better not leave me behind, mister," Liz said, a bit of the stereotypical redhead feistiness showing through as she thumped Damien's chest. "If you go to Europe some little French slut will snap you up and then what will I do?" The group laughed as Damien kissed her and whispered in her ear. By the way her face glowed afterwards, it was apparent to all he had reassured her against those fears.

After eating began the requisite wait time before swimming, though none seemed to think it precluded them from wading in the pool. It was during this time Mike's fears came to life as Deb looked right at Mike and asked what he had been dreading. "So, Mike, I hate to pry, but how on earth did Colleen track you down here?" As Mike stood there, caught off guard by the pointed question, Cliff came to the rescue.

"I think it may have been my fault," Cliff said quickly. "It appears my father has hired Colleen's father for one of his manufacturing companies. I never put two and two together even when they arrived yesterday. They are staying in our guest house until they make housing arrangements. Being close in age, my father thought I should act as Colleen's chaperone. When they arrived, and she saw those pictures from Fourth of July with all of us and Mike in it, the questions started. I was surprised she would know Mike, until I learned who she was. I had intended to tell Mike, but hadn't had a chance to when she showed up. She must have borrowed a car from the garage and followed me when I left. I'm very sorry things happened like they did." Cliff had put every bit of his considerable negotiating talent into convincing the group at large his story was true.

"It makes sense though," Mike added in, hoping to squash any further questions. "Colleen's dad was plant manager for a while where my dad worked. Those credentials get you noticed. How ironic Cliff's dad would have recruited him. Small world right?" Mike tried to be convincing, but lying did not come terribly easy to him. Deb shrugged, seeming to buy the story and Mike breathed a silent sigh of relief. Laurie, attached at his hip in the water, felt the shudder and leaned against him more fully. The group had taken up residence about halfway between the shallow end and the deep, so Mike's feet were planted firmly on the bottom of the pool, otherwise the added weight may have thrown off his buoyancy and caused them both to slip below the water. Mike, for his part, adjusted his hold on Laurie and kissed the top of her head. "So, who is up for another race?" Chad and Joey eyed each other before agreeing wholeheartedly. The two had found a common activity to be good natured rivals over and were willing to go against each other again. "Girls, will you do the honors?" They all agreed and Mike hoisted Laurie up on the side of the pool before swimming in long lazy strokes to the far deep end.

Anne started calling out there was about to be a rematch, and to please clear the pool. Everyone started to head for the ladder or the stairs on the shallow end. Once they were all lined up around the outside, the guys lined up in the water beneath their girlfriends. Except for Cliff, but a classmate of Anne's quickly stepped forward when she saw Cliff had no cheerleader. Mike was puzzled because she looked familiar, but didn't have time to ponder it long as Anne was counting down the start from her place above Joey's head. Mike knew this was really going to be a race between Chad and Joey, but he was determined to make a better showing then he had previously. When Anne reached one, Mike took a deep breath and tensed to push off hard from the wall. With a loud, "GO". The race was on.

The five friends started evenly, but it was readily apparent Chad and Joey were in a league all their own as they soon began to gain distance over the other three. Mike continued to push himself, determined to at least push ahead of

Damien, who he could see was also laboring hard to keep up. Rounding into the last turn, it looked like Chad was going to beat Joey this time. The assembled crowd cheered its encouragement for Chad as the local favorite. When his hand clasped around Deb's ankle a second before Joey's reached Anne, a loud yell went up around the pool. Mike never slowed, having mentally told Damien he planned to come in a solid third. The enthusiasm for the race was infectious and even Cliff managed to not fall too far behind his friends.

After Mike received his congratulations from a happy Laurie, he glanced over to see Cliff sitting and talking with the girl who had acted as his timekeeper. It took Mike a moment to realize it was Julie, the girl from the bookstore whose thoughts he had heard a couple months back before he had learned about his gifts. She looked different without her glasses; Mike was encouraged to see her laughing at whatever Cliff had said. He'd been worried for Cliff since he was the only one in the group without someone. Maybe things were turning around.

For most of the afternoon everyone swam or floated lazily about the pool. There were a few rematches between Chad and Joey where they traded wins back and forth. The other guys didn't join in on most of those, knowing the other two would be fighting for first and second. To Mike's great relief, the Colleen issue was not brought up again. Everyone seemed satisfied with the big coincidence of Cliff's dad hiring Colleen's dad. The party started to break up as dinner time rolled around and the buffet was mostly picked through. As the sun started to dip, the friends found themselves nearly alone in the pool house, lounging on some chairs in a corner. Cliff and Julie had picked seats nearby but a little apart from the rest of the group. It seemed they were hitting it off at least a little. Mike and Damien exchanged a look, "Good for Cliff," Damien thought to Mike, to which Mike agreed. The last few stragglers from the party waved their goodbyes to Anne and prepared to leave.

"Cliff looks happy," Laurie whispered in Mike's ear, having noticed where Mike had been looking a moment ago. "Julie is a quiet girl, but a good one. I think her parents own a bookstore. We have had a few classes together but we aren't close friends."

"I thought she looked familiar," Mike said, smiling at his girlfriend. "I wasn't sure at first. She offered to help me find a book once when I was at her parent's store."

With Laurie snuggled in his lap, Mike dozed as the evening progressed and everyone fell quiet. The exception was Cliff and Julie, who continued their whispered conversation until it was only the eight of them left. Suddenly Julie glanced out the window and saw it was starting to get really dark out. She jumped up quickly, "I have to get going. I was supposed to help my parents with the orders that came in yesterday late. I had a wonderful time Anne, thanks for inviting me. It was nice meeting you, Cliff," she spoke quickly and quietly, sharing a hug with Cliff before she took off to get changed and head home. With

Julie's departure it was like everyone realized what time it was and headed off to change as well.

# Chapter 13

As the guys filed into the men's changing room, they all began teasing Cliff. "So, did someone finally get your interest Cliff?" Damien said, slapping his friend on the back. "I say it is about time. You nearly gave Anne an aneurysm this summer because you wouldn't warm up to her. Good thing she seems to have set her sights on Joey or Julie might have trouble in her future."

"Yeah," Chad joined in. "About time you got yourself a girl there Cliff." Joey managed to get Cliff in a headlock and knuckled his friend's head. The other three were all laughing uproariously as the shorter Cliff struggled to free himself from his taller friend. Suddenly Cliff seemed to get his feet under him and managed to pick Joey up off the ground. Mike was surprised to see he did this without any spark of his gift. As Cliff twisted, Joey lost his grip and found himself dropped to the ground with Cliff half across his body.

"Ow," Joey said, rolling to the side and sitting up. "I forgot you wrestled in school. Well, I won't make that mistake again in the near future." He was laughing as he stood up and rubbed his chest where Cliff had pinned him. He extended a hand to Cliff who was laughing until he rolled over on the floor. Cliff took it and stood up with his grin still in place.

"Next time maybe you should keep your mind on your own business there, Joey," Cliff replied, "Or I won't go so easy on you." The grin on Cliff's face softened the harsh words into the teasing it was. The pair exchanged a hearty handshake before everyone started to change.

"Nice move there, Cliff," Mike found a moment to talk to his friend off to the side of the rest of the group. "I'm glad you and Julie looked to be hitting it off. As for the other thing we needed to do today. I think we better get it out of the way. Let's meet you know where." Cliff nodded, sending a message mentally to say he understood and would bring Colleen to the Council chamber. The friends had still unsuccessfully convinced the older members to move the meetings to a place less depressing. After all five guys had changed and bundled up their belongings to take home, they went in search of the girls.

* * *

"I am so glad Cliff has met someone," Deb said as soon as they had waved to Julie. She had been on her way out when the other girls entered. "I always felt bad he was the odd man out."

"Well, I tried to fix that for him," Anne said. "Can't blame me if the guy was clueless." Anne laughed and the girls joined in. They had all talked about Anne's inability to charm Cliff during the course of the summer. She had taken a fair share of good natured teasing saying perhaps she had lost her touch. The way Joey was taken with her today proved otherwise. "But it is good since I think I will be spending more time with Joey in the near future. Did you see how he kept pace with Chad in the pool? Too bad he isn't in our grade, they would be terrors if he has talent on the soccer field as well. Could you imagine those two racing down the field?"

"You are thinking about those soccer shorts is all Anne," Liz tossed her towel at her host. The annoyed looks Anne once elicited from Liz were gone since Anne's secret had come out. Finding out one of their friends had been raped brought all the girls closer. Only Anne and Laurie knew the truth of everything, especially the fact Mike had brought justice down on the offender. This had brought the two closer than they had ever been before.

Anne caught the towel and tossed it in a basket with her own. She had pulled a pair of jean shorts and a t-shirt over her dry suit, since the girls had not spent any time in the pool as the evening wore on. "Well, I cannot say it wouldn't be a perk. We all know it's why Deb doesn't miss one of Chad's practices unless it is life or death." She was then forced to dodge another towel as Deb had launched hers before breaking into a fit of giggles.

"Well, I'm glad we all have our guy to start the year with," Laurie chimed in. "Though I don't think any of us doubted Deb and Chad. Those two are attached at the lips." They all broke into giggles and, having finished changing, headed out by the pool. They were not surprised to see the guys waiting over by the nearly empty buffet table, drinking from soda cans and talking.

"Ah, here come our visions of beauty," Joey said loud enough for the girls to hear before they had crossed the distance. As one the guys turned to their respective girlfriend's, though it may be too soon to tell with Anne and Joey. It seemed to be heading that direction.

Laurie noticed Cliff was gone and wondered if he had rushed out to meet up with Julie on her way out. Laurie smiled at Mike and greeted him with a kiss. "Ready to go sweetie?" She entwined herself around Mike's arm and looked up at him. She could see there was a shadow to Mike's eyes and wondered if it had anything to do with their surprise visitor of the day. He smiled down at her and kissed her again, nodding. The friends said their goodbyes and retreated to their own vehicles. Since Joey had arrived with Cliff, there was a brief discussion of how he was getting home. It became clear Anne was going to take care of his transportation in Cliff's absence. Damien and Mike exchanged glances, knowing Joey didn't really need a lift, but they had to keep up appearances in public.

The ride home for Mike and Laurie was quiet. They didn't even bother turning on the radio as they enjoyed the silence of each other. When Mike pulled into her driveway a short time later, they knew their evening was going to have to draw to a close. The porch light was on and they both looked briefly for a curtain to twitch into place before they exchanged a long good night kiss. After a few minutes they separated to catch their breath and Laurie asked a question she wasn't sure she wanted the answer to. "Are you really ok, Mike? With her showing up and all?" There was no need to say who 'her' was.

Mike paused a moment, gathering his thoughts and feelings, especially those for Colleen. He began mentally stuffing them back in the box in the back of his mind where he had buried them. He looked deeply into Laurie's eyes, "I am as well as can be expected I guess. Shocked is all. To show up after three months and expect me to have been waiting, pining away. I know she and I are going to have to have a long talk, but hopefully that will be the end of it. She will need to see I have moved on, and she should to." The elation in Laurie's face at Mike's words gave him peace he was making the right decision. *'At least,'* Mike thought, *'I hope I am.'*

"I meant what I said Michael Keller," Laurie said, taking his face in her hands tenderly. "I love you and you are my hero. I am not giving you up." They then kissed again until movement in one of the front windows distracted them. Laurie glanced at the clock on the dashboard and nearly jumped. Mike grinned and quickly got out and went around the vehicle to help her down from the big SUV. She really didn't need the help, but it was an excuse to prolong their time together, as well as an opportunity to touch her again. Mike walked her to the porch where they exchanged a slight more chastely goodnight kiss before Laurie retreated into the house. Mike practically skipped to the SUV and climbed into the driver seat. With a sigh he put the vehicle into reverse and backed out of the drive. His night was far from over.

# Chapter 14

"So, explain to me again what the hell is going on?" Mike demanded as soon as he arrived in the Council chambers, scaring a whispering Colleen and Cliff out of their skin. Mike could already feel the anger and betrayal he felt earlier rearing its head, but it was in competition with the rush of feeling for Colleen. Mike knew if he wasn't careful he would end up in trouble.

"Mike," Colleen said breathlessly, stirring Mike's memories and feelings a little more. "You nearly scared me to death. I really cannot wait to master this teleporting thing. It seems so unreal. All of your headaches and the stuff that happened at school make so much more sense now." She came over to Mike as she spoke and tried, unsuccessfully, to wrap her arm around his. It was clear to Colleen that Laurie had her hooks deep in Mike, but Colleen was sure she could remove them given enough time alone with him.

"Sit," Mike commanded, pointing to a table off to the side setup with four chairs. "As soon as Damien gets here, we will go over a few rules if you are going to be around." Mike knew the only way he was going to get through this without breaking down was to stay hard as stone. If he gave Colleen an inch she would turn on her charm and take a mile. It was hard when she kept touching him. The feelings were nothing like the spark between him and Laurie, he noticed in a detached way. It didn't stop the strong feelings he had nursed for Colleen for years from rising up within again. He had to get her to accept they were over. It was the only way to put those feelings to rest forever. Mike watched as Colleen sat down with Cliff across from her, this meant that no matter which of the two seats left she would be able to reach him easily.

"Sorry for my tardiness," Damien said as he arrived and strode into the room. "I had to extricate myself from Liz before I could teleport here. Maybe you are right Mike and I should let her in on our little secrets. It would make things so much easier. I wish I had the spark thing of yours to know if she was the one or not." Damien froze, realizing what he had said and who he had said it in front of.

"Sparks?" Colleen's eyebrows seemed to be trying to climb up into her hairline. "What is Damien talking about Mike? You can't be serious about this Laurie. She's pretty, but we have years of friendship." She started to rise up, but Mike's tone of voice in his reply stopped her halfway from her seat.

"First rule," Mike intoned darkly, "You will not speak of Laurie in anything but polite terms or you will not speak of her at all. When I arrived here, torn up and confused, she was there for me. When I told her I wanted nothing serious because I might be going home in the fall, she was there for me. When I had finally decided to stay, and told her about my gifts, she was there for me. When I explained the attempt on her life had been orchestrated by a member of our kind in order to hurt me, she stayed with me. She has been supportive of my need for time and space to collect myself after you abandoned me. I don't want to hear excuses it was all orchestrated by the Council and you didn't have a choice. It doesn't matter anymore. It might have months ago, but not now. I am in love with Laurie, and even though I still love you Colleen, it is not the same." Mike had yet to take a seat. During Mike's tirade, Damien had retreated to the far chair and plopped down.

"See Mike, you still love me," Colleen said softly, pleadingly. "We can make this work. I still love you Mike, I always have. My feelings never stopped the whole time we were apart. My father said he had to keep messing with my memory to prevent me from contacting you the whole first month of summer. When I finally broke the block on my gifts and remembered everything that happened, I knew getting back to you was everything. I hurt you deeply, and though it wasn't anything I could have stopped, I am still sorry. I need you to forgive me." Colleen had finished rising and stepped towards Mike. Though his face showed no encouragement, his words certainly had. Colleen's heart felt like it was going to fly when Mike said he still loved her.

"I forgive you, Colleen. Forgiving you is not at issue here," Mike said, as coldly as he could manage. The longer he stood there with her staring at him with her blue eyes brimming with tears threatening to fall, the harder it was for Mike to remain impassive. The memory of her running into his arms the night he fought Kevin outside Tony's came unbidden to the forefront of his mind. He saw again the tears running down her face and the red tried to take over his vision. Blinking away the memory, Mike turned and walked to a small counter where coffee or snacks were laid out during long Council meetings. This time only the water cooler stood there, its stack of foam cups at hand. Mike filled a cup and chugged down the cool liquid. He then refilled it before turning and coming back to the table. He sat down cautiously, and raised a hand to forestall any comment or effort by Colleen to touch him again for a moment. Mike knew he had nearly lost control of himself and if he didn't regain his composure everything was going to fall apart.

"What I think Mike is trying to say," ventured Damien after a couple minutes had passed in silence. At no indication Mike was going to stop him speaking his opinion, he continued, "I think he is trying to say Colleen. While he is happy to see you well and alive, and perhaps even glad to know you are part of this world we are involved in; he has had a rough road the last few months and is happy with where his life is. If an arrangement can be reached for you two to remain friends, it would be great for us all. It is clear we will be running in the same social circles because of our powers. However, I think it best if it is clear there is nothing romantic between the two of you anymore." Damien, having heard

90

about the tantrums Colleen had thrown during her training, braced himself for her assault, be it verbal or otherwise. What happened was not what he expected.

Colleen drew herself up straight and looked Damien, then Cliff in the eye. She had tried apologizing. She had tried begging and pleading. There wasn't much else for her to do than to change her tactics. Then she turned her stare to Mike, "I may have been gone for a few months James Michael Keller, but mark my words, we will be together again. As soon as this Laurie realizes she cannot compete with what we shared, and do still share in the form of our powers, she will begin to resent you. She will see you staying with her as pity. When she finally breaks your heart and you come to realize I was right, I will let you tail along behind me." She then stood up and, after wavering a moment, managed to teleport herself back to her room in Cliff's house. As soon as she was sure she was there, she collapsed crying on her bed until she fell asleep.

* * *

Watching her go, Mike was stunned by Colleen's words. He looked across the table at Damien, then to his side at Cliff before speaking, "I am not entirely sure what happened there, but I don't think any of us have heard the last of this. Cliff, I hate to put you in this position but you are going to have to keep an eye on her. I am going to have to watch to make sure she takes no action against Laurie. I have no doubt she herself is going to try and turn Laurie against me and this world we live in so be careful what you say in front of her as well. I don't want Colleen left to run free." Mike sipped his water and sighed. "I would hate to have to take her powers like I did Derek."

It was Cliff and Damien's turn to be stunned. They were sure Mike must be joking. However, neither of them detected the slightest hint of sarcasm and Mike's mischievous grin was not present. Cliff swallowed hard, "Mike, you can't be serious. I get what happened with Derek and his father was necessary, heat of the battle and all. But you are talking about severing her powers because she spoke ill of your girlfriend. We have to be able to talk sense into her."

Mike nodded, "I hope so. I would not want to be the one responsible for it, but I made it clear. If anyone goes after my friends or family, I would see to it they were punished. The rule has to apply to Colleen as well." Mike stood up abruptly and sent his cup to the trash bin. "I'm going home to get some sleep. I will see you guys around." Mike then vanished himself, home to his Aunt and Uncle's.

Damien looked at Cliff, who was looking very sick to his stomach. "I know you were getting close to Colleen, Cliff. I also realize she has played you and it might hurt a little. You are probably our best bet to talk her out of any crazy idea she gets in her head." Damien made as if preparing to leave.

Cliff stood as well, nodding, "I know. No matter what Mike says, I cannot see him stripping Colleen's powers, or anyone else really. I hope I'm right." Cliff and Damien shook hands and then both zipped back to their respective homes.

Matthew stepped out of the shadows again. This time his eavesdropping had garnered even better information. He debated whether he would take a hand himself or merely report to his master. As plots and schemes swirled in the young man's head, he whisked himself home and to his bed. He was too tired from hiding his presence and following Mike around to bother with trying to watch on Mike the rest of the night, the likelihood he would learn anything more than he already had was slim.

* * *

Cliff knocked cautiously on Colleen's door. He had taken only a moment to gather himself before he went to confront the problem head on. As he paused before knocking a second time, he realized for the first time since Colleen arrived, he had thought about a girl other than her. Julie kept intruding into his thoughts. She was bright, well read, and seemed sincere in her efforts to get to know him. He smiled as he recalled their conversation, comparing their recent reading list and finding much more in common than he thought he would. He was so absorbed in his thoughts he almost missed the muffled, "Come in" from within Colleen's room. He cautiously pushed the door open and peaked inside to see Colleen curled up on her bed, her face buried in her pillow. One eye peeked over the edge of the comforter.

"What do you want?" Colleen snapped out before pulling the comforter back over her head. She did leave an ear outside so Cliff took it as a sign she wanted to actually hear his response.

He took another deep breath and figured he would start at the beginning, "Colleen, I need to warn you about Mike. When he came into his powers and had his battle with Derek, he managed to do what no one has done in centuries, at least, none we have been able to verify."

"I heard all about the stupid power stripping he did," Colleen spoke quickly, her head coming from under the blanket and the pillow falling to the side. "I don't believe Mike is capable of hurting me. All he needs to see is we are right for each other and he will drop that little bitch like a bad habit. He only needs time to realize we belong together. It would help if I could get him away from her for a while. Either way, I am not giving him up without a fight. If you aren't planning to help me be happy, then you can go away too." Even though she said the words, Colleen's heart was aching to have Cliff hug her again like he had when she was stressed and panicking over her trials. Although it tickled her mind she could not place what else was bothering her when Cliff began speaking again, breaking her concentration.

"He not only stripped their powers, Colleen, but he absorbed them into himself," Cliff said again. "What he did out of anger and spur of the moment, no one has been able to do in ages. His powers work in a different way than most, impulsive and untrained. He does things, without thinking, anyone else spends years to master. He also vowed anyone, and he means even you, from our world who harms his family or friends he will declare war on. If you go after Laurie in any way, shape, or form, he is going to consider it an act of war and take your powers as well." Cliff paused before continuing mostly to himself, "And I can't bear to see that happen." He froze when Colleen's eyes suddenly locked with his.

"What was that?" she asked, feigning she had not heard him entirely. It had been hard to make out, even with her enhanced senses. She knew Cliff had a crush on her, but she still struggled with her feelings, especially when he acted similar to Mike. She also couldn't decide a tactful way to bring up the spark she felt when she and Cliff touched. The lack of spark when she had touched Mike concerned her only a little. *'Is it significant?'* she thought to herself before Cliff interrupted her thoughts.

"Nothing, Colleen," Cliff said, his face reddening. Colleen could see he was nervous and embarrassed even in the dim light. "I think you should be careful threatening Mike, or Laurie. He is completely adamant in his stance. His friends and family are to be left alone. I fear he may see you as an enemy if you go after Laurie in any way. I don't think your history is going to make much of a difference on this one." Cliff shifted nervously from foot to foot, hoping his speech would make an impression on its target.

"Don't worry about me Cliff," Colleen replied. "I have known Mike since we were kids. He won't hurt me. It isn't like I want to hurt Laurie anyway. I intend to see to it she moves on and Mike comes back to me. That's all. She doesn't have to get hurt."

"Be careful," Cliff repeated before turning to go. He then said in a voice loud enough to make sure she heard, "I would hate to see anything happen to you. You are my friend and I care about you." He then left before she could say anything to stall him.

Colleen sat there on her bed for over an hour after Cliff left, thinking about what he had said. Not only the warning about Mike. Even as sure as she was Mike would come back to her, she could see the last few months had changed him. She supposed she wasn't the same either after having her powers restored. Colleen also tried to sort out her feelings for Cliff. He had been a great and true friend, and was only looking out for her. He would gladly be with her if she would give up on Mike. Colleen's head spun in circles until she finally collapsed, exhausted, and went back to sleep.

# Chapter 15

Since no one else was up when Mike got home the night before, he went to bed as quickly and quietly as possible. Saturday dawned clear and bright. Before joining his Aunt and Uncle in the kitchen for breakfast Mike took stock of the last twenty four hours. He had finally resolved and succeeded in telling Laurie how he felt. Mike believed wholeheartedly he was in love with Laurie. He had also been confronted with the one person who could mess with his mind and heart, Colleen. Not only was Colleen back, but she was gifted. She was nearly as powerful as he was before his taking of the Gohrs' powers if his assessment of her strength was accurate. Knowing he needed to do some last minute back to school shopping, Mike dressed and grabbed his phone, wallet, and keys. He headed out of his room and down the hall. Sure enough, his Aunt and Uncle were sitting around the breakfast table, Uncle Jim buried in the newspaper. Aunt Jenny, with her long brown hair pulled back into a utilitarian ponytail, was setting about dismantling a grapefruit, her usual morning routine.

"Morning Aunt Jenny, Uncle Jim," Mike said as he walked behind his Uncle's chair to get into the kitchen. After pouring himself a cup of coffee; Mike reached into the cabinet for a bowl. Coffee had never been a drink he really liked, other than the smell of it, but this summer had brought a change there as well. "I have to do a little shopping for school so I will probably be gone at least part of the day. I think Laurie is working a midday shift so I will probably be with her after she's done with work." He continued after they had said their good mornings.

"That sounds nice dear," Aunt Jenny said, having finished with her grapefruit dissection. She added a little sugar to it and took a sip of her coffee. "How was the party yesterday? Lots of fun? Everyone behave themselves?" She took a bite of her grapefruit and chewed while she waited for her nephew to respond. Uncle Jim appeared engrossed in an article he was reading in the paper.

"It was interesting to say the least," Mike said, pouring his cereal and putting the box back in the cabinet. As he went for the milk he decided to go ahead and get things in the open. "Colleen showed up yesterday at the party. Turns out she is gifted as well and has been training with Cliff's and Damien's dads since the day after I fought Derek." Mike kept no secrets from his Aunt and Uncle, knowing if anything were to happen to him, they should be prepared. "She seems to think everything is going to go back to like it was before her disappearance. I sent her packing, or at least, I made it clear I am with Laurie now. I cannot force her to go anywhere she doesn't want to. That's how Colleen has always been."

Aunt Jenny looked like she had tried to swallow her grapefruit whole the way her mouth hung open during Mike's revelation. "What does this young lady intend to do now? I will not have Laurie caught in the middle of a war again. She has done nothing to deserve it."

"Aunt Jenny, relax," Mike said quickly, coming over to the table and taking a seat. He arranged his cereal and coffee before continuing, "Laurie still has the pendant remember? No one with gifts can directly touch her. I will know immediately if they try. I also made it clear to Colleen, like I did the Council; any attempt on my friends or family will result in direct action from me. I also asked Cliff to talk to her. They have become friends since her family is staying with his right now. I think Cliff has a crush on her which should motivate him to keep her from doing anything stupid."

"And how do you feel about Colleen not only being back but being one of us?" Uncle Jim suddenly spoke up, spooking his wife and nephew, neither of which were sure he had been paying attention. Apparently he was. "I know when you arrived you were still pretty torn up about her disappearance. Where has she been and why has she reappeared now? Why didn't she show up right away if she has been in town for two months already?" Aunt Jenny nodded along with her husband's questions, obviously she thought they were all valid and deserved a response. She turned back to her nephew.

"I am not sure how I feel about Colleen," Mike began. "I know I loved her, and part of me always will. But I am in love with Laurie." Mike emphasized the difference. "Cliff and Damien told me she was kept away from public because her gifts tend to run towards fireworks when her emotions get out of control. There was concern about her exposing everything to the public eye. None of us want the publicity." Mike watched his Uncle nod. "Besides, I was, and am still, with Laurie. They didn't want to interfere with my relationship. I guess they thought Colleen might move on, or at least give up the idea of getting back together with me. She has made it clear she thinks Laurie and I are short lived and I will come to my senses."

"And what do you think is going to happen? Are you planning to end things with Laurie and get back together with Colleen?" Aunt Jenny pushed, making it clear her concern was for her Goddaughter. Over the last couple months, she had gotten the full story of Mike and Colleen growing up together. Their eventually getting together sounded like a fairytale turned horror after Mike's accident and Colleen's sudden transfer away. Aunt Jenny didn't want to see Laurie get dragged into any mess.

"I am in love with Laurie, Aunt Jenny," Mike repeated. "I may not know how I feel about Colleen's reappearance, but I am sure of my feelings for Laurie. Laurie has stuck by me even after she found out not only what I could do, but her having been a target because of her association with me. I don't know how I would have survived this summer without her." Mike tried to be as convincing as possible, and when he saw his Aunt smile, he knew she approved.

"I needed to hear you say it," Aunt Jenny said, reaching across the table and patting her nephew's arm. "I have seen the way you look at Laurie, and I cannot imagine you deciding anything else. Call it a woman's intuition." She laughed at the look on Mike's face. It dawned on him she was trying to get him to admit to his feelings, an act he had been struggling with. "You young men often have trouble admitting it to yourself, much less to others. I know your Uncle did." She giggled again at the look she got from her husband before he rolled his eyes at her and went back to his paper. "And I suppose you told Laurie this as well, did she see Colleen?"

"Everyone did," Mike admitted. "She showed up at the pool party. We told everyone it was a fluke Cliff's dad had hired Colleen's dad and they were staying with Cliff's family while they arranged housing. That was how Colleen found out about my connection to Cliff and followed him to the party. Everyone seemed to buy the coincidence. Cliff really sold it when Deb asked me about it. I hated lying to the rest of them, but it was easier than letting them all in on the secret. Laurie will know the full truth, but we didn't have much time away from everyone else to discuss it."

Aunt Jenny nodded and the two relatives settled into their breakfast. Mike chewed his cereal, and pondered what he was going to do now, with Colleen back in his life. The only recourse, he decided as he washed his cereal bowl and coffee mug about ten minutes later, was to make sure Colleen understands he has moved on. No matter how painful it was going to be for him. Grimly accepting his decision, Mike said his goodbye to his aunt and uncle before heading out to his SUV.

* * *

"Time to get up sweetie," Colleen's mother, Carrie, said after entering her daughter's room. "It's after nine and we have to go shopping for school on Monday. Get up, sleepyhead."

Colleen, for her part, was excited about going back to school shopping. She had not been looking forward to the new school after she had prepped for the one in Virginia after her father's transfer. There was small consolation in it being arranged for her to share a few classes with Mike. With any luck this would give her the opportunity to make him realize he belonged with her. Sighing and stretching, Colleen waved off her mother and got out of bed. She dressed quickly and headed to the kitchen to get breakfast before really beginning her day. Her mother was already waiting there.

"I love back to school shopping with you," Carrie said to her sleepy eyed daughter when she entered the kitchen. "Maybe we can get our nails and hair done and make it a real girl's day."

"Sounds like fun, Mom," Colleen replied as she got a bagel and stuck it in the toaster. While it warmed up she grabbed the butter and grape jelly from the fridge. She dug a butter knife out of a drawer and then went to get a glass of juice while her mother was already eating a piece of butter only toast.

"Honey, I know you are set on Mike," Carrie began, knowing her daughter might react negatively to the parental intrusion. Carrie had been brought up to speed on her daughter's gifts and the changes to the lives of the entire Nicholson family over the last couple months. She wasn't sure what to make of it, but she knew one thing was certain, her daughter was in love with the Keller boy and anyone who stood in Colleen's way was in trouble. "Maybe you will meet a cute boy this year. It is your senior year and it's supposed to be fun, not depressing, watching Mike be with another girl."

"Mom," Colleen said sharply, "I'm not going to be depressed. Mike will come to realize we belong together. We have so much more history than he could ever share with Laurie, not to mention we are both gifted. It is only a matter of time." Colleen grabbed her bagel from the toaster and began adding its toppings.

"I know you feel that way dear, and I would have been crushed if your father had moved on with anyone else during the summer I spent at my grandmother's in high school, but you have to be realistic. I know our situation was out of your control, but it sounds like Mike has finally put his life back together after his own revelations. At least the way your father tells it. I still can't believe I never knew about his powers before we got married. I guess it was important to be kept secret, but, he could have told me. It has been nearly twenty years." Carrie had drifted off into her own ramble and wasn't even noticing her daughter tuning her out. It had been quite the shock to find out what her husband and daughter could do. Even after two months of watching it, it still struck her how unreal it was.

"Don't worry, Mom," Colleen said cheerily as she took a seat across the breakfast table from her mother. "I know how I feel, and though he is trying to bury it, I know how Mike feels for me. As soon as this thing runs its course, we will be back together. So, where do we want to go first? Cliff was telling me about this mall with several good clothing stores. We could have lunch there and see if they have a little salon to get our hair and nails done. What do you think?"

"I think that will work great sweetie," Carrie replied, noting the certainty in Colleen's voice regarding her future. Carrie had learned all too well the chance you take when you pin all your hopes on one boy. She hoped her baby girl wouldn't get hurt. Carrie remembered the years watching Mike grow up and was unable to find any anger or dislike for him with regards to him moving on. He was always a polite and sweet boy. She watched her daughter attack her bagel and thought about the future.

# Chapter 16

It was nearly noon when Mike walked back into the mall near the food court. He had driven in the old fashioned way, enjoying the air through the open window on his SUV. He enjoyed acting normal and making a trip or two out to put bags in the car as he added to his already expanded wardrobe. Most of it was adding more winter items to go with what he already had. At a rumble from his stomach, he realized it was time to eat and began perusing the stalls to decide what to have this time. Over the summer he had probably sampled all the places at one point or another. He remembered his first trip, where Laurie had suggested the sandwich shop with fresh cut French fries. Feeling nostalgic he walked in the direction of the sandwich shop, where a long line was already forming.

As Mike stood waiting to pick up the order he placed a few minutes later he looked out across the food court and nearly choked on the sip of cola he had taken. Colleen and her mother were coming into the food court from the mall at large. At first, he was struck by the beauty of his childhood friend. It took him a moment to shake himself out of it, but he had paused long enough to be spotted. Colleen made a beeline for him even as he turned to grab the tray being pushed towards him with his food. He grabbed it and turned around, using it as a buffer against the opening arms of his former girlfriend. When she realized there was a tray between them, she paused and gave him a mischievous grin.

"Mike, it's so nice to see you," Colleen spoke brightly. "Doing some back to school shopping as well? This mall is so much nicer than our one back home, don't you think?" She brushed a hair behind her ear where it was loose from her ponytail. She knew it would set off memories in Mike's head and was secretly glad her mother and she had not gotten their hair done yet. If they had then it might not have worked. Her blue eyes sparkled as she smiled at Mike.

"Hi Colleen," Mike managed after her initial blast of speech. "I was, now I am having lunch. Then I have about an hour or two until Laurie gets off work. Hello Mrs. Nicholson, nice to see you again." Mike said as Colleen's mother joined her daughter.

"Nice to see you too, Mike. You're looking well," Carrie said as she stopped beside her daughter. She could see the slightly cornered and hunted look in Mike's eyes. She had also heard him affirm he had plans with Laurie. Carrie realized it had been meant to deflect her daughter. "Well, I am starving so I am going to get something to eat. Those fries look good, maybe I will have a sandwich too. Don't be too long Colleen, we have to eat and then we have appointments at the salon for our hair and nails." She waved to Mike and turned to go to the other end of the counter where you place your order.

"Are you excited for school, Mike?" Colleen asked, stepping to his side and following him towards a table when the next customers in line forced Mike to have to move or collide with them. "Senior year, high school is almost over. Going to be great, don't you think?" Colleen managed to lay a hand on Mike's arm until he set his tray down and pulled the chair out.

"Honestly, I don't know," Mike replied. "There's already so much going on. It doesn't feel like it would normally I think." The momentary contact had sent a shiver through Mike, but he was struck again how it was nothing like the electricity when Laurie touched his hand. "Are you going back to Virginia now you have control of your… condition?" He dropped his voice slightly, even though eavesdroppers were unlikely in the crowded mall. It paid to be cautious though.

"No, my Dad signed me up for high school here," Colleen replied brightly. "Looks like he and Cliff's dad are going to be working together a little more closely so they opted to keep us here. Looks like we will be classmates again. Just like old times." She accented the last of her speech with another blatant attempt to touch Mike's arm. To anyone passing by, they would look very much like a couple the way she had sat very close and kept her hands near to his when he wasn't actively eating. The average bystander would be oblivious to the rising tension between the two teens.

Mike could see what Colleen was doing and tried his best to ignore the effect it had on him. He finished a bite of his sandwich and picked up his soda with the hand Colleen kept attempting to hold. "So, you are staying here, huh? Remember what I said, Laurie is off limits. I would like us to be able to be friends but she means everything to me." Mike tried to make his voice as cold as possible.

"I agreed to your terms, Mike," Colleen protested in a shocked tone. "I don't see why we have to act like strangers. Is it so easy to forget about our friendship merely because I had to leave?" She batted her eyes and leaned a little towards Mike before swiping one of his fries and sat back in her chair. She chewed slowly, watching Mike for a reaction.

"I haven't forgotten anything, Colleen," Mike sighed. "That's the problem for me. I'm still trying to figure out how to act around you given everything I've been through in the last three months. Hell, you reappeared yesterday out of the blue. I'm still processing."

Colleen saw her mother waving her over to a table a short distance away and stood. "Well, at least can we try being friends again? Can I have a hug at least?" Colleen pouted, hoping it would do the trick. Mike sat impassive a moment, then nodded. Colleen came around the table and leaned heavily into him as she gave him a hug as he sat there. Her perfume filled his nose and Mike breathed deeply as he half-heartedly hugged her back. When she finally let him go, she turned her head and planted a peck on his cheek. "It is going to be nice to have one friend when I start school. See ya around, Mike." She quickly departed, leaving him momentarily stunned.

"Better not let Laurie see her do that," came a voice Mike almost didn't recognize in his distraction as Anne sat down across from him in the seat Colleen had vacated moments before. She had a sandwich wrap and a bottled soda instead of the normal fountain cups.

"Anne, great to see you," Mike recovered quickly; he was still touching his cheek where Colleen had planted her kiss. "I didn't know she was going to be here. We have known each other since we were kids. It's going to be hard to not even speak to her if we cross paths. I thought I made it clear to everyone where I stand."

"Oh, don't worry about me," Anne said after finishing a bite of her sandwich. "I said don't let Laurie see her do that. Colleen might find herself lacking hair or an eye." She giggled at the idea of Laurie attacking anyone. It brought to mind how Laurie had been possessive of Mike from the day they met. Anne smiled again thinking of the movie where they met and her failed attempt to insert herself into Mike's life. The two teens had become quite close since Anne revealed to Mike the real story of her rape. The inner wounds still stung at times, but she felt much better; it was not a secret between her and her friends anymore. The girls had all grown closer with the air cleared. It had helped Anne to come to terms with what happened to her those years ago. She still admired Mike for his role in punishing Derek.

"Well, I don't want any drama between the two of them," Mike said. He chewed a French fry before continuing, "Colleen says she's staying in town, so she's going to be a classmate of ours. Given our history, I know it might be difficult, but I would appreciate everyone not being too hard on her. A new school is bad enough, but the baggage she'll have will make it worse. She and I have been friends for a long time and I can't simply turn it off." Mike came dangerously close to saying he still cared for Colleen, at least a bit. There were things you don't say to one of your current girlfriend's closest friends. "It would be great if you girls could take her in a little. I know it won't be easy, but I think Colleen realizes she and I are not going to be together and she doesn't want to lose our friendship as well."

"I suppose we can give it a shot," sighed Anne, not sure if she believed Colleen was going to back off because Mike said so. With all she had learned about Mike's history, Colleen didn't strike her as one to give up easily. "I'll talk to Liz, but you're going to have to handle talking to Laurie. I'm not going to tell her to be friends with your ex. That's all on you, boy." She giggled as she took another bite of her sandwich.

Mike nodded and the two friends finished their meal in silence. As they both headed to throw away their trash, Mike glanced around but didn't see Colleen. "So, what are your plans for the rest of the day?" Mike asked Anne as they stood over by the garbage bins. Mike wasn't sure what was so funny when Anne burst into laughter so hard she clasped onto his arm and laughed into his shoulder. "What did I say?" he asked when she seemed to be regaining her composure.

"I was thinking about the first time we met here at the mall," Anne said, fighting off the last of her giggles. "I was so jealous of Laurie and you being paired up by your aunt I tried everything I could to spark your interest. I felt like such a slut for the way I acted, but you were so cool with it. And then there was everything that happened afterwards." Anne turned sad a moment. Her impromptu fashion show for Mike had turned into an evening where she had told her story and started the healing process amongst their friends.

Mike reached his arm around her and hugged her to his side, "It's ok, Anne. We are all past it. Besides, I wasn't complaining at the time. I can still look if you need to try on anything for me. Maybe some lingerie or a swimsuit?" He laughed when she turned to him and slugged him in the arm. Anne's small frame held a surprising amount of strength. He grinned and she started laughing.

"Laurie really would have a cow then," Anne said between giggles. "But no, sadly, I am all done with my shopping. I'm supposed to be meeting Joey for a movie this afternoon. What are you and Laurie doing? When I talked to her this morning she said she was supposed to meet with you after work."

"I don't know for sure," Mike replied honestly, shrugging his shoulders. "I know we have to talk, especially now I found out Colleen is staying in town. I think we will probably hang out and then grab dinner. I think it will be an early night because she has a full day tomorrow between church and work and choir rehearsal. Enjoy your date with Joey. Everything Damien and Cliff told me has been good. I'm happy for you. Maybe try to not be as forward right off the bat. Save the good stuff for the second date." He laughed as this got him another punch to the arm. The two friends then hugged and went in separate directions. Mike intended one more stop before he went to pick Laurie up, the book store.

\* \* \*

"Cliff," Julie squealed when she came out of the back room. Her mother had said a young man was asking about her and she had hoped it would be Cliff. After their introduction the day before at Anne's party she had been distracted all day with thoughts of him. They awkwardly hugged before they stood there staring at each other. "So, how are you today?" Julie asked, feeling nervous.

"I'm good," Cliff replied, not sure what to say. These were the moments he wished anything for Damien's or Mike's more outgoing personality. "How are you?" he asked back, stalling for time.

Smiling, Julie replied, "I'm great now. I wasn't sure if I really would hear from you so soon, much less see you again." She stopped quickly, realizing how desperate and pathetic she was starting to sound. She blushed and fidgeted with her glasses.

Cliff was struck again how cute Julie was, and the way she fixed her glasses drew attention to her light scattering of freckles. Recovering his senses, he spoke up quickly, "I was hoping you could help me find those books you mentioned I might like." He recalled they had spent most of the afternoon and evening discussing literature in all its myriad forms and sub genres. Finding much in common, Cliff was delighted to find out about up and coming authors who fit his normal reading criteria.

Smiling and taking his hand, Julie turned towards the shelves, "Right this way." The pair started off when a voice behind them called out. They stopped and turned around.

"Cliff my man," Mike boomed across the short distance. "Fancy meeting you here. Hello Julie." Mike clapped his friend on the shoulder and smiled. He had been pleased to see Cliff hit it off with Julie, since he hadn't seemed interested in Anne's advances. Mike wondered briefly if it would interfere with Cliff keeping an eye on Colleen but discarded the thought quickly. Cliff deserved any happiness he found.

"Hey Mike," Cliff and Julie said together before looking at each other. Cliff continued, "What brings you around here, I figured you would be glued to Laurie like usual. Or is she hiding behind you to jump out at me." He grinned at his taller, albeit slightly younger friend.

"She gets off work in a little bit, she's working a midday shift but we have the evening together. I wanted to pick up a couple books I had ordered last week. I have been so busy I almost forgot about them," Mike grinned. Then Julie's mother came out of the back room and saw the trio standing in the middle of the store. "Ah, I will ask your mother to get them for me, Julie. I wouldn't want to stand in the way of you making a sale. Nice seeing you again. Cliff, talk to you later or tomorrow right?" Cliff nodded and the two headed back into the shelves of books as Mike turned towards Julie's mother. When he gave his name she went to get his special order. Even after Mike had paid for everything, Cliff and Julie had not reappeared from the section she had pulled him off to. Mike smiled to himself as he headed out to his vehicle. He still had about an hour before Laurie was off and he intended to do a little reading.

# Chapter 17

Mike smiled to himself as he got ready for school on Monday morning. Saturday night with Laurie had been wonderful. They had an early dinner; then met up with the rest of their friends for dancing. Mike and Laurie cut out early in order to be alone. Laurie had handled the news of Colleen going to be at the same school this year surprisingly well. Mike recalled her final words, after he had asked if Laurie thought everyone could please try to coexist.

"Mike, unless you are telling me I have to worry about her, I couldn't care less," Laurie said. "I will try to be her friend for your sake, but she is going to have to behave herself." Laurie had then kissed Mike so deeply and firmly he was left thinking she was trying to obliterate the memory of every kiss he had ever had before, with either of them.

He chuckled as he strolled down the hallway to the kitchen for breakfast. He had to pick Laurie up and then head to school. Course, with his abilities, they could leave at the last minute and still be on time. Mike intended to do so. Then he could have extra time with her. Things were rapidly becoming more physical and Mike knew he and Laurie were going to have to decide if they were ready to take the next step in their relationship or not.

* * *

Colleen dressed in her best skirt and blouse combo and had her hair in loose curls about her shoulders. She knew as she looked in the mirror she was going to turn heads, she was familiar with being the focus of the school's attention. The only head she was interested in turning however, was Mike's. Suddenly there was a motion behind her in the mirror and she spun around to face a guy she didn't recognize. She watched as he stepped out of a shadow in the corner of the room and she knew he had powers like hers, before she could scream, he spoke.

"Don't panic please," Matthew Stenton said softly. "I am a friend, or at least, we have a common goal I think." He paused to study her with his piercing blue eyes. While not as tall as Mike, Colleen was struck with how much taller than her this guy was from her position seated in front of her mirror. "My name is Matthew Stenton, you can call me Matt. I am here about Mike Keller."

"I don't appreciate a strange person appearing in my room, Matthew Stenton," Colleen stated acidly. "How long were you hiding in my room? And how did you manage that trick? What do you want with Mike?" Colleen had tensed and was ready to strike out if she needed to. She had learned how to channel her pyrotechnics and with a little luck she thought she could manage to scorch Matthew before he could do anything to her.

"Calm down, Colleen," Matthew began again, "I only arrived a moment ago. I was hoping to catch you before school so we could have a little talk. As for my shadow walking, not many have the same talent." He grinned and flicked his head, his bowl cut blonde hair swinging slightly. "As for Mike, what I want, is him distracted. He is making enemies on the Council and it would be best if he found other things to occupy his time. I thought perhaps you might be willing to help me reach my goal. One look at you and I can see how you would distract any guy, but I am hoping for more. What do you intend to do about this Laurie of his?"

"I told Mike I wasn't going to do anything," Colleen stated simply. "I mean to hold to my promise. As long as I do not interfere in their relationship, then when it falls apart, and it will, I can be there to pick up the pieces. There is no way he can be truly in love with her." Colleen had stood while she was speaking and crossed her arms around her middle to stare down the interloper.

"I'm afraid you're wrong in your assumption," Matthew replied to her stance. He gave her a very obvious appraising look. "However, perhaps you will be distraction enough without doing anything overt. While it's true he struggles with his feelings for you, the self-righteous fool believes he is in love with Laurie. He's too honorable to break it off with her because of your history unless you give him enough reason to. So you can continue in your ignorance, or you can accept my advice."

"What did you have in mind?" Colleen said, unsure whether to trust Matthew's words. She knew in her heart she belonged with Mike and he with her. An image of Cliff's face, concern etched in his features sprang to her mind, along with the tingle in her fingertips when they touched. Again she was struck with how odd it had been. She still had not gotten up the nerve to ask Cliff or anyone about it. Damien mentioning Mike knew about it had caught her attention, but she wasn't sure if it was a topic she could broach with Mike yet.

"Well," Matt began, standing casually. "Start with little things. Don't do anything to draw undue attention to yourself. Especially since Mike can see a person's auras and know when they're using their gifts around him. If you can manage to make her think she is going a little crazy, or fearful of people with powers, all the better. If trouble were to be stirred up in his little paradise, it would pull his attention away from the Council and my master can counter his initiatives more effectively."

"I am not going to risk Mike getting upset with me and shutting me out of his life," Colleen said. There was a call from down the hall from her mother to come to breakfast. "I have to finish getting ready for school. You have to leave, now." Matthew inclined his head slightly and, still leering at her, stepped back into the shadow of her room. Colleen waited a minute until she was sure he was gone before heading down the hall to get breakfast.

# Chapter 18

As Mike and Laurie strolled into their homeroom class for the first day of school they took up seats next to each other in about the middle of the room. Neither were shocked to see Colleen not a minute behind them. Mike had figured Colleen would have found her way to most of his classes, but he intended to make sure she stayed on her best behavior. She exchanged a good morning with both Mike and Laurie before finding a seat near the edge of the room where she could better appraise her rival for Mike's attention.

When the teacher started taking attendance and handing out start of school paperwork, all three teens turned their attention to what lay ahead. When the teacher called for volunteers for the Homecoming Committee, Laurie and Colleen's hands both shot up simultaneously. The teacher noted their names on a form she had in front of her and told them the meetings would start after school the next day. Homecoming was about six weeks away, but the planning would have to begin right away. Finally it was time to head to their first period class. Mike was off to his AP Biology class, while Laurie was going to Spanish. The school was trying a different schedule this year and only doing five classes a semester, instead of eight the whole year. This would allow the students to take up to ten credits a year, but most would take one study hall so it should average out the same. Mike watched as Colleen stopped Laurie on the way down the hall, asking directions to the Spanish class they would be sharing. Mike hoped Colleen would behave herself.

"So it looks like we will have a couple classes together this semester," Colleen said as she and Laurie walked to their first class. "I am sorry about the other day. I really do hope we can become friends. Mike and I had a chance to talk and he made it very clear he is with you now. I want him to be happy and you seem to make him very happy."

Laurie retracted her initial prepared response, hoping Colleen's words were true. If Mike had been in love with Colleen for years, she had to be a good person. "I hope we can put that unpleasantness behind us. Mike and I are committed to each other."

"I understand," Colleen said smiling. "So, what is the school like? Is the football team any good? I was a cheerleader at the school Mike and I went to. I'm supposed to meet with the advisor after school."

"We're pretty good, made regionals last year with our sophomore quarterback. Now he has another year under his belt. He should be better," Laurie replied. "We have always had a small squad. My friend Anne is cheerleader captain."

"Oh great," Colleen spoke quickly. "Maybe you can introduce us at lunch?" Laurie nodded as they reached their classroom door. They both went in and found their seats. The teacher had assigned them based on last name to start with so this put the two in separate rows. This suited Colleen fine. Without Mike in the room, she had decided to test out what might spook Laurie.

As Laurie unpacked her books, Colleen sent Laurie's pen rolling onto the floor on the other side. It was small and petty, but she was trying to test Laurie's calm. For her part, Laurie barely registered any reaction. As she picked up the pen, Colleen tried to hold it to the floor but nothing happened. Her own pen however shot off her desk and bounced off the wall next to her before falling to the ground. Confused, Colleen grabbed her pen and studied her rival. When Laurie turned to glance at her, Colleen flashed her best smile. *Maybe this will be alright,*' thought Laurie as she smiled back.

\* \* \*

Mike and Laurie sat together in their English class and even managed to hold hands during the reading assignment. When they parted for Mike to go to his AP History class and Laurie was off to her Chemistry class, they shared a brief kiss in the hallway. Their English teacher, Mrs. Baker, called out to them, "Mr. Keller, Ms. Sterling, keep it clean in the hallways please. Save that for after school." She then giggled and went back into her room. Mike knew he was going to like this teacher. So far he had had two good teachers. His Biology teacher, a short balding man named Mr. Rodgers, seemed to have too much energy trapped in his small frame. He moved about the room rapidly as he talked about the experiments they would complete this semester and where to find the equipment. Laurie laughed when Mike told her.

"Yeah, he is a great teacher. He taught a biology class I took last year. And," she said, holding onto Mike's hand even though they would be cutting it close to get to their classes at this point. "Colleen seems nice. I think I can understand why you cared about her so much, and still want to be her friend. I promise to try."

Mike kissed her nose and smiled, "I cannot ask for more from you. She and I may not be a couple anymore and won't be as long as you want to keep me." Laurie looked about to speak but Mike continued, "Which I know you say is forever. But she was and still is a good friend. We have shared a plethora of memories and I want us all to get along. Life is too short and we are supposed to be having fun this year right?" When the warning bell sounded, Mike gave Laurie another brief kiss, on the lips this time and they turned down opposite sides of the hallway.

Mike walked into his AP History class to see Colleen sitting by herself at a table in the back. Most of the classrooms on this side of the building had two person tables and had doubled as science labs at one time or another. Mike saw

Chad sitting at the next table with another member of the soccer team so he went over and stood by Colleen. "Is this seat taken?"

"Mike," Colleen breathed, putting every effort into caressing his name. "Please sit. I was hoping we would have a class or two together." She smiled her best smile. She thought she caught him looking at her a little like he would when they were together. She had had time to think and she remembered now often seeing him staring at her glass eyed during the years they didn't associate much. It had slipped her mind before she had decided to reconnect with him at the end of their last school year. She hoped to provoke the same look often enough she could loosen Laurie's hold on Mike.

"Trade with me so I can sit on the same side as Chad," Mike smiled. He knew Colleen had dressed special for the day. It was nice to see parts of her had not changed. Even though he knew he was in love with Laurie, it didn't stop him from remembering his time with Colleen, as short as it really was. He waited while Colleen swapped seats so Mike could sit on the side with Chad and his teammate. They exchanged greetings as the bell rang.

Throughout class Colleen found ways to touch Mike's arm or push her leg against his under the table. Mike stoically ignored it when it was clear telling her to stop was only encouraging her. He started to think this was a bad idea when the bell for lunch rang and Mike sprang out of his seat. He turned to Colleen and gave her an exasperated look before he followed Chad out of the classroom and towards the cafeteria, leaving Colleen to quickly gather her things and follow in his wake.

True to her word, Laurie did introduce Colleen officially to Anne at lunch and the two girls sat at the end of the table to talk about cheerleading. Anne had pulled Mike to the seat next to her so Laurie took the one on the other side. This left Colleen diagonal across the table from him. After the third time Mike had had to push Colleen's foot away from his leg, he leaned to whisper in Laurie's ear, "I am going to go get a soda, do you want anything from the vending machine?" Laurie nodded no, smiling as she fiddled with her can of soda she had brought in her lunch. She didn't often eat school food, preferring a sandwich or a salad from home.

Colleen thought this would be a perfect time to try her powers while Mike was away. She concentrated on the can of soda in Laurie's hand, willing it to become as if it had been shaken violently. When Laurie popped the top of the soda, Colleen expected it to spray everywhere. To her disappointment there was no explosion. Sighing to herself, she reached for her own can of soda which shot out as soon as the seal was breached. She jumped to her feet and backed away as Anne did the same. Mike reappeared, grabbing a stack of napkins off the table next to them and quickly beginning to mop up the mess. He discreetly used his gifts to help. Laurie had slid over into Liz who was on her other side busily texting away with Damien by her lack of attention to the world around her.

"There, that should do it," Mike said once the mess was cleaned up. "Here, take this one Colleen, I will go grab another after I throw these away." He ran his fingers on his free hand through Laurie's hair as he walked away. When he returned a minute later, everyone had regained their seats, but no one was talking. Jokingly he asked, "So, did you drop it or what?"

"I don't know what happened," Colleen replied, then took a sip from the can he had left for her. She paused with the can to her lips and batted her eyes at Mike.

Laurie was engrossed in a debate with Deb about the syllabus from their chemistry class and had missed the exchange. She felt Mike stiffen next to her and turned to look at him. He had managed to push Colleen's foot away from his leg again, this time using his powers. He smiled at Laurie. Before she could wonder what was going on he kissed her nose lightly and she turned back to listen to what Deb was saying. Mike cut his eyes towards Colleen and pushed a thought to her, "Cut it out Colleen."

She paused, having practiced this with Cliff a little. She sent back, "What? A girl can't let a guy know what he's missing out on? I said I wouldn't take action against Laurie, but that doesn't mean I can't fight for us in other ways. Besides, it is fun to get you riled up."

"Well, cut it out," Mike snapped mentally before closing the connection. He turned, wrapping an arm around Laurie who responded by leaning back against him. He spent the rest of lunch enjoying the smell of his girlfriend's hair while listening to her and Deb discuss what project they were going to do for the first quarter.

After lunch Mike, Laurie and Colleen all had an advanced calculus together. Mike found himself thinking about his last math class, and how he had been forced to fake an illness to save his teacher from a falling blackboard. Mike pondered his lack of visions since his powers had fully come to him as he copied down the formulas the teacher wanted memorized to start the semester off with.

When he concentrated, he was able to see the last two they were supposed to copy and quickly jotted them down. He looked up to catch Colleen watching him again. He was struck by the similarities between this and another fateful day where he had used his gift to work ahead of the teacher. Colleen had caught on to Mike being off that day. He grinned and pretended to follow along with the rest of the class.

"Cheater, that's not fair, or is this teacher going to be the victim of an accident as well?" came Colleen's voice clear in his mind. He looked back at her and saw her suppressing a giggle as she pushed a loose curl of her blonde hair behind her ear. No one else noticed the exchange.

When the bell rang, Mike gathered up his belongings and took Laurie's from her once she was packed. He had arranged his schedule with a study hall at the end of the day so that he could complete any homework, or best case, sneak into the back of her Choir class and hear her sing. Since this was the first day of school, he had already arranged with the teacher to sit in on Laurie's class. They walked together to the room for Laurie's class and paused outside while there was a spare minute to talk, but mainly to share a quick kiss.

"Hey, get a room you two," Anne called as she passed in the other direction on the way to her class, causing the couple to separate as if they had been shocked. They laughed and shouted back at her to get to class before, giggling to themselves, they went into the choir room. Mike took a seat in the back, out of the way. He watched as the teacher passed out sheet music for the Fall Fest concert program and arranged the returning students into their sections. There were a few newcomers who had to run through practice exercises to place them appropriately. Mike had hoped he wouldn't be a distraction but he quickly noticed he had nothing to worry about. Laurie was all business in class. She rarely spared a look his way the entire period.

\* \* \*

Colleen sat in her car and wept after school. She had watched Mike walk out with Laurie, hand in hand, smiling as they went to the big black SUV she had learned was his. "That should be me," she whispered to the steering wheel.

"You are right," stated Matthew as he appeared in the passenger seat next to her. "I take it our plans for today did not go as well as hoped?" He produced a tissue from his pocket and handed it over to Colleen, who took it hesitantly.

She dabbed at her eyes slowly and sniffled. "No, they did not," she said after a calming breath. "I was able to roll her pencil across the desk, but when I tried to pin it to the floor nothing happened. At lunch I ended up exploding my own soda instead of hers. I don't think this is going to work." Colleen felt like her heart was breaking when she watched Mike with Laurie throughout the day. She had been encouraged by his edict to his friends to try and accept Colleen into their circle. It had to mean he still cared about her.

Matt sat, thinking over Colleen's report. He had had other things to contend with so he was not able to keep tabs on her progress throughout the day. "I am willing to bet Keller has protected her with a ward. Which means we have to separate her from whatever is granting her his protection." He tapped his lips, deep in thought while Colleen shifted nervously in the driver's seat. "It has to be an object or piece of jewelry. Was she wearing any rings or necklaces you saw?" Matt turned to face Colleen, shaking her from her own thoughts.

"I didn't see any rings, but she had a silver chain on. I couldn't see what was in it as she kept it tucked in the top of her shirt," Colleen replied. "It reminded me of the chain I would wear my ex's class ring on." The thought of another girl wearing Mike's ring burned inside of Colleen and her hands where she gripped the steering wheel started to smoke. As the smell of burning rubber from the grip began to fill the car she jerked her hands away, but Matthew was already gone. Shaking her head, Colleen started her drive home.

# Chapter 19

Things grew tense as the week went on with Colleen making every effort to make Mike's life more difficult. She was the picture of innocence whenever Laurie was watching. However, the Chemistry class Mike shared with Colleen became unbearable. Halfway through class on Wednesday, Mike shielded their voices from the rest of the room.

"Cut it out, Colleen," He shouted. If it had not been for the wall constructed the next classroom may have heard him. "I have made it clear to you I'm with Laurie now."

"Mike," Colleen said breathlessly, marveling at the ease with which he had constructed their little bubble of privacy. "Whatever do you mean?" She continued to run the toe of her shoe up his calf. "Are you thinking inappropriate thoughts about me? I don't think your girlfriend would like that." She winked at him. "But I might."

Groaning in frustration, Mike lowered the wall and tried to focus on the lesson for the day. He couldn't understand what Colleen's end game here was, but it was only serving to make him angry. Mike felt sure in his decision to stay with Laurie, but Colleen's constant flirtations affected his concentration. The feelings and memories he carefully buried kept bubbling to the surface. When the bell rang, Mike ran out the door before Colleen even finished zipping up her backpack.

\* \* \*

After school, Colleen sat in her car, a smile on her lips despite the glare in her eyes as she watched Mike walk to his SUV with Laurie. "That will be me before too long." She muttered to herself.

"I take it you are making progress?" Matthew said from his spot in the backseat where he appeared. He had watched from time to time Colleen's attempts to befriend Laurie while simultaneously flirting with Mike. Matthew was impressed with how easily she pushed Mike's buttons.

"I wish you wouldn't sneak up on me," Colleen scolded. She wasn't sure what to make of this Matthew Stenton yet. She had been too worried to try and bring him up with Cliff in case it would set him off. "And yes, I am getting under his skin. I can tell I am chipping away at the wall he put between his love for me and the rest of his life. Laurie is coming along. Before long she will trust me and I will be able to find out what protection Mike has on her and then can convince her it won't protect her from those with powers. If I can scare her enough with what is out here, then I shouldn't have too far to go for her to drop Mike and move onto a guy more her own level."

"Sounds like a splendid plan," Matthew said encouragingly. "I hope to see more concrete results soon. My master is awaiting the opportunity to make his move. I'll be in touch." Matthew disappeared and Colleen headed home.

* * *

Before their shared Spanish class Thursday morning, Colleen stood talking with Laurie in the hall. Mike took a phone call before his next class so the girls walked to class together. "So, doesn't it scare you a little what Mike can do? What others can do?" Colleen asked, pushing all the friendly concern she could manage into her question.

"No," Laurie said quickly. She still wasn't sure what to make of Colleen. She was trying to be friendly, if only for Mike's sake. She thought she had seen looks pass between the two of them in the last two days. Laurie wasn't sure she understood. Her quick response was followed with, "Well, not really. I know Mike won't let anything happen to me. Anyone who comes after me is in for a big surprise even if Mike isn't there." Laurie said proudly, touching the talisman through her shirt. She had wanted to wear it publicly, proud of Mike's gift. Mike had said it was more effective when the pendant touched her skin so she wore it underneath her clothes from then on. When she touched it, Laurie was sure she could feel Mike smiling at her.

Colleen had watched how Laurie's hand often went to a silver chain hung around her neck. Colleen speculated it had to do with Mike but the shape didn't resemble a ring so she didn't think it was a class ring. She wasn't quite confident she had won Laurie over enough to ask point blank about it, yet.

"It's obvious Mike would move heaven and earth, literally, for you," Colleen said. "I don't know how I would feel knowing about this other stuff when I couldn't defend myself. That accident over summer sounds horrible."

Laurie weighed the words and body language of her classmate. She kept telling herself she had nothing to worry about, but it seemed clear Colleen had an ulterior motive to how friendly she was being. She said instead, "It was scary when I thought it was merely an accident. When I found out it was a targeted attack, I nearly fell apart. Mike risked his life to save me and I knew my heart was his then. He then went further to punish the one who attacked me. It was all I would need to know about him to know how great he is. Nothing, no gifted or otherwise, will stop me from loving Mike."

Colleen nodded, "That's the Mike I know. Even before he knew what was going on with him he did whatever he could to save people." The bell rang and the girls turned to go inside. "Did he tell you about our prom night?"

"He told me parts of it," Laurie whispered as the girls were taking their seats. "Maybe we can talk about it later." Laurie began unpacking her book and Colleen smiled.

*'Whatever keeps her safe is definitely around her neck,'* Colleen thought to herself. *'I'm sure I'm getting in Mike's head. He won't be able to resist me forever. But Laurie is so nice.'* Colleen was starting to feel torn about trying to break them up. *'Mike is happy with her. Shouldn't I be happy for him?'* By the end of class Colleen felt farther than ever from sorting out her feelings.

The events of the Homecoming Committee meeting in the afternoon made her decision to sabotage Mike and Laurie's relationship harder. It became clear from the opening talks Laurie and Colleen were born to lead and they quickly had a rough outline of the preparations they would need to make.

Mike hung out in the back of the room during the meeting so he could take Laurie home afterwards. As everyone wrapped up to leave, he came up to the front of the room where Laurie and Colleen checked over the notes they made. He was impressed with how the two girls had worked in tandem. Watching Colleen lead the meeting like she handled the popular clique at their last school brought back fond memories. Mike forced his emerging feelings back below the surface by focusing his attention on Laurie. She had grown up with most of the other committee members and they all seemed to follow her lead naturally.

On the way he passed Anne, who attended as a representative of the cheer squad. She grabbed Mike's hand as he came by. "Mike, I have to say, I'm impressed with Colleen. She's a pro at this stuff."

"She was in charge at our old school. I am glad she's fitting in so well already," Mike replied grinning. He was proud of how well Colleen was doing with the adjustment to her gifts and a new school. *'If only she would move on and stop her flirting with me before Laurie catches on,'* he thought to himself.

Anne noticed the darkening of Mike's expression but let it go. She knew looks passed between Colleen and Mike, but had not said anything to either of her friends because she didn't want to cause problems if there wasn't anything to worry about. "Well, I gotta get going. But see you tomorrow, Mike." She gave him a brief hug and then turned to wave at Laurie, who had her head together with Colleen and didn't notice.

Colleen let Laurie talk and so she could pick up on the exchange between Anne and Mike. *'Mike is glad I am fitting in so well,'* she felt warm inside before a measure of ice returned when he leaned over Laurie and kissed her softly on the neck.

"You ladies about wrapped up for the day?" he asked, resting his chin on Laurie's shoulder. Laurie's hand had gone up immediately to lightly touch his cheek. Her eyes however, never left her notes.

"I think so," Laurie said, smiling. "Unless there is anything you want to talk about before we leave, Colleen?"

Colleen shook her head in the negative, "I think that's about all we can do today. By Friday afternoon we should have the numbers from the football boosters about how much funding they expect from concessions this year we can use towards the dance."

The trio gathered up their belongings and left the school. The parking lot was mostly empty as they waved goodbye and went their separate ways. Mike took Laurie home and then headed to get ready for a meeting tonight with the Council. He only hoped tonight wouldn't run too late. He had questions for his financial adviser as well. *'Going to be a busy afternoon,'* he thought to himself as he drove home.

# Chapter 20

Colleen lay on her bed in her room, absentmindedly chewing on her pencil eraser when there was a knock at her door. She was so startled she nearly bit the end of the pencil before she called out, "Who is it?" She figured it was her mom checking on her again. She felt an odd rush of warmth when it was Cliff who poked his head in her door.

"Colleen," Cliff began, "Can I come in a minute?" Halfway through the door, the sight of her made his pulse race. He was concerned with her adamant stance she and Mike would be back together quickly. Busy with the Council and his family's business dealings, there was no real chance to catch up with her since school started on Monday.

"Sure, Cliff," Colleen replied brightly as she sat up, shuffling her books and papers to the side. "You have been hard to find the last couple of days. You aren't avoiding me are you?" She knew to tease him was wrong but she realized how much she missed all the time they spent together before the previous weekend.

"No," Cliff said nervously as he sat in the chair across from her bed. It was a big cushioned affair which could almost seat two, if they didn't mind sitting really close. "It's been a busy few days with meetings. My father is pushing me to take a more active role. How do you like the school? Everyone playing nice?" He instantly regretted the poor word choice.

Colleen caught the meaning in his question and almost snapped at him. The nervous way he shifted his feet and hands made her smile return. "It's great. My teachers are great and everyone seems really nice. I think Laurie and I are going to be good friends one day."

"You aren't causing any trouble for Mike and Laurie, are you?" Cliff took his task of keeping Colleen from angering Mike seriously, but he wasn't sure exactly how he was supposed to keep her in line. Especially when being around her caused reason to fly out of his head.

"I said I wouldn't attack Laurie or anything," Colleen replied angrily. "I actually like Laurie. I still don't think she belongs with my Mike. I get he saved her life from Derek, but that's Mike. He would have done it for anyone. What he and I had is special and it will prevail."

Cliff stood up and walked over to stand near Colleen. "I really wish you would drop this Colleen. He moved on. You should too. I," He stopped suddenly as he had reached to take Colleen's hand and the ensuing shock froze his tongue.

As Cliff stood and approached her, Colleen momentarily lost herself in watching him instead of what he was saying. She seemed distanced from her body as she saw him reach down to take her hand in his. When the pulse ran through her, she felt her body react, closing her eyes and tilting her head back. Her lips parted all on their own as she pictured the night of Mike's fight with Kevin outside of Tony's. She remembered crying and running into Mike's arms, waiting for him to lean down and kiss her.

Cliff saw and felt Colleen's reaction to him taking her hand. He had always felt very self-conscious around girls, especially pretty ones. When she tilted her head back and closed her eyes, he hesitated a moment before leaning forward to kiss her. It was like the start to all the dreams plaguing him since the night they got a little drunk and made out.

As their lips touched, Colleen flashed back to reality. Pulling away, she left Cliff standing there awkwardly leaned toward her. "Cliff, we shouldn't," Colleen said breathlessly. She wanted to. The feeling she got when Cliff touched her was like electricity running up from her hand into her brain. "I am going to be with Mike." For a moment she wasn't so sure Mike was what she wanted as the memory in her mind wavered between Mike and Cliff. Cliff knocking out the pushy guy at the club was winning more and more in her mind, even though she still felt her heart belonged to Mike.

"I won't push you, Colleen," Cliff said, releasing her hand reluctantly. The crestfallen look on his face almost made her regret pushing him away. "I want you to be happy. If you keep down this road after Mike, I don't think you are going to be happy." He turned and left quickly before she could respond.

For nearly an hour after Cliff left, Colleen alternated between anger and sadness. She got angry at Mike, at Laurie, and especially at Cliff. She knew Mike belonged with her, why couldn't he see it as well? Then she was sad and crying at the frustration of the situation. The next minute she was comparing the way she had felt when Mike touched her with the electric feeling caused by brushing up against Cliff. "What does it all mean?" she asked the walls of her room.

"What does what all mean?" Matthew said as he stepped into her room from a shadow in the corner. "Forgive me for not knocking but I would rather not run into Cliff or his family. I have a meeting to attend soon but I wanted to get an update from you real quick."

"I don't know if I can go through with this," Colleen said, drying her eyes with a tissue from her nightstand. She had decided she liked Laurie and didn't really wish her harm, even if it freed Mike. She wasn't sure what she felt about Cliff, but she was almost ready to ask what the connection between them seemed to be.

"What do you mean you can't go through with this?" Matthew asked, his voice hardening. "Don't you want your precious Mike back? I thought getting him was the goal of all this. You get Mike back, and my master gets his way with the Council. Do you think it's too hard to shove aside a pathetic normal?"

"She isn't a pathetic normal," Colleen railed back. Now she was getting angry again. This stranger who could come and go from the shadows at will was pushing the wrong buttons. "Laurie is a nice girl who has tried to be my friend even though she knows I love Mike as much or more than she thinks she does. She has been nothing but understanding the last couple days as I have tried to settle into a new school with my ex-boyfriend as the only person I knew. Leave me alone."

"I'm sorry," Matthew quickly backtracked. "Have you figured out what protection Mike has put on Laurie?"

"She has something on a necklace preventing any powers from coming near her," Colleen replied without thinking. She instantly regretted her words. "Now leave, I don't want to see you again. I'm not going to do anything to Laurie and Mike." She gathered her gift, prepared to make him leave or be torched.

Having gained confirmation of what he already suspected, Matthew bowed politely. "I'll take my leave then, Colleen. It has been a pleasure seeing you, as always." He then stepped back and disappeared. Colleen's small burst of flame appeared where he had been standing.

"GRRR," Colleen groaned to the wall. She then buried her face in her pillow and cried. She waved her mother off when she was called to dinner and ignored Cliff's tentative knock on her door in the evening. Ignoring her friend was harder than ignoring her mother, but Colleen wasn't done sorting the maelstrom of emotions in her head and heart.

* * *

Cliff turned from Colleen's door. She hadn't responded to his knock like she normally does when he returned home after a Council meeting. Colleen was always interested in anything concerning Mike. Disappointment filled Cliff. He looked forward to these visits with her, even if another guy was the focus of conversation. The spark he felt each time they touched bothered him. He didn't feel the same with Julie, even though he was extremely attracted to her. He turned down the hall in search of the one person who could advise him, his father.

"Come in, son," Clifford responded to his progeny's knock. He came to be very impressed in the work his son and friends were doing. His perusal of the financial data and reports from those members who had gone along with their plans looked promising. All participants reported as being optimistic of future changes.

"Dad," Cliff started, before plopping down in a chair across from his father. "I need to ask you about when you met mom. How did you know she was the one for you?"

"Well, your mother is a unique woman," Clifford replied smiling. "I went to college rather full of myself, prepared to run the campus. It went well for the first year. Even as a freshman I had status and wealth, which put me ahead of most of those in the higher grades. My Sophomore year there was a freshman who tested into an English Lit class I was taking. She was infuriating. She debated every interpretation I put forward." He smiled thinking about those days.

"So mom drove you nuts?" Cliff asked. His parents had always appeared very much in love. He felt odd he had never asked how they met before.

"Oh, certifiably," Clifford laughed. "Finally, after the semester exams were over, I stopped her in the hallway to ask her what her problem was. When I grabbed her arm I was taken clean off my feet. I thought she had hit me, but she looked as surprised as I was. It took us both a few minutes to catch our breath."

This is what Cliff had hoped to hear; something akin to what he felt when he touched Colleen. "So there was a spark? Like a physical manifestation of your gift?"

"That is what I figured out it was after I talked to my father about it. He said it happens often with those of our kind when we find a person who would be a match," Clifford paused. "Is this Julie you have been talking about causing you to feel sparks?"

Cliff shook his head, "Not really Dad. Julie is great. She is intelligent and funny. Beautiful in a subtle way. But I don't know what my feelings about her are."

"Then what is it, son?" Clifford asked, taking a sip of his drink while the younger man responded.

"Well, Mike had talked about a spark between him and Laurie. Damien brought it up saying he had not felt it with Liz but didn't seem concerned about it. It made me think, should I be looking for it?" Cliff looked up from his lap to his father, meeting the older man's gaze.

"If you find it, hold onto it, son," Clifford said, already thinking this had everything to do with the Nicholson girl. "I have never heard of a time it wasn't a good thing when one of our kind feels the connection with another person, be they gifted or not."

Cliff stood up slowly. "Thanks, Dad. I'm going to get some sleep. Tomorrow, I'm going to try and find office space we can present as a new meeting place. The dungeon has seen better decades."

"Good night," Clifford replied, watching his son go. "It has, I agree with you there. Good luck, on both counts."

# Chapter 21

After a stressful evening of negotiations the night before with the more stubborn members of the Council, Mike looked forward to his morning drive to school with Laurie. They didn't say much and Laurie could tell Mike was chewing heavy thoughts over in his mind. She traced a swirling pattern on the back of his hand and let him think. By the time they arrived at the school, Mike appeared to be smiling more and they were nearly late from sharing their good morning kiss.

Mike's elevated mood deflated a little when he saw Colleen in his biology class. He began to worry what she was going to try today. He sat down heavily and turned his side towards her. He looked up when she pushed a small note towards him which read, "We need to talk." Mike looked up and could see the red in Colleen's eyes meaning she had been crying. He nodded to her and they waited for the teacher to begin his lessons.

When they were given time to work on their partner project, Mike asked, "So, what do you want to talk about?" He hated to see her upset, but whatever it was had put a stop to her flirtations. It had been refreshing to not have to fend off her advances all class period.

"It's about you and Laurie," Colleen began and could almost feel Mike tense up. "I'm sorry for how I've acted. I've been unfair to our friendship and to her. I was so caught up in getting back what we had, I missed the fact we are not the same people we were when we were together. I like Laurie and I think she is good for you. She seems to keep you calmer than you were when you woke up from the accident."

"I'm glad to hear you say that, Colleen," Mike replied, stunned. He had been prepared for a long battle with her over his decision. "Are you really ok? I still do care for you, but as a friend. I'm worried about you."

"I'm going to be fine," Colleen said softly. She had come to terms with Mike moving on during the course of being up most of the night crying. She knew they were no longer the same people. "I still need my friend. And maybe a hug once in awhile?" She smiled.

"I think we can keep being friends. As long as it doesn't go any further," Mike grinned. Things were going better than he expected. "Was there anything else you wanted to talk to me about? Because I think you should have this talk with Laurie too." Before Colleen could reply the bell rang and it was time to get going.

\* \* \*

Colleen's Friday morning confession eased Mike's mind considerably. She and Laurie talked after school while Mike was on the phone with Damien. This seemed to put things to rest. The fireworks Mike had been anticipating between Laurie and Colleen never came. The two seemed to even be bonding due to their shared class and the planning for the homecoming game and dance they were both working on. Mike sat in the back of the room during a planning meeting on Friday afternoon and watched his first love and his current love in control of the committee.

"So, if we can get a few corporate sponsors from the local area, then we can make up for the shortfall in the fundraising efforts. Anything extra and we can maybe host a winter formal as well. Might be nice to have different activities this year," Laurie said, holding a ledger book in her hand. Her weekends spent dancing had made her want to try and have an extra event at the school this year. She knew there really was no shortfall in the budget as Mike had already pledged to cover anything she wanted. It was important to keep it anonymous though, so arrangements had been made for several businesses to hand over checks as soon as they were asked. They left it up to the committee members to do the legwork so it didn't look like it had been orchestrated by Mike.

As Colleen voiced her agreement with Laurie's statement, Mike's cellphone went off, as well as he heard the mental call from Cliff indicating it was him calling. Mike quickly silenced the phone and walked to the doorway to talk, "What's going on Cliff?" Mike knew Cliff and Damien were going to be having a status session with other members of the Council today. Mike had chosen to skip it in order to be here to give Laurie a ride home after the meeting.

"Mike, I think you might want to get over here," Cliff said, panic seeping through his tone. "There is a call for your removal from the Council. It is a very little used vote but they are using your absence as an excuse. Damien is stalling so I could call you and tell you to get here now."

Mike froze, indecision striking his mind. On the one hand, he didn't think he would miss the bickering and politicking which usually went on at the Council meetings. On the other hand however, he knew his removal wouldn't be the end of it. It would make him a target for everyone who had voted his removal. It would also make Laurie or his family fair game in their minds. This made the decision easy for Mike. "I'll be right there." He hung up the phone and went into the room where Laurie was handing out the carefully prepared lists of businesses for the committee members to approach.

He slipped up behind her and put his hand on her waist. She turned and smiled at him, but then frowned when she saw the serious look in his face. "How soon can you wrap this up?" Mike whispered. "There is a situation I need to go handle and I want to make sure you get home safe." Laurie could see in his eyes it wasn't a situation she wanted to know the details of. While her mind raced over the memories of Derek Gohr's attack on her life at church, both of them failed to remember Colleen standing there.

"I can take her home, Mike," Colleen spoke softly. Her enhanced hearing had made it easy to hear what Mike had said and she thought this might be the perfect opportunity to further bond with Laurie. Colleen wanted to ask her about the shock Damien had mentioned in reference to Mike and Laurie. She had been thinking over how she reacted to Cliff and knew she needed more information. She wasn't comfortable asking Mike about it, even if they were back to being only friends and classmates.

Mike looked from Colleen to Laurie several times, unsure about putting the two of them in an enclosed space together. He was glad Colleen had said she was moving on and accepting his commitment to Laurie. He still worried. He knew Laurie was protected as long as she didn't give up the talisman and he didn't believe Colleen would ever try to take it anyway. When Laurie nodded, Mike turned to Colleen. "Thanks Colleen. I appreciate it." He turned back to Laurie and gave her a quick kiss, "I'll call you later. I gotta go."

Mike nodded to a couple others as he left the room. Once he was out of the room he glanced down both ends of the hallway. Seeing no one, he transported himself to the Council chambers. After Mike left, Matthew Stenton stepped out of a shadow, excited he had once again fooled the mighty Mike Keller. Chuckling to himself he settled down to wait until the school meeting was over; then he was going to make his move.

# Chapter 22

"This is ridiculous bullshit," Damien shouted as Mike appeared in the room. "Ah, Mike. Now you're here and we can squash this nonsense about removing you from the Council."

"Calm yourself, Damien," Blake Kosgrove said in his usual flat tone. "Mr. Larsen and Mr. Parker are allowed to voice their concerns and bring a vote on the matter if they wish. Our laws state it takes only two members to bring forth a topic for discussion. Everyone has been patient with the initiatives you and Mr. Keller have been proposing so we will hear out their arguments and you will get your chance for rebuttal."

Damien looked about to argue, but closed his mouth and sat down. Mike took stock of the mood in the room. He was quick to notice the encouraging look from Corey Dawson, Joey's father, who sat to his right. As Mike took his seat, Mr. Kosgrove turned to the far end of the table past Damien. At a nod, Matthew Larsen stood, "I propose a censure on Mr. Keller. His initiatives, while well meaning, are the fantasies of a child. He does not have the business experience or education the rest of us here have. He has not even finished high school. I agree his talents are considerable, and he deserves to be one of us. However, I feel he needs to finish his schooling and gain experience in the world before he carries a vote within this Council."

A few other heads nodded along with Larsen's opening speech and Mike counted among them all the biggest opponents to his initiatives. Joseph Parker stood and echoed Larsen's comments, giving the measure weight enough to be voted upon. Blake turned to Mike, who was seated on his right, "Do you have anything you wish to say Mr. Keller?"

Mike stood slowly, making eye contact with every other member of the Council. Support seemed to shine from the eyes of those Mike had seen embrace the ideas he and his friends had proposed. He addressed his reply first to them, and then to his detractors. "I know I am not as experienced as most of the members of this Council. I also know I came to my seat merely as a fluke. My ignorance of this organization and its laws has been at the top of my list of items to correct. I have tried to remedy these shortfalls the last couple of months. I feel I understand the reticence of members here to embrace change. I am well aware of the old adage, 'if something isn't broke; don't fix it'. I also think to not move with the times is a recipe for disaster. We have all been slaves to custom and the way things have always been. I for one have seen an increase in employee morale and a drop in losses since I implemented the changes I called upon each and every one of us to make. I am confident the returns on this little investment will reap dividends for years to come. I agree I lack decades of training and experience most of the rest of you possess." Mike glanced at Cliff and Damien at this point, seeing understanding in their eyes. They were freshly come to their seats as well, Clifford's father having all but officially turned over his to his son.

"So," Mike continued, eyeing the two who had called for his censure, "If I remember my training on the Council's laws, a vote of censure needs a simple majority to pass. I also know I am not allowed a vote as it is my right in question. I call for the vote here and now so it may be put to rest one way or the other. Mr. Kosgrove, as a member of the High Triad, will you call the vote?"

Blake was taken aback by Mike's comments. Oh, he still believed the boy was a threat to his own power, but he was surprised Mike did not lash out violently. He stood, hiding his unsteadiness with a palm down on the table. Before he could speak, Mike stood back up, "My apologies Mr. Kosgrove, but I have one last thing to add." Blake nodded, wondering what the youth had up his sleeve. Blake knew the measure would fail, he had calculated who would support it and knew even with his vote it would merely end in a deadlock. He intended to abstain and leave the majority in Mike's favor, for now.

At Mr. Kosgrove's nod, Mike smiled. He was glad for all the study sessions of Council law he had had Damien and Cliff put him through. He turned to face Parker and Larsen. "If the measure fails, I invoke my right to request the same restrictions be placed on those who called the measure in the first place." The room fell silent. Joseph Parker looked like a fish out of water as his mouth worked but no sound was forthcoming. Matthew Larsen jumped to his feet, a retort hot on his lips, but Blake put up a hand to forestall any more comments.

"Everyone take your seats," He said, abandoning his normal tone of voice for one more full of command and authority. He was getting angry now. He had not counted on the Keller boy to know much about Council law. The Rule of Reciprocity was used even less than the Rules of Censure. "Mr. Keller has every right, as the accused, to call for Reciprocity. First the matter of his own censure must be addressed. All those in favor of censuring Michael Keller for a period of five years will now declare your vote before us all."

Blake turned first to Matthew Larsen, who had retaken his seat only a moment before. He of course declared in the affirmative. Stephen Conner, to his right, was quick to throw his support behind Mike. Stephen had seen things improve at his businesses as well. Joseph Parker was next and gave his agreement for Censure. Damien and Cliff were supportive of Mike, but as he occupied the highest seat, Cliff was restricted unless there was a tie. This left the vote against censure at the moment. Blake turned to the other end of the table where Gary Denison was already giving the signal against censure. Gerald Barklen and William Stenton were next and both were against Mike. Stenton was one who Mike had unloaded on more than once for his stubborn refusal to even try Mike's proposed reforms. Corey Dawson even went so far as to clap Mike on the shoulder in support.

The vote stood at four to four. With only Blake himself to vote, and of course Cliff. Blake knew if he abstained, then Cliff would vote in Mike's favor and the measure would fall. Making brief eye contact with all the detractors, Blake signaled his support for Mike. "The call to censure Michael Keller fails. Now, to the measure of Reciprocity. Mr. Keller, this is your last chance to rescind your call before a vote is taken." He waited a moment while Mike gave his intention to see the vote taken. Blake sighed and began again.

When this second vote was taken, the picture was different as two of Mike's biggest opponents were not allowed to vote. Though not in favor of censuring Mike, Conner and Denison hesitated before abstaining from the vote to censure their colleagues. Mike had expected they would, but he knew who his supporters were. Corey Dawson and Damien immediately voted for censure. Barklen and Stenton, who opposed Mike at every turn, voted against censure. Mike, unsure at times how Blake felt about him and his friends, abstained, forcing the vote to the older man. If Blake failed to vote, then it would be up to Cliff and the measure would surely pass on a simple majority.

Blake had calculated the odds already and correctly guessed he was being checked out to gauge his feelings. "I vote against censure. I understand Mr. Keller's request for Reciprocity and cannot disagree with his feelings, were I in his shoes. However, I assume by his abstaining he is merely making a statement, instead of intending to cause any real rift within the Council. As such, the measure then fails and we will continue as we have." He glanced at his watch, "Shall we move onto other matters? I would like to wrap this up before too late tonight. I am not as young as the rest of you." His laugh at his own expense like sandpaper.

The rest of the meeting was as fruitless as many the last few weeks. Those opposed to Mike's ideas were still against them and not budging at all. They even seemed to take his failed bid to censure two of his opponents as a victory. The only thing they could all agree on was to move forward with looking into moving their meetings into a location less dungeon like.

\* \* \*

Laurie and Colleen wrapped up the planning meeting for the Homecoming committee and headed towards the parking lot. Laurie realized she came to like Mike's first love over the course of the week. Colleen might never be her best friend, but at least Laurie felt the two of them could coexist for the sake of Mike. "I appreciate the lift," Laurie said as they piled into Colleen's car. "If it's any trouble, I'm sure I can get a hold of Anne or Liz. And Chad's practice should be over soon, so I can wait with Deb if you needed to get going."

"No worries," Colleen said as she put the key in the ignition. "I'm a little surprised you agreed. I know I'm not your favorite person in the world" Colleen really hoped the two of them could be friends.

"I didn't think we would be able to get along," Laurie said. "It's . . . been a pleasant surprise." Laurie was trying to give Colleen the benefit of doubt, but struggled with liking the person who had hurt Mike so deeply. 'If she hadn't though, I wouldn't have him now,' Laurie thought to herself.

"Listen," Colleen said as she cranked up the car. "I'd askMike but . . . I overheard Damien talk about a 'spark' between you two. I thought he was speaking figuratively, but given this world we are both in . . . Has, um, Mike ever said anything to you about a feeling of, like, electricity?"

Laurie thought a moment, "Mike mentioned once about feeling as if he knew we were right for each other. He attributed it to his gifts."

"That's great," Colleen said, and actually meant it. 'Now I have to talk to Cliff.' Colleen started to head out of the parking lot, "I'm happy for you and Mike. And you have to know, I never intended to hurt him the way I did."

"I don't think Mike blames you for it," Laurie tried to sound reassuring. "He knows these Council people messed with both of your lives. And it sounds like he is making progress to change things so this doesn't happen to anyone else-- at least from what little he's told me."

"That would be great," Colleen agreed. "I hope . . . I hope I can still be a part of Mike's life. I know neither of us are the same person we were, and he has you and I don't want to come between you, but I also don't want to lose my friend."

"I don't think you have to worry about losing Mike's friendship," Laurie said.

Matthew had been listening although neither girl knew he was there. Their exchange angered him. 'Who does Colleen think she is? We were supposed to have a deal. Here she is making friends with her rival instead of distracting Mike.' Matthew briefly debated taking them both, but decided to stick with his original plan. He would have another conversation with Colleen later and see if she can be swayed back to the original course of action. He zipped back to the Council chambers in time to assist his master, Blake Kosgrove.

The girls, unaware they were being observed, continued their drive. Colleen dropped Laurie off at her house and then returned to her current home at the van Doornick's, her mind turning over her thoughts of Mike and Cliff.

* * *

"What of your plans to distract Mr. Keller?" Blake asked his apprentice during their evening meeting. Mike appearing so quickly at the meeting this afternoon had been a test of sorts. Blake Kosgrove had orchestrated the entire exchange to see if Mike would be slow to respond or not. Damien's outburst while Cliff alerted Mike to the situation had been prepared for.

"Colleen is proving less than cooperative," Matthew stated simply. "She has resigned herself to Mike's moving on with Laurie. I suspect her friendship with

Cliff has everything to do with this. I think I'm going to have to take a more active role than I can from the shadows."

"Do not stray from the plan at this time," Blake cautioned before a coughing fit stopped him. After a moment he was able to recover his breath. "Soon we will make our move and I will be able to rid myself of those annoying upstarts."

Matthew nodded before leaving. He intended one more stop before going to bed himself.

\* \* \*

"Cliff, can we talk?" Colleen asked after knocking on her friend's door. She had waited for him to get home and was glad it wasn't too late when he did.

"Just a sec," she heard his reply, muffled by the door. When the door opened, they stared at each other. He was torn between the budding friendship with Julie and his feelings for Colleen. Julie was definitely interested, but the charge he felt with Colleen weighed on his thoughts.

"How was your day?" Colleen asked, only slightly put off by his not inviting her in right away. The moment's pause while the question hung between him was all it took for Cliff to then open the door and turn to go farther into the room.

"Long day arguing with stubborn old people," he laughed as he plopped down into a chair. "Getting used to it though, which I don't think is a good thing. How was school?"

"Long," she laughed. "It looks like Mike and you guys are going to be funding our Homecoming, Winter Formal, and Prom in the spring if we don't get better fundraisers going."

"It isn't a problem," Cliff replied. "I know Damien will do anything because of Liz, and of course Mike for Laurie." Cliff winced and looked askance at Colleen to see her reaction. To his surprise, she didn't look upset.

"They are really good together," Colleen said thoughtfully. "I know my disappearing on Mike is inexcusable. I'm glad to still have his friendship. Believe it or not, Laurie and I are really getting along. Maybe we can all be friends with time."

"That's good news." Cliff felt like a weight had been lifted. Colleen seemed sincere, which made it better. "I'm glad things are going well. I was worried about you." Cliff shifted but decided not to reach out to her.

"I know you worry about me, Cliffy," Colleen teased. "How is Julie? You two discuss anything other than books?" Colleen felt a little jealous of Cliff finding another interest. Part of her had enjoyed having him doe eyed around her. She felt guilty she hadn't reciprocated his feelings sooner and may have lost her chance with him.

"Things are going alright," Cliff admitted, sitting back in his chair. "She really has a handle on the up and coming author scene. I like her, but I don't know if either of us are really in it for more than friends at this stage."

"Well, give it time, if it is meant to be things will click," Colleen replied.

"Colleen," Cliff began, reminding her of Mike went he turned serious. "There is. I do need to talk to you about something. I, don't know how exactly to ask this so I am going to say it. Do you feel anything for me?"

Colleen was knocked reeling by the direct approach. She was even more surprised it was Cliff who brought it up first. "I guess I would have to say I really like spending time with you Cliff. I am so happy you are my friend and have been so nice to me since I came here. I have to process moving on from Mike before I can be with anyone else."

"That's," Cliff stammered, "Not exactly what I meant. I really like you Colleen and I am glad we are friends too. What I mean is, do you feel anything when we touch?" For emphasis he reached over and took her hand in his, the resulting surge rocked them both. Cliff felt drawn forward towards Colleen and he moved closer.

For her part, Colleen had been caught off guard by his sudden movement. The shock pulsed through her at their contact, bringing the memory of their drunken kissing weeks before to the front of her mind. She leaned into Cliff reflexively and they pressed their lips together. Colleen was first to pull back for air and the two friends stared at each other. "Cliff," she whispered breathlessly.

Cliff retreated to his chair, blushing furiously. "I, shouldn't have done that," he stammered quickly. "I'm sorry Colleen." Each time the two had gotten close like this before, Colleen would pull away and affirm their relationship as platonic.

Taking a deep breath, Colleen got up and plopped down on Cliff's lap. She took his face in her hands, "I am not sorry." She then kissed him again, the shock which usually ran through them settled into a steady hum and bounced back and forth between their bodies.

Minutes later they came up for air again and Cliff spoke, "What about your feelings for Mike?" Instantly regretting his words when he saw Colleen's face turn pensive.

"I am always going to love Mike," she replied, feeling a crestfallen Cliff tense up beneath her. "But," she emphasized with a brief kiss, "I know it is only love for a friend now. Maybe it always was and we were trying to be more than we were meant to be out of stubborness. We are both different people from who we were before we discovered we have these powers. I'm not completely sure what it is I feel for you Cliff, but I know I cannot hide behind Mike's memory anymore."

Wrapping his arms around her, Cliff smiled, "I'm very taken with you Colleen Nicholson. I'm willing to wait and see what this between us is."

"But what about Julie?" It was Colleen's turn to wince. Here she was sitting on Cliff's lap, professing feelings for him she wasn't even sure of, when he had been talking with another girl.

"Julie and I are book aficionados and I think becoming friends," Cliff stated simply. "I don't think I really looked at it as a romantic interest because of my feelings for you. I had hopes this would happen eventually."

"You hoped I would plop down on your lap and kiss you?" Colleen giggled. The two shared a few more minutes of passionate kisses before there was a knock on Cliff's door.

"Cliff, Is Colleen in there?" her mother's voice came through the door. "I went to check on her and she isn't in her room. I am hoping she didn't use the trick you guys have of disappearing whenever she wants."

"I am here, Mom," Colleen said, pointedly not getting up from Cliff's lap. "We are talking about our days. I'll be heading to bed shortly."

"Ok, dear," her mother replied, smiling because she was certain they were not talking about their day. At least not anymore by the sounds she heard before she knocked. "Maybe tomorrow we can have lunch and you can tell me all about school."

"Sounds great mom," Colleen called back. Cliff had slid his arms tighter around her and had pulled her head to his shoulder. "Good night."

"Good night, you two," her mother replied as she retreated back to the room she and her husband shared. A huge smile lit her face as she thought for sure her daughter must be happy.

"That was close," Cliff said, shifting slightly to settle Colleen more comfortably.

"Mom will be glad I am not pining away over Mike," Colleen replied. "What is your father going to say?"

"Doesn't matter, but I think he suspected and approved all along," Cliff replied. "Now I have to figure out how to tell the guys. You don't think Mike will be against it do you?"

"If he is, too bad for him," Colleen said before nuzzling into Cliff's shoulder. The two sat there enjoying holding each other for a time. They both awoke with a start a couple hours later, the house still and quiet. Grinning sheepishly at each other, they untangled themselves and Colleen left to go to her room.

# Chapter 23

Saturday morning dawned bright and clear. A little colder than the previous week; almost as if Summer was finally passing the torch to Fall. It gave no indication of the significant change coming to Mike's world. Cliff had called him first thing to tell him they needed to talk. Mike was apprehensive as he went to meet with Cliff at an office building they had been looking at for the Council meetings. Cliff had been dodgy about the whole thing, insisting it be the two of them alone. Mike hoped it was a matter they could handle quickly because he wanted to spend his Saturday with Laurie. She wasn't working at all this weekend so they were supposed to spend the entire day together.

"So what's on your mind, Cliff?" Mike asked when his friend arrived. Mike had been early, taking the opportunity to take a closer look at the meeting and conference space this property offered. The risen sun poured into the glass windows stretching all the way around the floor.

"It's about Colleen," Cliff said, deciding to get the real reason for the meeting out in the open.

"What did she do now?" Mike rumbled. "I thought she was giving up this play against Laurie. I'm not breaking it off with Laurie to get back together with her."

"It isn't what you think at all, Mike," Cliff said nervously. He had expected Mike to react on the offensive given the last week. "She and I are, well, as of last night, dating." Cliff braced for Mike's reaction.

Mike rushed over and hugged his friend tight. "I'm so happy for you two. I didn't expect her to move on quickly given what she had said when she came back. This is great news though."

Cliff, taken back by Mike's reaction, said "So, you aren't upset or anything?"

"Upset?" Mike asked incredulously. "I am ecstatic for you two. Did you tell Damien?"

"Not yet," Cliff admitted. "I... wanted to talk to you first. Make sure it wasn't going to cause a problem between us."

"Why would it cause a problem?" Mike asked, really looking at his friend and seeing how conflicted he was. "You were there when I told her. I will always love, Colleen. We have been through too much to not have those feelings for each other. But it is strictly friends. With you and her dating I don't have to worry at all about her. I think you two will be great together."

"Thanks, Mike," Cliff was struck by how much Mike's endorsement of his decision buoyed him. Having Mike's blessing made the next part of things easier to talk about. "Colleen wanted to go over to Laurie's this morning to talk to her. I think the two of them have really hit it off."

"I've made the same observation," Mike replied. "This day keeps getting better and better. Two of my best friends are happy and I have a whole day with Laurie planned out. Maybe we can get everyone together for dinner. It could be fun," Mike trailed off as he realized he didn't have Cliff's full attention.

"I will talk to Colleen when I get home then," Cliff said. "She said she has left Laurie's. I guess Laurie was already getting ready for you to come pick her up." Cliff laughed.

"Well, I better get going then," Mike responded. He waved before he zipped back home. Cliff left soon after.

Matthew stepped out of the shadowy corner, disgust twisting his face. "That bitch," he said aloud in the empty office building. "She is going to ruin everything if she doesn't do her part."

* * *

Cliff and Mike managed to round up everyone else from their little group for dinner that evening. The girls all seemed quite pleased to see Colleen happy with Cliff, none more than Laurie. She leaned over to whisper in Mike's ear halfway into the evening, "I think they are cute together. It's about time Cliff found a match right?"

Mike looked at his two friends across the table. Colleen was practically sitting on Cliff's lap and the two of them were sharing their entrees back and forth. He smiled and put his lips close to Laurie's ear, "They do, don't they?"

Laurie shuddered at the feel of Mike's breath on her ear before whispering back, "And you are ok with everything? With seeing her with someone else?" Laurie had worried about this part ever since Colleen's surprise visit in the morning to tell her about her dating Cliff. She worried seeing Colleen with anyone else would snap Mike back to his feelings for Colleen.

"You are my angel," Mike whispered back before planting a kiss on Laurie's earlobe. Then the two noticed the table was silent. They both blushed as they looked around at all their friends staring at them.

"You two really should get a room," Anne said laughing. The others joined in.

"You and Joey aren't much better," Liz commented after her fit of giggles.

"Pot, this is kettle calling," Chad chimed in before he had to duck a thrown napkin. Liz had been practically wrapped around Damien since he picked her up earlier in the evening.

Mike laughed as the tables turned on Chad. He looked around the table and knew he had a great group of friends. Things were finally starting to settle down with the Council after the failed attempt at Censure. Sure, there were opponents to Mike's initiatives but he knew it was only a matter of time before they would see the wisdom in what he was proposing.

The rest of the night filled with laughter as the five couples headed en masse to the dance club after dinner. They looked like an invading army when they came in together and took over a set of tables in the back.

Several times throughout the night Mike thought he felt powers being used nearby but tried to ignore it. When Mike excused himself to the bathroom, Cliff and Damien caught his eye and began to disentangle themselves from their dates. They followed Mike to the restrooms and checked all the stalls before shielding the room.

"Have you felt anything weird tonight?" Mike asked them both. "I can't place it, but it feels like we are being watched. I don't mean because we are the largest group together in here, but like someone is really watching us."

"I thought something seemed off," Damien replied. "It was like the other night when we thought we felt a teleport away without the person coming up and saying hello. Coincidence once, twice suspicious." Cliff nodded along.

"Keep your eyes peeled then," Mike commanded. "I don't want any trouble tonight with the girls all here. There are too many non-gifted around for trouble of our kind tonight."

"Speaking of non-gifted," Damien began. "I plan on telling Liz what's really going on. I think I'm falling for her and I want her to know, before it goes any farther, what she's getting into. Are you ok with me telling her about you guys as well? Joey and Anne gave their blessing earlier."

"Certainly," Cliff said the same time Mike replied, "About time."

* * *

While the guys were having their brief meeting, Matthew finally managed to catch Colleen's eye without alerting the rest of their little group. Colleen's breath caught in her throat. She glanced around but the other girls were all laughing at Joey who had been telling a joke while the other guys were gone. She looked around for Cliff or Mike, then licked her lips nervously. "Tell Cliff I needed to get some air ok?" Colleen said to the rest of their group. Anne at least looked like she was going to come with but Colleen waved her off. "I only need a minute." Anne turned back to Joey as Colleen slipped away towards the entrance to the club.

"Colleen," Matthew called her name once she stepped away form her friends. "So nice to see you out and about. How is it going? Tearing holes in Mike's love life?" He motioned towards a shadowy corner of the club.

"I told you," Colleen spat through gritted teeth as she followed. "I'm not messing with Mike and Laurie. In fact, Cliff and I are celebrating our first outing as a couple so if you don't mind, you can buzz off."

Matthew grabbed her arm as she turned to walk away, "I will not buzz off. You are going to do as I tell you. When Mike returns to the table you are going to ask him to talk outside and then try to slip back into his heart. I am sure you can figure out how." Matthew pointedly looked Colleen up and down.

"I will not," Colleen replied. "I think you forgot they call me a pyro." She channeled her power through her arm and into Matthew's hand. The smell of burning hair struck first as his arm started to smoke. Matthew pulled his hand away quickly but then slapped Colleen across the jaw.

"Bitch," he barked, rubbing his arm furiously. "I'll get you for that. You'll pay for crossing me."

"Colleen, is everything ok? Matthew, what are you doing here?" Cliff asked as he came stepping out of the crowd towards them. He arrived back at the table to find out Colleen had gone outside for fresh air. He saw her standing in a corner talking to Matthew Stenton. Cliff saw Colleen jerk away but had not put together Matthew struck her until he got closer. He watched Colleen rub her jaw. Then he got angry, "I think you better leave, Matthew. I'll be taking your conduct up with Mr. Kosgrove, and your father. There is no tolerance for this behavior. Did you learn nothing from Derek's actions?"

Matthew smirked. "Whatever Cliff, go running to your daddy. Or maybe that's why you latched onto Colleen? She's more powerful than you so you hope she'll protect you? Pathetic. See you both around." Matthew quickly stepped into the shadow of the corner and disappeared. He noticed Cliff's fists were clenched tight as he vanished.

"Cliff," Colleen panted, wrapping her arms around him. "I'm so glad you came to find me."

"What was going on here?" Cliff asked, holding Colleen, but still unable to make his fists relax fully. "How do you even know Matthew?"

"It is a long story, can we go outside and talk?" Colleen asked. Cliff nodded and led her outside and away from the noise of the building. Once they were outside, Colleen gathered her scattered thoughts. If Cliff hadn't arrived when he did, she was sure she would have torched Matthew right there in public.

Taking a deep breath, Colleen began her tale, "It was right before school started. Matthew appeared out of nowhere and started talking about distracting Mike, and getting Laurie to dump him because of his gifts. You know how much I wanted Mike back, so I listened. I listened and I tried to pull Laurie's influence away from Mike. It wasn't working, and I kept thinking about you instead of about Mike. That was when I realized Mike and I were over and I had to move on. I realized how much I like you Cliff. You have been such a great friend."

"Ok, but what does Matthew being here have to do with anything?" Cliff pressed. He liked hearing Colleen talk about her feelings for him but he knew there was more to the story.

"I," Colleen started, "I told him I wasn't going to cooperate with him. I like Laurie and I think she is good for Mike. He got angry but then went away. I saw him here and he wanted to talk. When I tried to walk away, he grabbed my arm and I burnt him. Then he slapped me."

This enraged Cliff, "When I get my hands around his neck." Cliff looked dangerously close to Mike's eyes when he threw his doctor across the room. Colleen was struck by how it looked similar to when the guy at the club tried to grab her a couple weeks ago.

"Cliff," Colleen repeated a few times until he focused back on her face. "It's alright. I nearly set him on fire in public. I think he got the message to leave me alone. Can we please keep this between the two of us? I don't want to upset Mike and Laurie since we have put this all behind us."

Cliff looked deep into her eyes and it softened his anger. "Alright," he said, kissing her softly. "Let's get back to the gang. We will have to mask that mark." He touched her cheek tenderly. "I can fix it." He channeled a small amount of power to mask the light bruise caused by Matthew's hand. No matter what he promised Colleen; he was going to hunt down Matthew and make him pay. The two went back into the club to rejoin their friends, a furious Matthew watching from the shadows.

The couples enjoyed another hour of dancing before it was time to go home. As they headed their separate directions, Mike caught Damien's eye as his friend was walking Liz to his car for their drive home. Mike gave him a smile and a nod, knowing Damien was going to be bringing Liz into the circle of people who knew about his gifts. It had been a huge step for Damien to make and Mike was happy for him. Mike waved to his friends before climbing into the vehicle, having already situated Laurie in the passenger seat.

* * *

"Liz," Damien said later as they sat in her driveway. He had driven her home like normal while he built up his confidence to spill his secret.

Liz sat nervously the whole ride home. The mood changed when the guys came back from the bathroom, like something weighed on Damien's mind. She worried he would eventually tire of her. His mysterious wealth combined with her having yet to see his home or family concerned her more when he seemed distracted like this. Now he was the most serious she had ever seen him. She braced for him to tell her it was over.

"Liz," Damien repeated, licking his lips nervously. "I have to explain something to you but I need you to hear me out before you interrupt."

"I knew this was going to happen eventually," Liz said calmly. "You don't have to say it, I won't call you anymore."

"Wait, What?" Damien stammered. "No Liz. Just no. Listen," he grabbed her hand and placed his other hand on her knee. "Hear me out, it isn't what you're thinking. No way is it anything like what you're thinking." He waited for her slow nod before continuing. "I have a secret to share with you. But it isn't my secret alone so I had to talk to the others before I shared it with you. I'm not like other people you know."

"I know that, Damien," Liz began, confused about what he was stumbling over. She used her free hand to stroke his cheek. "Tell me your feelings for me are as strong as mine for you, the rest are unimportant details."

"They are Liz," Damien breathed quickly. "Believe me. But, I have the ability to do things not many other people can." Remembering his conversation with Mike about how Mike had told Laurie, he quickly fished a few coins out of his pocket, letting go of her hand to do so. He placed them on the dashboard, confusing Liz even more. She watched as the coins started to float and spin in the air above the dashboard.

She giggled and waved her hand above the coins, looking for strings. "Air vents?" She ran her hand between the dash and the coins. "How are you doing this?"

"With my mind," Damien replied, watching her reaction. "I guess you could call it psychic powers." He watched her face twist in thought. "I can move things like this. I can teleport, which is how I come to see you most of the time. I can also talk to people telepathically."

"A psychic?" Liz stared in disbelief. She had never been one to believe in the paranormal, even though the girls had gone to a fortune teller at the fair their freshman year.

"It is the easiest way to explain it," Damien replied. "Unless you want to call it magic. We prefer the term gifted."

"We?" Liz's eyes got big and round. "How many of you are there? Is this why you won't let me see where you live? Is it a gypsy camp or secret commune?"

Damien laughed, "No, nothing like that. I haven't lied to you about where I live. My father is a very wealthy businessman. Until recently we did not get along very well at all. I owe the better relationship with my father to Mike. I'll have to remember to thank him for helping." Before she could interrupt again, he continued, "Yes. Mike is like me. Although much stronger I should say. So is Cliff, Joey, and your friend Anne, though in a much more limited way. Not all of us can do the same things or as strongly as others."

"Anne can do what?" There was no stopping Liz's interruption this time. "Why hasn't she told me? I'm her best friend, even with her and Laurie patching things up. She tells me everything." Liz stopped when she remembered the other big secret Anne had not told anyone, even her.

"There are strict rules about telling anyone who isn't like us," Damien began. "For their own protection. Mike and Laurie said I can tell you the accident at her church during the summer, was no accident. Another like us, jealous of Mike's ability; tried to kill Laurie, and Anne, in order to get to Mike. Mike managed to save them both."

Liz thought about the organ pipe incident Laurie had talked about being the moment she knew Mike and her were destined to be together. Liz had heard all about Mike's heroics. Learning it was an attack on her friend was shocking. "So, you didn't tell me. No one told me. In order to protect me from others? Shouldn't I know what I am getting myself involved in?"

"That's why I'm telling you now, Liz," Damien said softly, trying to keep himself from getting lost in her eyes so he could finish what he wanted to say. "I wanted you to know what I am and the world I am part of before I told you I am in love with you."

It took a moment for Liz to connect everything, as distracted as she was by Damien's revelation about not only himself, but her other friends as well. Then her face lit up and Damien knew he was gone. She pulled his face close to hers and kissed him soundly. "I love you too, Damien."

Damien was relieved with Liz's reaction. His worry over whether his revelation would push her away had dragged him down more than he thought it would. Taking a page out of Mike's book, he produced a pendant from his pocket where it had been resting all night. The dark, blood red stone flashed in the moonlight coming through the windows, reflecting back the little bit of dashboard lights. While Liz gave him a puzzled look, he looped it over her head and gently pulled her hair out from under the chain.

Liz picked up the stone, which was heavier than she thought it would be and stared into the reflective surface. It gave her face an eerie red tint. She looked up at Damien, unable to keep a tear from falling from her eye. "It's beautiful," she whispered.

"Not as beautiful as you," Damien replied, wiping away the tear from her cheek with his thumb.

* * *

Mike's elated mood filled the car as he drove Laurie home from the club. Even her curfew had been relaxed a little on non-school nights when she was spending time with Mike. Laurie could see from the grin on Mike's face he was either up to mischief, or had a secret he was dying to share. After a couple of minutes she had had enough and asked, "What is with the stupid grin of yours, Mister? What are you up to?"

Mike tried to look innocent. "Nothing at all." He then squeezed her hand. "Damien is going to bring Liz into our circle tonight so she will know about all of our gifts."

"That's so great. He must really be serious about her then." Laurie had been skeptical when Damien and Liz started dating, knowing what she did about the gifted people around her. Damien had proven himself to be a good friend to Mike and their friendship was all Laurie had cared about. Now not having to tip toe around things with Liz would be an added bonus. "Wait, what about Deb and Chad? They are the only ones left in the dark."

"I will have to ask Damien and Cliff about it," Mike said thoughtfully. "I would certainly trust them with my secret, but I don't know how everyone else will feel about it." Mike squeezed Laurie's hand. "I don't think it will be an issue though."

\* \* \*

Matthew paced in his room, muttering to himself. "That little bitch. All she had to do was crook her finger at Michael and he would have tumbled like a house of cards." He kicked the trash bin from next to his desk, a few scraps of paper floated in the air. "Now Cliff is going to be stupid because he thinks he loves her. I can handle him easily enough, but will he draw in Damien and Mike or come at me on his own?" He sat down in a leather arm chair and pondered how he was going to handle this disruption to his plans.

# Chapter 24

Cliff awoke Sunday morning still ready to kill Matthew Stenton for slapping Colleen. The blinding rage had been lost in holding her until they both fell asleep but returned with the rising sun. Scenario after scenario played through his head, but knowing Matthew outmatched his own gifts kept Cliff from going after him right away. It also didn't help Colleen stirred in her sleep, distracting him before she opened her eyes to look up at him.

"Were you watching me sleep?" she smiled. "That's creepy you know."

Cliff leaned down and kissed her. He wasn't sure what either of their parents might say about the sleeping arrangements but for the moment he didn't particularly care.

"Promise me you won't go after Matthew," Colleen demanded, knowing it had to still be playing in Cliff's mind. "I don't care about what happened. It's behind us all now. OK?"

Cliff nodded and pulled her to him so she couldn't see the lie in his eyes. *'He will pay my sweet Colleen.'* Cliff was glad she couldn't read thoughts or he would have been in trouble long ago.

"Good," Colleen said as they separated. "Now, I'm starving. Time for breakfast." She bounced out of the bed so fast Cliff thought she had teleported. She laughed at the expression on his face as she headed for the hallway to find a bite to eat. Cliff was quickly behind her and the two raced, giggling, to the kitchen. The staff weren't aware of everything happening but they were glad to see Cliff happy.

\* \* \*

Mike sat in the front row of the church as Laurie filed into the choir loft with the other members. There had been a large, anonymous, donation to the church which allowed them to upgrade the sound system and increase their outreach programs. Uncle Jim, seated behind his nephew, put a hand on Mike's shoulder briefly. He knew where the money came from and was proud of his nephew for what he had done.

As the opening hymns were finished and the choir sat down, Mike received a warning. It took him a moment to realize it was from his sister's necklace. When everyone stood up to greet their neighbors Mike turned to his uncle. *'Something is wrong with Connie. I have to go. Cover for me?'* he thought quickly. At his Uncle's nod Mike slipped down the row and out the side door.

"He said his stomach is acting up," Uncle Jim said to a concerned look from Colleen's parents as Mike exited the church.

Out in the hallway, Mike quickly shifted to his room at his mother's. He quickly headed for his little sister's room. He briefly wondered where their mother was as he could clearly hear Connie screaming as soon as he was in the house. He pushed open the door and had a flashback to Anne's room and Derek's attack during the summer. There were two masked figures attempting to pin down his sister. Mike roared even as he used his gifts to snatch both of them up in the air.

Even with the mask Mike saw their eyes go wide as he slammed them together once, twice, three times. Then he let them fall to the ground. They didn't move. As the rage faded Mike ran to his sister's side. Connie was shaking, her pretty pink comforter pulled tight to her chin.

"Connie, it's me," Mike tried to sit on the edge of the bed next to her but Connie reacted by swinging wildly. Her eyes were glazed over in fear and she had yet to look away from her two assailants.

It took another moment but she finally recognized her brother's voice. "Mike, thank God you're here." She hugged to her brother so tight he thought she would crack a rib. Then she held him at arm's length, "Wait a minute. How did you?"

Mike touched the chain around her neck. "I made sure I would know if you were in danger as long as you had it on. I hoped no one would ever try attacking my family or friends again."

"Again?" Connie tensed up.

"My friend, Anne," Mike began. He had told his sister before all about Derek and the attempt on Laurie's life at the church. He hadn't shared the details of Anne's near assault. "Derek. The guy who attacked Laurie. He tried to do this with Anne. He sent thugs into her house to attack her."

"But, you said you dealt with Derek," Connie was starting to panic. "Why would anyone come after me?"

"I guess I have made an enemy who thinks my threat doesn't apply to them," Mike was getting angry again as he stared at the two figures, neither of which had moved as of yet. Mike knew he hadn't killed them, though he had considered it while in the depths his rage. It felt too reminiscent of the Darkness buried within him.

Connie saw a change come over her brother and grew fearful of what he might do. She touched his arm gently, "Mike, thank you saving me but don't be like them. They are trying to goad you into doing what they want you to do."

Mike turned to his sister, the concern in her eyes granting him a reprieve from the stirring Darkness. It was easier to push it away since his powers awakened fully, but there were times he wanted to give into it. Times like these. He saw a flash in his mind of Kevin's dead eyes staring at him again from the school bathroom. Shaking it off he turned to Connie, "I'm going to take them to a safe place and ask them a few questions. I have to know who sent them. I won't go too far though." He then hugged his sister tight. "Let's keep this away from Mom ok?"

Connie nodded and watched as he stood up and walked over to the two knocked cold assailants. Mike reached down and grabbed a collar in each hand. With a last eye contact with his sister, he vanished. Once she could stop shaking, she ran to find her old softball bat in the garage. It was going to find a new home next to her bed.

* * *

"Let's go over this again," Mike said to the two thugs who had tried to attack his sister. He had gone to the home he had inherited from the Gohr's as it was the only place he could think of where he would be free from interruption. He bound the two with his power to chairs. Mike then wove shields around them both to prevent them from using their gifts. "Who sent you to attack my sister after I specifically said any attempt on my family or friends would result in all-out war?"

When he had removed their masks, Mike had not recognized the two. Blonde and Black, as he had come to call them from their hair color, stubbornly refused to share their names. They continued to stare at him in stony silence. Then Blonde leaned forward like he was going to speak, but instead he spit at Mike. It fell short but it was enough to snap Mike's frayed nerves. Mike stepped forward and hit Blonde so hard with his fist there was an audible crack as he and the chair tumbled on their side. Mike only realized after the third or fourth kick he had augmented his strength and could have killed the guy with blows of that strength. Blood gushed from Blonde's mouth. It was obvious his jaw was broken and he had probably lost a few teeth as well. Black went white when Mike turned to him.

"We don't know who it was," Black started, flinching when Mike stepped towards him. "I swear man. We were sent a text from a blocked phone number with instructions of where to go and a dollar amount. We were told it was a game. We were supposed to kidnap the girl, hold her for a few days in a safe house, and then release her. We were supposed to scare her. Like an intervention thing. Then we would get paid as long as she was unharmed. Like one of those scared straight things."

"The girl you attacked was my sister," Mike repeated. "Do you know who I am?"

"Yeah," Black responded. "We didn't know it was your sister man. I swear. We all know what you said. I swear we were told it was like an intervention thing."

Mike struggled with the Darkness. He reached back like he was going to strike Black and saw his eyes go wide. Blonde coughed from his spot on the floor, spewing blood. The image of Kevin's broken and bleeding body came to Mike and he paused. Taking a deep breath Mike unbound both of them. "Leave me the phone you received the message on. Get him help. Then I suggest you both get out of town for a while. If I see either of your faces again neither of you will walk again." Mike's clenched fists sent Black springing into action. He quickly put his cellphone on the chair he had vacated and reached down to grab his friend. The two of them disappeared seconds later.

Mike roared and kicked the overturned chair Blonde had been bound to. It sailed across the room to break against the wall. He snatched up the phone and scrolled through the message.

"Need you to pick up a girl in need of an intervention. If she doesn't change her ways she is going to be in real trouble. Hold her a few days and then let her go. If anything untoward happens to her, there will be consequences." Then there was Connie's address and a picture of her standing around at school. Mike recognized the brick wall behind her. Black had not lied, the number was blocked. Mike put the phone in his pocket, in hopes the organizer of this little stunt would contact his hired help to check the status of their assignment.

\* \* \*

Matthew laughed to himself as he saw Mike smash the chair. The two low ranking minions he had hired were expendable in the grand scheme. He needed to test if Mike had placed a ward on his sister as completely as Laurie was and had not been disappointed.

Matthew slipped back to his own room to find Cliff waiting. "We have a matter to discuss Matthew. Sit down."

Matthew laughed out loud this time. "I think you should go home, Cliff. You are in my home, and outmatched even if we were in yours. Don't embarrass yourself like you do at all the Council meetings. Your daddy handing you his spot will not last long."

Cliff was on his feet and in Matthew's face in moments. Matthew was stunned the slightly rounder young man could move so fast when Cliff pinned him against the wall. "Listen carefully, Stenton. Go near Colleen, I will end you." A flash in Cliff's eyes reminded Matthew of Mike when he started beating on one of his hired thugs. Then Cliff was gone and Matthew was left rubbing his lightly bruised neck from where Cliff's arm had been pressed against it.

"Well, that's interesting," Matthew said to himself as he went to retrieve a bottled water from the kitchen and wait for the next step in the plan.

\* \* \*

"So, are you ready?" Damien asked. "Are you sure you are ready?"

"Of course silly," Liz responded. "Do you still want to do this?" When Damien had showed up at her door Sunday afternoon with plans to show her more of his powers and his life, Liz was able to banish the lingering doubts his revelation the previous night had been a dream.

"Good. Come here." Damien took her hand and after a moment transported them both to his study.

"Incredible. I didn't fell a thing."

"That was only the beginning," Damien grinned. "Welcome to my home. This is my study. My room is beyond the door there. Now, let's go to lunch. My father is anxious to meet you." He took her hand in his and led the way to a small dining room.

"Damien, you're back already," Leonard said, standing to greet his son and Liz. "And you must be the beautiful Liz. Damien has talked about you often. I see his talent for exaggeration does not do you justice." Leonard smiled and shook Liz's hand.

"Father, you will embarrass me in front of my girlfriend."

"No, Mr. Mauston, go on. I want to know everything Damien has told you about me. Especially since until yesterday I barely knew you existed for all he talked of you. You don't seem anything like the tyrant he painted you as."

Damien laughed at the expression on his father's face. "Part of my putting her off from visiting was telling her you were a wealthy businessman and we didn't see eye to eye on pretty much anything."

"Well, I would say it was mostly true, Liz. Lately Damien and I have become closer than we were for most of his growing up days. But let's sit and eat instead of standing around in the doorway." Mr. Mauston took both of the teens by a shoulder and guided them to seats side by side, but across from the one he had vacated earlier.

On the table was a spread of sandwich fixings for any appetite. The trio settled into loading up their plates with their chosen lunch. Conversation remained light. Leonard asked general questions about Liz's family and school. What she liked to do in her down time. She answered in between glances at Damien and little bites of her food.

Damien devoured two sandwiches piled high with turkey and Swiss cheese while Liz picked at hers. Damien was concerned she wasn't eating. "Is everything ok?"

"I was thinking," Liz tried to fake a smile. She could see right away it wasn't working. Damien's father could sense the teen's uneasiness and quickly excused himself to the bathroom, leaving the couple alone. After a moment, Liz continued, "I feel like this is so surreal. I always feared you would get bored with me. You are rich, handsome, funny. I didn't think I could hold your interest. Now I see the rich part for myself. I always thought maybe you were making this part up. Top it off with you having these special powers and I don't have any ability like yours. Is this really happening or am I asleep at home?"

"It is completely real, Liz." Damien moved his chair a little closer and took both of her hands in his. "I wasn't looking to fall in love when I tried to befriend Mike. Hell, I wasn't even sure if he would be friends with me. Then I met you and I couldn't deny the connection we made. As long as you will have me, I am yours. Don't fear I am going to leave you simply because I have money, or power. None of it matters when compared to you."

A tear began to fall down Liz's cheek. They embraced and held each other. This was how Damien's father found them when he returned to the doorway. He watched the two of them a moment and then went back to his study to read. For the first time in a long time he did not worry about his family carrying on after he was gone. Damien had grown to be the kind of man he would be proud to hand everything over to. A tear of his own dropped onto the page he was looking at but not really reading.

# Chapter 25

By Monday morning Mike was no closer to finding out who the mystery attacker was. Connie had reported nothing strange the rest of the day but promised she would be on her guard and keep her necklace close. Mike was reassured his warning system had worked as he hoped. With nothing to go on, he managed to keep his temper and the reawakened Darkness in check. When talking to Laurie Sunday night he tried to not say too much. Mike thought over their brief conversation, not happy he'd lied to her.

"She saw what she thought was a mouse and it scared her. Her panic set off the necklace I gave her. It is warded like yours. I guess it was too sensitive."

Laurie had giggled almost uncontrollably for several minutes. "So she saw a mouse and it alerted you to her panic? The poor girl must have been so embarrassed to see you show up right then."

"Well, she did take a swing at me." Mike laughed. "I don't want to embarrass her any further so please don't say anything to her. OK?"

"Of course not. I may have to use the same stunt if I'm ever missing you though. Seems like a good trick to get you to come running." The couple shared a goodnight kiss and then Mike went home.

His recollection was interrupted by Laurie coming down the stairs from her room. Mike had waited in the living room for her to finish getting ready for school. Laurie's parents weren't aware of Mike's abilities, but they were going to be cutting it close to get to school on time and not seem suspicious. Laurie quickly said good bye to her mother and Mike carried her backpack out to his SUV.

"Are you worried about getting to school on time?" Laurie teased as Mike had jogged around the vehicle and jumped into the driver seat after he had seen her into her side.

"I don't want your parents suspicious. I don't know if telling them would be a good thing or not at this point. I know you say they adore me but I don't want to freak them out."

"Big softie. You could sprout another limb or a third eye and I don't think they would pause a moment." Laurie again thought about how cute it was when Mike worried about her parent's opinion of him.

"Yeah, I know. By the way, I think we can tell Chad and Deb what's going on, but let's wait until the weekend so they have a few days to process ok?"

"Sure." Laurie took Mike's right hand in hers as they drove to school.

\* \* \*

The week passed fairly quickly. Mike confirmed with Damien and the others they should bring the final two friends into their circle and everything was set for the big reveal on Friday night. Colleen and Laurie continued to grow closer and actually joined forces to pick on Mike during lunch. Everything seemed less tense than the start of the year.

Friday afternoon, Mike was once again sitting in the back of a Homecoming Committee meeting while Colleen and Laurie discussed the shortfalls from the football boosters and the progress of the solicited business donations. Mike's phone beeped once before Cliff contacted him telepathically. "You coming to the meeting? Looks like Parker and Stenton are gearing up to attack your absence again."

Sighing Mike responded in kind. "Be there in a few minutes." He got up and quietly walked around the outside of the room to behind Colleen and Laurie. They had their heads together as they went over the items in their notes. Mike lightly touched Laurie on the shoulder and both girls looked up. "I have to run. Are you alright getting home without me?"

Laurie nodded as Colleen spoke up, "I can take her home when we get done here. Give us a chance for more girl time."

Mike thanked Colleen and gave Laurie a kiss before leaving. When he stepped into the hallway he saw a couple fellow students about to turn the corner. Mike waited impatiently for them to get out of sight but as they did, a teacher stepped out of their classroom where they must have been working late. Mike grumbled in frustration and headed for the bathroom where he hoped he would be able to get a moment alone to teleport to the Council meeting.

When he came through the door he was relieved to find the bathroom empty. Mike quickly shifted to the meeting and took his seat. He glanced around the room to find all eyes on him. Mr. Parker was standing, his eyes clear in their hatred for Mike. "Now that Mr. Keller has deemed our meeting important enough to attend, let's get down to business." Mike knew this was going to be an annoyingly long night.

\* \* \*

Colleen and Laurie left the classroom after their Homecoming meeting about fifteen minutes later. The girls moved on to discussing plans for the night and wondering if Mike and Cliff would be late. They both knew Mike's sudden departure had to have to do with the Council. Laurie had learned little more than Colleen, aside from it being a constant annoyance to their boyfriends.

The two girls were watched from the shadows by Matthew Stenton. He still fumed over Colleen's failure to disrupt Mike's life.

Then he made his appearance in the backseat of the car. Matthew was pleased the plan worked and the two of them would be in the car together. Frustrated with Colleen's backing out on her part, Matthew jumped at the chance to take a more active role in the plans of his master. His job was to secure Laurie and distract Mike with her disappearance. "Hello ladies," he said calmly as he reached over the seat and plucked the necklace from around Laurie's neck. "I will take that. Now, before your boyfriend shows up, we are going to have a little chat. Then you are going to come with me."

Laurie was shocked, first by the newcomer's arrival, and then by the casualness with which he plucked her pendant from around her neck. Her close friends knew about the talisman Mike had given her, but she didn't display it to the world. It made the pendant all the more special because only a select few knew of it. "Give it back!" she shouted, panic snatching her voice. "What's going on here?" Laurie looked imploringly at Colleen, who sat there through the exchange.

It was Matthew who responded, "I will not give it back. As for what is going on here, Colleen has been my little spy. However, it's time to take matters into my own hands. We're going to go somewhere safe and secure from your boyfriend. When he shows up here looking for you, Colleen is going to give him this trinket and a message from me." Matthew grinned at the stricken look on Laurie's face before turning to Colleen. "You will tell Mike I have taken Laurie and he will have his precious love back when he resigns his seat on the Council, as well as his fortune, to me. If he does this, I may let him live. He can figure out the price of failure if he wants."

After his speech, Matthew laid a hand on Laurie's shoulder and the two of them disappeared from the car. Colleen was left staring at the swirled necklace Matthew dropped on the console between the front seats. She knew Mike was not going to be pleased and braced herself for his anger. She had not had any idea Matthew's plans would involve a kidnapping. Colleen sat in the parking lot, crying softly and waited for Mike to show up.

She didn't have long to wait before Mike arrived in the backseat. "Colleen, where is Laurie? And why do you have the necklace I gave her? She is never to take it off except at home. She knows that," Mike was frantic. He had been so focused on the Council meeting he had barely noticed the change in his connection to Laurie which signaled her having removed the necklace. He knew she would when she was at home, but Mike had placed other protections there for her. When he realized the connection said the necklace was still in the school parking lot, he left immediately.

"Mike," Colleen began, her voice cracking through her sobbing. "It was this guy, Matthew. He had said he would help me to be able to explain to Laurie she didn't belong with you. He asked me to try and make her fearful of those with gifts like ours. I told him last Wednesday I was done with him and done with trying to separate you two. I had no idea he was going to take her. I swear I had no idea." Colleen reached out to Mike, tears rolling down her face. She could see the look in his eyes and it scared her.

Mike clutched the swirled disk in his hand so hard it hurt his palm. The pain kept him back from the edge, but the Darkness within reached for control. Venom filled his tone as he spoke, "You were warned. They were all warned. I thought this was settled. I am going to end this now." Mike reached towards Colleen both physically and with his will, intending to strip her of her powers right then and there. As he latched onto her gift, Colleen screamed as if her soul were being ripped in half.

"Mike, stop," Colleen pleaded through the pain. "Please. Stop. You're hurting me." She could feel her gifts slipping away, her senses dulling from their heightened state. She grabbed Mike's wrist and did what came naturally to her, scorching his skin. When Mike yelled in pain and pulled away, Colleen felt her powers returning. "Mike, I'm so sorry, but you were hurting me."

Panting and holding his burned wrist, Mike met her eyes and Colleen was relieved to see him and not whatever was looking at her when he was trying to hurt her. "I," Mike said softly, "I'm sorry Colleen. I should have figured someone might try to use you against me. Who is this Matthew? Matthew Stenton?" At Colleen's nod, Mike continued, "His father has been opposition from the start. Did he say he was acting on his father's instructions? If so, I can put an end to their threat quickly."

"I think he was acting on his own," Colleen said quickly. She knew there would have to be further discussion. She wasn't going to forgive Mike so easily for attacking her and she was sure he wouldn't be this forgiving once he had Laurie back. "After he took the necklace from Laurie, he said he was taking matters into his own hands. He said you will turn over your seat and fortune to him or there will be consequences. He said you can guess what the price of failure would be."

Mike nodded as he grappled with the Darkness inside. It was still trying to reach out and strip Colleen's powers. Mike felt he had this part of himself under control until now. The attack on Connie, and now Laurie's kidnapping, had sent him spiraling closer to losing control than he had been since Kevin's death. Even during his fight with Derek he had been calmer. "Go home Colleen. Stay there until I come talk to you. I have to handle this immediately before anyone else is in danger." The pain in Colleen's eyes nearly made his resolve weaken. She still had an effect on him regardless of his feelings for Laurie. Before he found himself taking her in his arms, Mike wrapped the chain of the necklace around his fist and went in search of the Stenton family.

# Chapter 26

Mike reappeared in the Council chamber where most of the members were still milling around and talking. Mike strode up to William Stenton. Before anyone even realized Mike was back, he had the older man pinned against a wall with the collar of his shirt balled in his fist. The burn Colleen had given him had begun to blister but the rage was fully in control and Mike did not feel it. "Where is your son, William? I am going to end his miserable existence and yours if there is one hair on Laurie's head harmed. For every tear she has shed in fear I will inflict on you and your son a month of torture before I finally strip your powers and leave you empty the same way I did Derek and his father."

Cliff and Damien heard the tone of Mike's voice and knew their friend was lost in his anger worse than they had ever seen him. Rather than try to touch him physically, Damien reached out with his mind to try and talk to his friend. *'Mike, calm down. What happened? Tell me. Talk to us. We will help you get it sorted out. This is not our way.'* William Stenton had turned white when Mike assaulted him, but now he was getting angry himself. If he lashed out at Mike, things were going to get out of control fast.

"Mr. Stenton," Cliff said with every ounce of authority he could muster. "You will stand down and do nothing. Everyone will take a breath and we will discuss this like gentlemen. As we always have. Mike, as leader of this Council, and your friend, I order you to release Mr. Stenton so we can get to the bottom of this." Cliff surprised himself with his speech and several of those who had supported the younger men's initiatives were nodding in approval.

Mike could hear his friends calling for him to release Stenton, but all he could picture was Laurie's panicked face from the day Derek attacked her at the church. Mike was at war within himself like he had never been before. He wasn't sure if he was going to win or if this was going to end up like the fight he had with Kevin over Colleen's honor. Thinking of Colleen along with the images of Laurie in his head gave him enough of an edge on the anger to release his hold on the older man. Before he turned away, he said menacingly, "If I find out you had anything to do with this, not only your son is going to lose his powers."

"I don't know what my son is doing," William said, recovering his breath. "I also will not stand for this threat. Once we resolve your little problem, you will answer for your actions. I will see you removed, I guarantee you that." William set about straightening his clothes and regaining his composure.

"My little problem," Mike began icily, trying to hold back from strangling the older man, "Is your son. He has kidnapped Laurie, my girlfriend. I believe I made it clear. Any act against any of my friends or family would be seen as an act of war and I would abolish this Council one person at a time. I have reason to believe Matthew is acting on his own, at least for now, so I will spare you the fate awaiting your son. Make no mistake, once I lay hands on him, he will wish for death." Mike then turned to the others gathered. He was sure he knew which ones were on his side and which could be co-conspirators in this act. What face he didn't see was Blake Kosgrove, the third member of the Triad and a required voting member to call Matthew to account. He sent his question to Damien and Cliff mentally.

"Mr. Kosgrove said he had a matter to attend to, but I will call him and get him back here so we can address this issue formally," Cliff said quickly to the look in Mike's eyes. "In the meantime, Mr. Stenton, can you think of anywhere Matthew would have gone? It is important we do not cause any more harm to the truce we have here. None of us want any open warfare. Especially if it is the jealousy of a single member of our world."

"My son and I have very little to do with each other since he was apprenticed to Blake," William admitted as everyone took their seats. "I know a few of his old hangouts, but I do not know if he is currently using any of them." He mopped his face with a handkerchief. Mike's anger slipping during meetings the last couple months was one thing, but the young man's eyes moments ago were almost lifeless.

Mike took his seat two down from Stenton when he realized he was still clutching Laurie's necklace in his left hand. He carefully pried his cramped fingers open to see where he had imprinted the swirl pattern in his palm he had been holding it so tightly. Inscribed on the back was a set of numbers which looked like GPS coordinates. Without warning Mike simply vanished from the Council chamber.

* * *

"Stop your sniveling," Matthew yelled at Laurie, who was huddled in the corner of the room he had brought them to. She had cried almost nonstop for the hour they had been waiting while Matthew paced the length of the sparsely decorated room. Once or twice he paused as if about to speak again, but then he continued his walk.

"Perhaps your boyfriend doesn't care about you after all," Matthew said suddenly, ceasing his pacing and turning to his captive. "He should have discovered my little message attached to your pendant by now. Maybe he and Colleen are consoling each other over your impending departure from their lives. With you out of the way I'm sure Colleen will have him wrapped around her finger within a day, if not hours. Doesn't the idea of their reuniting warm your heart?"

"You bastard," Laurie yelled back as defiantly as possible through her tears. She trusted Mike with her heart but she was worried. She had been in this room for a long time. "Mike will come for me and then you will really be in trouble. You know what he did to Derek for attacking me. What do you think he is going to do to you?"

Matthew stepped close and smacked Laurie across the cheek with the back of his hand. "Shut up or I will." He was interrupted by a sound from the other side of the room as Mike appeared.

"I am going to kill you, Matthew," Mike roared, seeing how Laurie's captor was standing over her with his hand in the air. He didn't need to see the red welling on her cheek to know what had happened. Mike targeted a ball of air and launched it at Matthew, careful to make sure it wouldn't affect Laurie. Mike paused as his opponent turned towards him and started laughing.

"You didn't think I would be stupid enough to leave myself open to your attacks did you?" Matthew taunted. "I know all your tricks. I have studied you ever since your little fight with the Gohrs. I know your strengths, and your weaknesses."

Mike focused and could now see the shield his enemy had woven around himself and Laurie. Anything he did to it was going to only make it stronger. Before he could come up with a new plan, two figures stepped out of the shadows of the room and approached. Mike noticed one had a knife and the other a bat. Mike braced himself for their assault, momentarily taking his eyes off of Matthew.

Matthew knew his plan was working, the appearance of his two minions distracted Mike. He quickly lowered his shield and launched his own ball of air at Mike, taking the younger man off his feet to crash into the wall. Matthew turned triumphantly towards Laurie, knowing his servants would truss Mike up so he couldn't retaliate. At first, he was confused as Laurie was not huddled in the corner where Matthew had last seen her. Suddenly he was on his knees as Laurie had kicked him from behind between the legs.

Gasping for breath he looked up as his prisoner stood over him, looking ready to deliver another kick. He quickly wrapped her in air. Trying to fight down the pain her kick had inflicted, he turned to see his cohorts were about to finish up things with Mike, who still had not moved. Matthew smiled.

His smile turned to a frown as Mike gave a roar and both of the two assailants went flying across the room. Mike was on his feet quickly, the rage and Darkness in full control. He could feel every current of power in the room. The knife wielding thug was first on his feet and had miraculously managed to hold onto his weapon. As he cautiously approached Mike he formed a small shield with his gift in order to protect himself from future attacks.

What the thug did not count on was Mike's strength. Mike, burning with anger, simply reached through his opponent's shield and stripped him of his meager powers with barely a thought. Turning to look for Matthew, the source of his rage, Mike barely noticed when the glow of the other man's power seeped into his skin, bolstering Mike's own. The thug screamed in agony and fell to the floor.

Mike bellowed, "You are next, Matthew." However, the momentary delay while Mike dealt with the knife wielder was the opportunity Matthew needed to reestablish his shield around himself and Laurie. Mike stopped a couple of feet from the shield. He could see the bluish glow as it hung in the air, waiting for him to step forward and set off its countermeasures. Mike looked to Laurie to make sure she was alright, which dulled the edge of his anger momentarily. Laurie's eyes were open wide in fright as she stood stiffly.

The look in her eyes was similar to Colleen's when the Darkness had taken over and he had tossed his doctor across the room with the wave of an arm. Mike didn't have long to ponder the look in her eyes as he was struck on the back of his head and he began to black out. The last thing he saw were her eyes as he heard Matthew start laughing.

"Good, force the drink down his throat and tie him up," Matthew said to his minion. It had been lucky the second thug had been smarter and had lain in wait for Mike to turn his back before striking with his bat. Things might have gotten ugly if Mike had tested the shield. Matthew had no desire to match his strength against Mike's, at least until he could work out the trick of taking another gifted's power.

The thug propped Mike up as he pulled a water bottle from his pocket. He poured a bit of the bitter drink down Mike's throat and held the fallen youth's head until he reflexively swallowed. Confident his captive would give him no gifted trouble, he set about binding Mike's hands and feet with zip ties. Once done he looked to Matthew for direction, who signaled he could go with a nod. The hireling went over and helped his friend to his feet and then both of them disappeared. Matthew stood over Mike, and gave the young man a kick to the ribs.

* * *

"This is exactly what we are talking about," Joseph Parker said in the Council chambers. Mike's sudden arrival had been bad enough, but his departure had turned the chamber into anarchy. There were calls for his immediate removal and banishment. Cliff and Damien, as Mike's closest friends, were unable to get the room back into any formal order.

"That is enough," Blake Kosgrove said as he appeared in the room and took his place to Cliff's right. "Now, what is the meaning of all this. I thought we were done for the day. Now I receive a summons to return and find all of you screaming at each other like little children." The room fell silent as the older man turned to Cliff. "Tell me what is going on, and stick to the short version. No interruptions," he continued as he eyed the room.

"Mike came back after we had wrapped things up," Cliff began. He told how Mike had pinned William Stenton to the wall, yelling about Matthew having kidnapped Laurie. "Mike demanded to know where Matthew was. As we all sat down to discuss the matter, he suddenly disappeared. Several members are calling for another vote on his competency to be a member of the Council. I was trying to establish order until you arrived and the Triad was at full strength. Due to my close association with Mike, it appears a few here were disregarding my position."

"It does appear to be the case," Blake turned to the room at large. "You all know our traditions. You all know our laws. Whoever sits as High Triad is our law. Disrespect of this sort is treasonous. What do you all have to say for yourselves?" There was mumbling and shifting of feet until Blake spoke again. "I think the time for silence is over."

With his words, chaos launched anew in the Council Chambers. Matthew Larsen turned to his right and grabbed Stephen Conner. Barklen began grappling with Gary Denison. William Stenton smiled as he clubbed Corey Dawson over the head with a solid mass of air. Dawson slumped forward on the table. Blake himself turned and began to shield Cliff, a fire in his eyes the younger man had not seen before. Damien was unable to help his friend as he was locked in a battle with Joseph Parker to his left. It was clear to the two teens the uprising the Gohr's had tried to launch was still alive and well.

Seeing no hope of overcoming the blitz attack, Damien reached behind him and grabbed hold of Cliff's arm, teleporting them both out of the chambers and back to Damien's study. Damien looked to his friend, who was having a hard time getting his breath. "Go to your father, tell him what happened. We have to find Mike, he may be the only one who can salvage this." Cliff nodded and promptly disappeared. Damien ran in search of his father.

Damien found him in his study, playing chess with David Nicholson. "Father, sorry to intrude, but Mr. Kosgrove has taken over the Council. It appears Barklen, Stenton, Parker and Larsen are in on it. Cliff and I barely escaped. The others are prisoners. I am sure they are going to move on our homes next. I sent Cliff to his father, he should be able to collect your family as well Mr. Nicholson. I just hope we aren't too late."

Several figures appeared in the room. Damien didn't wait for them to get their bearings but struck at the closest one as soon as he could. He barely pulled back when he saw Cliff's face. Next to Cliff were his parents as well as Mrs. Nicholson and Colleen. Damien breathed a sigh of relief.

"I almost put you through the wall there, Cliff," Damien said, a little breathless. "How did you get back here so fast? And manage to get everyone together?"

Clifford's father spoke first, "Ungrateful bastards came into my home and attempted to attack my family. Needless to say they will not be making the same mistake again any time soon. Now, what is the meaning of this? What is going on?" Clifford van Doornick the Second was not a man to be trifled with. His temper may not even come close to rivaling Mike's, but he was still a force to be reckoned with.

"I didn't have time to explain Father," Cliff spoke up. "Mr. Kosgrove has led a coup against everyone on the Council. He looks to be taking over for himself. Matthew Stenton has kidnapped Laurie, and Mike has gone missing to look for her. I haven't been able to reach him by cell or by telepathy. I know something is wrong, but how did Matthew get the jump on Mike?"

"In any case," Mr. van Doornick replied, "We need to get everyone to a safe place and collect any families still loyal to us. Leonard, do you still have the protected estate?" He looked to his old friend, who had continued to casually sip his drink. Leonard nodded. "Then we have little time to lose, everyone, take a hand."

Everyone gathered around the older man. At the last moment, Damien and Cliff dropped their hands while everyone else disappeared. "Alright," Damien began, "We have to find Mike and take back the Council while our father's keep everyone else safe."

"True, but we should get Mike's Aunt and Uncle, and his family back east. I am sure Mr. Kosgrove isn't going to leave them alone for long. We may already be too late," Cliff responded. "I think we will have to split up, but what do we tell them?"

"Let me handle that," Colleen said as she reappeared. "His mother and sister know me. I am sure with their help I can convince Mike's Aunt and Uncle to go with me back to your father's estate Damien. I feel so horrible Matthew used me to get to Laurie. I need to do this to make it up to Mike."

Damien nodded. "Then we have our plan to get everyone safe. We need to find a way to track down Mike. Where do you think Matthew would have taken Laurie, Cliff?"

"I have no idea," Cliff began, but then a thought struck him, "Remember those warehouses his family bought when they thought they were going to get to handle the new Pacific trade? They have been sitting empty for a few years now haven't they?"

"Sounds like the perfect place for an ambush," Damien agreed. "We could be walking into a trap, but it's the only way I know to rescue Mike. Let's get to it then." The teens all separated on their separate missions.

# Chapter 27

"Mrs. Keller? Connie?" Colleen yelled as she entered the Keller home from the garage. "It's me, Colleen. We need to talk about Mike. Where are you?" She found them in the living room, bound while two men she didn't recognize were standing over them. Connie had been crying, but Sally stared defiantly though a bruise forming on her cheek. The two guards had been deep in conversation and not paying attention so even though she had been calling for the Keller family, Colleen's arrival caught the captors by surprise.

Colleen's own anger exploded as she lashed at the two figures the only way she knew how, setting them both ablaze. As they screamed in pain, she realized she could burn down the whole house if she wasn't careful. She acted quickly to encase the two in shields of air to smother out the flames. It was too late to save their lives however, as they were already twitching their last. As their motions ceased, their powers let go of the Keller women. Sally and her daughter collapsed on the living room carpet and turned their heads to look at Colleen. Both had been bound wrists and ankles as well as wrapped in air. A cloth gag had been wrapped around their heads and stuffed in their mouth.

Colleen quickly untied Sally and Connie, but before she could say anything else Sally spoke up, "What are you doing here, Colleen? What's going on? I was in the kitchen and these two showed up and attacked me. Then they brought us in here and tied us up."

"Mrs. Keller," Colleen began, "I have an explanation but not enough time to explain. I doubt the failure of these two will go unnoticed and we have to get out of here so we can get to your brother's house. The short version is, those like Mike and myself, are at war. We have to get out of here before more show up."

Colleen was right as another figure suddenly appeared in the room and looked at the crispy corpses of the first two. He yelled and launched himself at Colleen both physically and with his power, knocking her to the ground. Colleen struggled against the bindings of air but was suddenly free as the newcomer grunted and fell face down on top of her. Connie was standing behind him, holding the metal baseball bat the earlier assailants had left casually lying around.

"Talk later, do whatever we have to do to get out of here," Connie said, not relinquishing her hold on the bat. "But believe me Colleen, we will talk about what you did to my brother." Connie emphasized her stance by pointing the bat at Colleen's chest.

Colleen nodded sadly, tears falling down her face at the mention of Mike. She took the hands of both of the Keller women and whisked them to the home of Jim and Jenny Johnson, steeling herself for another confrontation with Mike's family.

When the trio appeared in the driveway of the Johnson cabin, Colleen knew already she was too late. There were crashes and sounds of a struggle from inside the home. She had a moment of panic and then a figure came flying out of the front windows. She knew right away it wasn't one of the Johnson's. She bound the figure before it could recover and ran up the steps as Jim Johnson threw the front door open. His intention to finish off his assailant was thwarted when he came face to face with a young blonde girl.

"Now they are sending girls to attack me?" Jim yelled and raised his hands to try and pin Colleen's arms. Then he noticed his sister and niece only steps behind. "Sally? Connie? Is it really you?" He stepped past Colleen as if she wasn't there and rushed to the Keller's. He pulled them both into a hug.

"You must be Colleen," Jenny Johnson said from the doorway where she held a large skillet in her hand like the weapon it had become. When the people appeared in her home, she was washing up the dishes and happened to have it in her hand. She had heard her husband yell from the living room and had turned quickly and struck immediately at the figure appearing behind her before he could react. It was only her quick action which saved her from being trussed up like a Thanksgiving turkey. "We will have words later young lady, but what is going on here?"

Jim turned around from hugging his sister and niece, placing himself between them and Colleen. "I think it better if you explain what you are doing here, and if you know anything about them." He nudged the one in the yard with his foot. "Then you better explain them too."

Connie came to the rescue, "Uncle Jim, Colleen saved our lives. Two guys broke into our house and had mom and me wrapped up while they were waiting for orders from a higher up. Colleen, well, she set them on fire and rescued us. We were coming here to warn you. Apparently they are after Mike."

Colleen was caught off guard by the sudden support from Connie and was unable to respond right away. Everyone looked at her expectantly and she finally found her voice. "Yes, Mr. Johnson, Mrs. Johnson. The Council Mike is a part of, is in revolt. It looks like the rebels are making their move. This means those like Mike, and his friends are in danger. I am betting they were going to use you as a bargaining chip with Mike. Right now no one knows where he is. Damien and Cliff let me come to you because I at least know Mike's family so I thought I could convince you all to come with me where you would be safe."

Uncle Jim knew right away Colleen was being sincere. He detected a measure of regret and sadness when she talked about Mike which swayed him even more in her favor. "Alright," he said nodding, "Let's get out of here before anymore show up. Where are we going?"

"Best if we don't talk about it," Colleen said quickly. "Everyone, join hands." As she teleported everyone back to the estate Damien's father had setup, she saw more figures appearing in the yard. Thankfully none of them were fast enough to catch on to where they were going. It was only a matter of time before they were caught.

* * *

"Think this is the place?" Cliff asked telepathically as he looked around the warehouse he and Damien were in. The first two they had searched had revealed nothing. The two had thought it prudent to be as silent as possible and only communicate mentally.

Damien nodded noncommittally before responding in kind, "I don't know but this is the last one they own, so if he is here, it shouldn't be too hard to find him." There was a sound from the back corner of the warehouse and the two friends stayed crouched down behind a crate.

"Are you kidding me?" Matthew yelled into the phone. "His mother and sister rescued? By Colleen?" A pause as the person on the other end must have replied. "She did what? She set them on fire? I knew she was a pyro, but she killed the two I sent?" Another pause as Matthew listened to the line. "Fine. Send everyone to his uncle's. She will take them there to get the rest of his damned family. I want them all dead. Forget prisoners. I already have Mike so I don't really need them as hostages. I want his line ended." Then there was a beep as he must have shut off the cell phone.

Damien and Cliff looked at each other and nodded. Mike was captive but at least his family seemed safe for the moment. Cliff felt a little proud of Colleen. She had come a long way in her time at his family's home. They cautiously crept from shadow to shadow towards the direction Matthew's voice had come from. The two stopped when they could see Matthew, standing over Mike who was bound and lying on the ground.

"So, the high and mighty Mike Keller," Matthew accented his speech with a kick to Mike's ribs. "Look at you now. Powerless, friendless, and my prisoner. I think once I am done with you I will do a little brainwashing of Laurie here. She will make a nice trophy. Mr. Kosgrove will reward me for bringing you down." He kicked Mike again and stood laughing.

Cliff and Damien looked at each other. They knew Blake Kosgrove had been behind the coup at the Council chambers, but to hear he had actively pursued ruining Mike like this was another matter entirely. Cliff was suddenly angry. He had always liked Kosgrove, and the older man had been nothing but nice to Cliff with his limitations.

Cliff stood up and strode towards Matthew, who as yet wasn't aware he had an audience. "Matthew, you and your master are finished." Cliff reached out toward Matthew's aura. He had seen Mike do it twice, and since he could see the aura around Mathew, he felt he could manage the trick once. As long as he could win the battle of will with his opponent.

As Cliff grabbed hold of the aura, Matthew screamed and started fighting for his power. Being stronger than Cliff, it wasn't long before he was pulling the other way, drawing Cliff's power to himself. Elated he yelled back, "Oh, is the little crippled Cliff going to take down his betters? I always knew you were little better than a Normal." As Cliff started to cry out in pain as his gift was being pulled away, Matthew grew triumphant.

Damien stood up and battered Matthew with a rapid fire barrage of projectiles. His concentration interrupted, Matthew lost the connection to Cliff's gifts as he was knocked off his feet. Breathing heavily, Cliff struggled to regain his feet even as Damien wordlessly advanced. Matthew attempted to rise as well.

Damien was about to wrap Matthew up when he heard a roar behind him and Cliff ran past him towards their foe. Cliff raised his hand and pointed at Matthew, who began to scream. To Damien's surprise, Cliff then yelled, "Normal? A Normal? I will show you what a Normal can do to you, Matthew. This is over." As Cliff finished speaking, Matthew went still and Cliff fell to his knees, panting heavily.

Damien checked quickly to see if Matthew was still breathing before returning to his friend. "What happened, Cliff? What did you do to him? He is out cold. The color is drained from his face the same as Derek and his father were…" Damien stopped as he realized Cliff was laughing and staring at his hands.

"I did it, Damien," Cliff said, looking up at his friend and smiling broadly. "I took his powers and added it to my own. I did what Mike did to the Gohrs." Cliff alternated between hugging himself and staring at his hands. He was laughing even as tears rolled down his face.

"But how?" Damien asked. Not for the first time he wished he could see auras like Mike and Cliff could. Then he could understand what they were talking about. Mike and Cliff had both tried to explain what stripping a gifted's powers had looked like, but he couldn't see anything.

"I," Cliff began, then paused and took a breath. "He called me little better than a Normal. You know how I hate it. Well, I got so angry and suddenly I felt like a weight fell away and I was stronger than I had ever been. Taking his power was easy. There was no struggle at all. I had to be at least as strong as he was, or more to be able to do it." Cliff continued to stare at his hands.

The two looked at each other a full minute before a sound behind them drew their attention. "Mike," they both chorused and ran over to their friend. They quickly sliced his bindings and rolled him over. Once they had him sitting up, Damien spoke, "Mike, you alright man? We got here as soon as we could. Kosgrove has made a power play. We are at war."

Mike rubbed his head groggily as Damien's words sank into him. He saw Cliff had moved over and was kneeling next to another figure. He saw Laurie's legs from beside his friend and rushed over to her as she opened her eyes. "Laurie, I'm so sorry." He kissed her softly while Cliff and Damien went to get Matthew on his feet so they could take him to the safe house. Damien took the cellphone from Matthew's pocket and put it in his own.

"I knew you would come, Mike," Laurie whispered. She wasn't sure why she said it, but she continued, "Don't be mad at Colleen. I think we were finally starting to work past our issues when Matthew took me. She had no idea what he had planned." Mike kissed her again and slipped the pendant back over her head, having removed it from his pocket while she was talking. He helped her to a sitting position and started to rise so he could help her to her feet.

Mike glanced towards his friends and saw them lifting a shaken Matthew between them. The Darkness was suddenly in control and Mike drew upon his power to rip Matthew apart. The power didn't seem to want to come and the blast was a pathetic imitation of what Mike had planned. It was a small shock when it was Cliff's aura flaring to life and blocking Mike's assault. As the Darkness turned to lash at Cliff for interfering, Mike struggled to regain control.

"Mike," Cliff began, "Matthew is beaten. I have taken his power during the fight. We are going to take him to an estate Damien's family owns. Once this war is settled, we will then decide what is going to happen to him. See to Laurie, she needs you now. We will leave when you two are ready."

The mention of Laurie's name sent the Darkness fleeing as Mike was overcome with his concern for her safety. During the exchange she had regained her feet and quickly wrapped herself in Mike's arms and began crying softly into his shoulder, much like the day at the church a few months ago. Mike nodded to his friends and held Laurie close.

Mike tried to reach out to his power but it was weak and fleeting. He looked up at Matthew, held between his friends. "What did you do to me? Why can't I use my powers, Matthew?" Mike tensed but couldn't seem to draw enough power to light a candle, much less burn Matthew to cinders like he wanted. The Darkness was dancing in the edge of his consciousness, confused without the power to latch onto.

Damien then picked up the water bottle lying nearby. He gave its contents a sniff and his face turned grim. "He drugged you. This smells like Mutewort. Rare, but it can dull or block the powers of one of us. It should fade, but without knowing how much he gave you, I don't know how long. It could be hours, days, or longer." Matthew had begun chuckling lightly. He knew he was finished, but he was glad Mike was inconvenienced and might still be taken by another member of the rebellion. Cliff elbowed him in the ribs and he quieted down.

"Well, then I am going to need a lift to get Laurie's family and then to this safe house of yours," Mike said. "I don't want to imagine what will happen to them when Matthew's failure gets out. Once my powers are back, I am going to end every single one of them. Starting with Blake Kosgrove." Mike's eyes flashed dangerously. He could feel his power, and though he might be fooling himself, it felt like he was a miniscule amount stronger than before. Maybe the effects would wear off sooner than later. He did know he was a long way from teleporting himself alone, much less Laurie and her family.

"Cliff, you take Matthew to our fathers," Damien said. "I will leave it up to you if you tell him how Matthew got the way he is or if you want to wait until Mike and I get back. I'll go with Mike and meet you there as soon as we can. With any luck we won't have to fight." Damien laid a hand on Mike's shoulder as Cliff nodded and disappeared with Matthew in tow. Then the trio disappeared as well.

\* \* \*

"Laurie, what happened, why is your face all red? Why are you crying?" her mother, Missy, was near hysterical when the three young people came down the hall. She had noticed Mike's disheveled appearance but dismissed the other young man temporarily as she didn't recognize him. When she saw the bruise on her daughter's face from Matthew's slap she lost it. She ran to embrace Laurie.

"Mrs. Sterling," Mike began, "Is your husband home? I need to explain something to you both and it would be best if we didn't have to go over it twice." He flinched when her eyes flashed to him as if he had done whatever had hurt her daughter. Mike hoped his meager power would be enough to stop her from killing him if she thought he was responsible. He definitely could feel his strength returning.

"He's in his study," She said curtly, not releasing her hold on Laurie. She led the way, dragging her daughter with her and leaving the two young men to follow or be left behind. On the way she kept glancing back at the two of them to be sure they were keeping up. "I intend to get to the bottom of this young man." Mike nodded as they reached the door to the study and Laurie's mother pushed the door open.

Damien and Mike reacted quickly to the presence of two other figures in the room; one was holding Bill Sterling by his collar. Damien lashed out, shielding and binding the one holding Laurie's father. Mike, not trusting his gifts to do both, wrapped the second figure in a shield and ran into him shoulder first. They both collapsed on the ground in a tangle of legs and arms. Mike was pleased the shield was holding, albeit barely, as he could feel his opponent trying to reach his powers.

Missy and Laurie screamed and ran to their family patriarch while Mike wrestled with his opponent. The two young men rolled about on the floor, trying to land a blow which would lend them an advantage. After a few moments Mike felt his powers slide back into place and he bound his opponent tightly. Standing, he adjusted his twisted shirt and looked around the room. Laurie's parents stared as Laurie wrapped herself around Mike and hugged him tightly.

"Mr. and Mrs. Sterling," Mike began. "I have something to tell you and it is going to be hard to believe." Mike floated a chair from across the room and sank into it as he started telling the story of his powers, the Council, and the current war escalating hourly. He even told the real story of the accident at the church which had nearly took Laurie's life a few months earlier. It took nearly an hour to get it all out. "Now we come to where we are," Mike ended with a sigh. It was up to them if they believed him.

Mr. Sterling stopped his wife from speaking first. "So," he started, "You are telling me you have saved the life of my daughter and my family several times now, with powers right out of a comic book or movie? We will talk more later, but what do we do for now?"

"We need to get to my father's estate until this war is settled," Damien spoke up, causing the Sterlings to jump in their seats. They had forgotten anyone else was there. Damien turned to Mike, "How are you feeling? Everything back to normal?"

"Close enough," Mike nodded. "Let's get out of here and figure out our next move." Mike stood and took Laurie's hand. She knew what was coming and quickly took hold of her mother's hand who was still clutching her father. Mike nodded to Damien and then the five disappeared from the room.

# Chapter 28

"Father," Damien called and ran to his elder as the group appeared in the room. When he embraced his father, the older man was overcome with emotion and tears started down his face. Damien fought back his own tears. "What do we do now father? The Council is destroyed and right now I am sure Kosgrove and the others are consolidating their power. It is only a matter of time before they discover where we are."

"It will be alright son," Leonard Mauston said. "We have not been idle. We have our own allies, and if Blake thinks he is going to push me out this easily, he is in for a rude awakening." Several voices behind the father and son voiced their agreement.

Damien was pleased to see so many supporters behind them, but worried about treachery from within. It was Cliff's father who put his mind to rest. "Everyone has been triple checked," Mr. van Doornick said softly. "All those in this room are loyal, and willing to fight if they have the means." There was a loud boom which rocked the entire building.

"Sounds like we are going to have to fight sooner than later," Mike said quickly. "Laurie, take your parents and the other non-gifted and go into the basement or cellar. A few of the gifted will go with you to keep all of you safe. The rest of us are going out front to face this." Laurie gave Mike a long kiss before she grabbed her parents and started leading the way. Leonard Mauston told off a few of the gifted to follow and cover the families. Mike noticed his mother, sister, aunt and uncle, standing off to the side with Colleen.

"Bro," Connie started towards him, then Mike was wrapped in the arms of both his mother and sister. "We were so worried about you. Colleen saved us. She has powers like you, but I guess you knew already. I'm so glad you're safe."

"Connie, Mom," Mike stumbled over his words. "I need you to take Aunt Jenny and Uncle Jim with you to the cellar. Things are going to get bad up here."

"I am going with you, nephew," Uncle Jim said, his eyes on fire. "They came into my home, and attacked my wife. I couldn't fight before, but I am going to fight this time." He glanced significantly in the direction of Leonard Mauston. "Nothing is going to stop me from defending my family." Leonard nodded grimly.

"Sounds great, Mr. Johnson," Cliff said, speaking for the first time since Mike and Damien arrived with the Sterlings. Then another boom shook the house's foundations. "I think we better get a move on, the shield and defenses aren't going to hold much longer." Everyone nodded.

As the Keller women and Aunt Jenny headed towards the cellar, Mike turned to Colleen. "Thank you for saving them," he said. "I don't know what I would have done if anything had happened to them." Colleen nodded through the tears in her eyes. She knew Mike was lost to her romantically, but still couldn't face him being hurt. Mike turned to everyone else who seemed to be looking to him for leadership, "Let's do this people."

\* \* \*

"I want Mike taken alive," Blake Kosgrove told his lieutenants. "The rest are expendable, but he is mine." The assembled men, both old and young, nodded. They knew their leader had a special fate in store for the Keller boy who had caused them so much grief. Blake smiled, seeing victory in his grasp, "Attack."

There was a resounding boom as the shield around the Mauston estate finally collapsed. The resulting cloud of dust from the crashing forces obscured the front lawn momentarily. When it cleared, Blake and his army faced an equal army with Mike at its head. He was flanked by Damien and the newly empowered Cliff.

"Blake Kosgrove," Mike projected his voice over the impromptu battlefield. "You are hereby charged with insurrection and treason against the Council of Elders. You are stripped of your titles as a member of the High Triad. Your sentence is loss of your powers and banishment. We can do this the easy way, or the hard way."

"I choose to end you," Blake said, pointing a finger at Mike. He launched a mass of air at the younger man and the battle was joined. The rest of his army began firing as well. Several were throwing balls of fire.

Those beside Mike struck back, throwing shields against the oncoming weapons while the rest returned fire. After the initial volleys, the opposing forces came together. They began to break off into smaller combats ranging all over the grounds. The smell of burnt grass and shrubs had started to fill the air from the pyros.

Colleen found herself facing off with another pyro she didn't recognize throwing fire as well as she could. They traded blows as they dodged around the lawn until she found herself back to back with Cliff. He was facing off against two former Council members, Gerald Barklen and Matthew Larsen. They had thought he would be easy pickings, but with his unlocked and boosted powers, Cliff was turning out to be a tougher opponent than they bargained for.

"Holding up ok, Colleen?" Cliff asked as they were at a standstill with their enemies. "I know this isn't what we taught you."

She smiled over shoulder, barely taking her eyes off the pyro across from her. "I'm doing great, but how are you? Aren't two of them going to be too much?" She could feel Cliff was different since that morning, but hadn't had time to talk to him after her arrival with Mike's family. Cliff had been helping to bring in other families and then closeted with his father talking strategy.

"I'm doing great," Cliff said, blocking a rapid blast from Larsen and sending return fire of his own. The older man went to his knees briefly and Cliff reached out to snatch his aura. Before he could complete his goal, Barklen began firing at the pair of young people. "I will explain later, shall we finish these three off?" He shielded against the combined assault of Barklen and Larsen as the former regained his feet.

Colleen nodded and ducked to her right, Cliff following around as they spun to face opposite sides. The change in opponent momentarily caught their enemies off guard. Having been trained at dodging and deflecting missiles of air, Barklen and Larsen were completely caught off guard by Colleen's firestorm. As they both began rolling about trying to put out their clothes, Colleen shielded them both.

Cliff was having a harder time as his opponent had been younger and reacted faster, shifting tactics. As he heard the screams of the two older men behind him, he finally got a hold of his foe's aura and wrenched away his powers. With a scream, the young man fell to his knees, clutching his hands to his face. Cliff thumped him with a club of air and left him lying in the grass.

He turned to see how Colleen was doing and looked into her eyes. "We did it," Colleen exclaimed even as the battle raged around them. She wrapped him in a hug and they both felt the surge of electricity from previous occasions when they touched. Without thinking, Colleen leaned in and the two kissed. An errant missile of air struck a little too close, snapping them out of their victory.

"Umm," Cliff stuttered. "We haven't won it yet. We need to go help the others. First I am going to deal with these two traitors." Cliff walked over to the bound older men and rolled them over to stare into their eyes. "You two will never trouble anyone again." He reached out and casually pulled their powers out of them. The two men screamed soundlessly from behind their bindings. Cliff then knocked them out and turned to survey the battlefield raging around him with a fury in his eyes.

* * *

Meanwhile, Damien was embroiled in his own battle back to back with his father. The two Mauston's made a formidable team and moved through several groups of lesser members, leaving unconscious foes behind them. "Glad to see all your combat training sank in, Son," Leonard said as they dispatched another pair of traitors. "There were times I wasn't sure if I was getting through to you or not."

"It sank in, Father," Damien laughed. "How could it not with how you beat it into me since I was old enough to spar. We need to get to Blake though, he is the key to this whole thing." Leonard agreed, seeing the wisdom in his son's words. He was very pleased with his progeny.

"You two are done for," William Stenton said as he squared off with Leonard. Joseph Parker stood next to him. "I have had enough of the Mauston family power and plan to take it for myself. When I am through, no one in either world will ever remember your names." He began his assault by launching a wave of air at the older Mauston.

Joseph did the same, focusing on the older of the two in front of him. Leonard pushed Damien aside but it was too late to save himself. He was hit dead on and his smaller shield collapsed. As he was taken off his feet, the ground underneath him erupted upward. Damien rolled away from the blast and watched his father fall to the ground.

He crawled in the direction of his father and was pleased to see the man struggling to shake off the effects of the combined attack. Damien turned his attention to the traitors. "I'm going to kill you both," he roared as he came to his feet, launching everything he had at the two older men.

Secure behind their shields, the two men laughed as they deflected his all-out assault. "You never were subtle, Damien," Joseph said between chuckles. "That's going to be your downfall today." The two men prepared to deal the same blow to the son they dealt to the father.

Before they could unleash it, James Johnson was suddenly by Damien's side. "I think you've got it wrong," he said, putting a hand on the younger man's shoulder. Returned to full strength, James knew the one thing he was superior at was shields as that was the only thing he had been able to do for years. "On the count of three, Damien." He then reached into the small weakness in his foe's shields and brought them down. As the two wondered what had happened, Jim turned to Damien, "Three."

Damien launched everything he had at the two, and he felt movement behind him. He turned slightly to see his father had gotten at least to a kneeling position and was throwing his power into the assault. The two traitors were knocked to the ground and quickly shielded and knocked out. Damien turned to James, "Thank you Mr. Johnson. How did you do that?"

"Please, call me Jim," he said quickly. "All I was able to do for years is weave the shield around my property. I got very good at shields, and at seeing their weaknesses. A wall built improperly can be toppled with the removal of a single brick." He smiled and clapped the younger man on the shoulder. He then turned and helped Leonard get the rest of the way to his feet.

"Thank you, James," Leonard said shakily. "I am grateful to you for helping my son." The two former enemies shook hands. "Now, let's see to the rest of this riffraff." Grinning at each other, the trio went off in search of Blake Kosgrove.

\* \* \*

The object of their anger was in a fierce battle with Mike. The younger man appeared to be winning from the start as he was driving the old man back by steps with his relentless assault. "Give it up Kosgrove. I am stronger than you," Mike taunted. He had been surprised at first the Darkness had not taken over, but was pleased to be controlling himself. He wanted Blake to suffer for what he allowed Matthew Stenton to do to Laurie.

"Be that as it may boy," Blake spat back. "But I have decades of experience on my side. A fledgling bird like you would do well to avoid the talons of the old hawk." He suddenly changed tactics and it was Mike on the defensive, dodging smaller but more precise shots.

As Mike was driven back now by the older man's assault, he didn't see the appearance of Cliff's father. He had been bouncing around the battlefield striking small blows in the confrontations so they would turn things to his side's favor. Now he had come to Mike's struggle with the man he had once thought of as a friend.

"Blake," Clifford van Doornick the Second screamed, drawing the older man's attention briefly. "This is over, your army is nearly finished. Surrender and I will see to it there is mercy in your case. It is the best I can offer you, old friend."

"Mercy?" Blake laughed. "I don't need your mercy or your pity." A coughing fit suddenly took Blake and he put all his power into a shield around himself while he was vulnerable. When he recovered he switched to an attack on his former friend. "Your time is over, Clifford." His blast took the former highest of the High Triad off his feet and sent him sailing through the air. Blake then turned back to Mike.

"You're going to wish you hadn't done that," Mike roared, feeling the Darkness having tried to creep in while he was watching the exchange between the older men. Instead of fighting it, he grabbed hold of it and rode the anger and rage as if it was a wild bull. By seizing control like he did, the Darkness only fought for moments before realizing it was no longer in charge. Smiling, Mike launched his attack and watched Blake shielding and deflecting as if his life depended on it. The way Mike was attacking, it very well did.

It was to this spectacle the others arrived. Blake fell to his knees, using everything he had to maintain a shield to keep Mike from taking his body apart. He looked around and saw his army fallen. They were either bound or unconscious. Cliff, Damien, their fathers, Colleen and even James Johnson all came to stand around him as Mike continued to batter the old man's shield.

Finally with a cry of pain it shattered and Mike stopped his assault. The young man walked slowly towards the man who had orchestrated so much misery for him. "Was it all you Kosgrove? The accident that killed my father and grandfather? The Gohr's? Did you plan all this? Answer me." Mike said the last bit right into the older man's face as he grabbed him by the collar.

"Yes," was all Blake got out before another coughing fit seized him. He reflexively brought the handkerchief to his mouth and it came away bloodier than ever before. Everyone saw the blood but Mike was not moved to compassion. He gripped the older man's collar tighter in his first.

"Blake Kosgrove," Mike intoned formally. "I charge you with treason against the Council of Elders. I charge you with the murder of James Johnson Senior, and Thomas Keller. I charge you with orchestrating the assault on Laurie Sterling. The penalties for these crimes is clear. You will be stripped of your powers and banished from our world."

Everyone standing around watched, though most couldn't see anything. Cliff watched as Mike drew out the older man's powers and absorbed them. The others merely watched as Blake stiffened, crying out in pain. A moment later he collapsed and a trickle of blood ran from the corner of his mouth. Without his powers to sustain him, Blake succumbed to his illness and died at Mike's feet.

After several moments, a cheer began to go up all over the lawn of the estate. Amidst the smoke from the burned grass and shrubs, the victorious forces began to gather together the losing army. Those left were gathered together where they could be shielded easier. There were those who wept openly, while others continued to stare defiantly. Those who had lost their powers in the struggle, either from having them taken or merely burning out, sat without moving. They appeared lost to whatever they found in their fractured minds.

The non-gifted and their protectors came up from the wine cellar to join with the victors out front. They brought along with them a few prisoners of their own. There had been a small attack on them but it was thought they would be without real protection. The presence of gifted among the non-gifted had caught the assailants completely by surprise.

Mike rushed to his family and struggled to hug his mother, sister and Laurie all at the same time. Aunt Jenny wrapped her arms around her husband. The women were all crying.

Colleen watched as tears streamed down her face until Cliff nudged her. She turned to him and collapsed in his arms. The resulting shock confirmed for them both what had developed during their time together. "I love you, Colleen," Cliff said softly into her hair.

Colleen smiled, "I love you, Cliff. I don't know how but I do. I'm so damaged. You deserve," Cliff silenced her with a kiss. Her father and Cliff's watched, grinning at each other.

"Colleen, stop it," Cliff said when they finally ended their kiss. "You beautiful mess of a pyro. How could I resist you? Does this mean you are ready to move on?" Colleen nodded and the two began kissing again.

"Hey, get a room you two," Mike yelled from nearby with his arm around Laurie. He laughed as the new couple broke apart, blushing. "I think you two are a good match, but Cliff, something is bothering me. About your powers?"

"It was during the fight with Matthew," Cliff began, hugging Colleen close. "He kept yelling at me, calling me little better than a Normal. No offense," He said, turning to the non-gifted in the vicinity. No one said anything. "I got so angry, which made me think of you. Suddenly, I felt this surge of power like a dam had let loose. I was so angry at him I lashed out and took his powers."

"Impressive son," Cliff's father said from where he was standing with Damien's father. Leonard looked like he might collapse at any moment. The battle had taken its toll on him and it looked like it would be some time before he fully recovered. Damien hovered close by.

Damien smiled at his friend. "It all worked out in the end, I guess. Now we can get down to the business of cleaning up this mess. What should we do with all of them?" He indicated the huddled mass of shielded gifted who had made up the insurrection.

"They made their decisions. We can either strip them of their powers, or extract oaths and put them to use doing charity work. Their choice," Mike stated. "There are no second chances. Anyone who refuses the oath is stripped of their powers. Anyone who takes the oath will be bound to the orders of the High Triad until the end of their days." Everyone nodded in agreement. "We need to find the rest of the Council, the ones they took prisoner."

"That won't be necessary, Mike," Corey Dawson appeared with his son and the other members of the Council. "When things wrapped up here, our shields came down. We freed the others and went looking for our captors. It wasn't hard to trace the remnants of the battle here. It is like the sun in the sky to those who can feel it, or see it." He ended with a nod to Mike and Cliff.

"Excellent news," Mike replied. "I'm glad everyone is safe then. I think we need to move quickly. There are going to be a host of companies and power bases changing hands. We are going to have to elect a new member of the High Triad and several new Council members I think. Mr. Mauston, Mr. van Doornick, do you think you could come out of retirement until we get things settled?"

"I think we have our High Triad, Michael," Leonard said as he leaned on his friend and son. After a moment it sank in for everyone. "I will have to respectfully decline your offer to come out of retirement. I feel now I need it more than ever."

"I agree," Cliff's father said. "I have far too many books to catch up on. I think the Council is in good hands with the three of you. Raise whoever you feel will be of assistance to the cause and continue to do the good things you were planning."

Mike took a moment to absorb the older men's words, then he nodded. "Colleen, Joey, I think you both need to take your places on the Council. Cliff, Damien, what do you think?"

Cliff smiled and Damien replied, "I think they make a start. There are several here who proved their loyalty and worth today. I would also say Mr. Johnson should take his place amongst our kind."

Mike and Cliff agreed wholeheartedly over the protests of James Johnson himself. At least until his wife smacked him in the arm. "You're going to work with your nephew, instead of him working for you this time," she said forcefully. Her husband rubbed his arm in mock pain and nodded in Mike's direction.

The newly reformed Council began gathering up its traitors and detractors. They transported them in groups back to the Council chambers and gathered them in the middle of the room. Several began pleading to take whatever oaths were required as soon as their bonds were loosened. Mike took his place to Cliff's right and the new High Triad held its first session.

After the new members were put in their places at the table, Cliff, Damien, and Mike began selecting others who had fought along their side to finish out the table. Many were minor families who had believed in what the boys were trying to do with helping the less fortunate. It took a surprisingly short amount of time to bring the Council to full strength so they could take on the matter of the rebellion.

"We will now come to order to address the rebellion of these before us," Cliff said, rising to his feet and looking around the room. "It is sad so many lost their way over jealousy. I want nothing more than to end these threats with all the brutality they tried to inflict on us. But that would make us no better than they are. We will offer them the terms previously stated. Oaths, or stripping of powers and banishment."

There was a commotion as those eager to retain at least a little use of their powers pushed to the front. Those who would rather die than give up their powers sat sullenly and stared at the Council members. It took several hours to sort everyone out, with Cliff and Mike having to strip the powers of the last three holdouts.

It was nearly midnight before the last of the rebellion was settled and shipped off to their new lives. Mike looked at Cliff and Damien, smiling wearily. "I'm glad that's over guys," Mike said softly, gathering a stack of handwritten sheets in front of him into a semblance of a reasonable pile. They had all been taking notes of who did what and where they were sent.

"I agree," Cliff replied in a low mutter. "I hope sorting the individual estates of our former Council members will go as relatively smoothly." Cliff yawned deeply and put a hand to his mouth. It had been a long day for everyone between the multiple meetings and then the battle.

"It's going to take a long time to root out anyone who sympathized with Kosgrove's ploy," Damien stated grimly. "Any low level members will probably fall back into line now the head of this snake is cut off, though." The three friends nodded in agreement and quickly went to their respective homes.

# Chapter 29

Mike appeared in his room to find it wasn't empty; as he should have expected. He dropped the stack of documents on top of his small file cabinet as he watched Laurie asleep on top of his bed. She must have been waiting for him to get home. Mike knelt next to the bed and gently shook her shoulder. "Laurie, I'm home," Mike whispered when her eyes fluttered.

Laurie came fully awake and flew into Mike's arms, knocking him back against the wall near the bed. She covered his face and lips with kisses before collapsing against his chest. "I was so worried I would never see you again," she whispered before tears overtook her.

Mike fought back tears of his own, the adrenaline rush he had maintained even through the Council meeting finally leaving him. He could have been killed today. It certainly appeared to be Matthew's goal eventually. To never see Laurie, or his mom and sister again. The implications were overwhelming and the two teens clung to each other, eventually falling asleep in each other's arms. When Aunt Jenny checked Mike's room in the morning she laid a blanket over them.

\* \* \*

Cliff appeared in his darkened study and stifled another yawn. He, Mike, and Damien had stayed long after the other Council members had retired for the night. As a result he wasn't paying attention as well as he normally would have. When Colleen suddenly stood up from the chair she had been sitting in, Cliff was spooked and the papers he carried fanned out around him.

"Cliff," Colleen whispered. "I think we need to talk about what happened. About us." She was nervous. *'Sure, heat of the battle they had said some things, but did Cliff really mean them?'* Colleen was wracked with self-doubt. Her feelings for Cliff had been growing steadily over the few months they had spent in close quarters. She realized her efforts to win Mike back once the school year started had been her last effort to hold onto her old life.

"I do love you, Colleen," Cliff stated simply. "I think I loved you the moment I met you. The spark between us, it's what my dad always said he felt for my mother. I never thought I would feel it. I can only hope you might come to feel the same for me one day."

"I do Cliff," Colleen said as she approached and wrapped her arms around him. "I didn't think I would ever love anyone but Mike. I didn't think I could love anyone but Mike. But you taught me different. You have taught me so much since we met." The two stood there, holding each other for several minutes before they both had to stifle yawns.

Cliff laughed lightly at their shared exhaustion. "I have to go to bed, Colleen. I'll see you in the morning, right? We will have to get your family settled in their new estate. No sense sharing this house when you have your own now as part of the Council."

"Can I," Colleen stumbled over her words. "Can I stay with you tonight? I feel safer when you're around." Cliff nodded and took her hand. The two shared a tender kiss before he led her through the door to his bedroom. The two climbed under the covers and promptly fell asleep in each other's arms.

* * *

Damien came home to a different homecoming. His father was waiting, a half empty tumbler of scotch sitting on the table next to him as he slept in one of Damien's big leather chairs. Damien smiled, knowing he had to wake his father up and give him a report. He gently shook his father's shoulder and the older man's eyes fluttered open.

"Damien, son," his father started. "How did it go? Is everything resolved now?" The old man had been worried as the night wore on, but had forced himself to stay away. He wanted his son to know he trusted him and had faith Damien could stand on his own without his father being there.

"It went well, Father," Damien whispered. "Everyone is sent off to their new homes. There is still more work to do on consolidating the holdings of those who are gone, but Cliff, Mike, and I have a fair start on it. Beginning with rewarding a few of those who stood with us today." He glanced at the clock, "Well, I suppose I should say, stood with us yesterday." He laughed briefly.

His father chuckled along with the joke. "You made me very proud today, Damien. I know I was not always the most supportive father, but your work the last few months has shown me how wrong I was about you," Leonard said as he stood. He extended his hand out towards his son. Damien laughed out loud as he pushed away the handshake and threw his arms around his father. The act further healed whatever remained of the rift between them.

After a few moments the two separated, suddenly embarrassed by the show of emotion. "I guess it is a new age, Son," Leonard said, picking up his half-finished drink. He raised it, "Here is to your continued success." He drank the last of the scotch and smiled. With a nod he left for his own rooms, leaving Damien feeling euphoric.

* * *

The next morning, Mike came awake not knowing where he was at first. He had not even opened his eyes but he could feel the stiffness in his back and a body

174

laying half on top of him. He shifted and looked around the room. He was lying against the wall on the floor next to his bed. He looked down to see Laurie curled up alongside him, her head snuggled where his chest met his abdomen. He gazed at her until her eyes slowly slid open.

"Morning sweetheart," Mike whispered before leaning down and kissing her forehead. Laurie smiled and then stretched like a cat. "How did you sleep?"

"The best ever," Laurie whispered. She slid up until her face was level with Mike's and they shared a deep kiss, clinging to each other as the late morning sunlight streamed through the cracks in the blinds.

Mike winced and Laurie froze, pulling back. "It's nothing," he said reassuringly. "A little stiff from sleeping against the wall like this. Next time we do this, let's stick to the bed." He smiled at the look on her face.

"I don't know," Laurie grinned mischievously. "I slept like a baby. Would you take away the best night's sleep I've ever had?" She even went so far as to sit up and cross her arms in mock anger.

Mike's response was to start tickling her and soon the two of them were rolling on the ground laughing as Laurie tried to return Mike's assault in kind. Their laughter drew the attention of Aunt Jenny who stood in the doorway for a few minutes watching the two. When they realized they had an audience, they both stopped, blushing lightly in embarrassment.

"Glad to see you two up and about," Aunt Jenny said with a smile on her face. Her attempt to look stern was a lost cause. "I'll warm up breakfast for you. Laurie, your mother and father expect a call as soon as you are up. They want to know you are alright. I told them you're fine, but your mother insists on speaking to you herself." She smiled again and turned to head down the hallway towards the kitchen.

The two teens reluctantly separated and Mike tried in vain to work the cramp out of his back. Laurie laughed at the pained expression on his face, but she patted him consolingly. He turned to her and kissed her nose softly, "Tell Aunt Jenny I'm going to take a shower. Maybe the hot water will ease my back." Laurie nodded and walked down the hall towards the kitchen. Mike grabbed a change of clothes and headed for the shower. He knew he was going to have to visit his mother and sister today.

"Mike says he's going to take a shower," Laurie said as she entered the dining room and dumped herself in a chair. "He claims sleeping against the wall with me on his chest hurt his back"

"I doubt the boy has ever slept so well," Jenny replied laughing. She was pleased to see her god daughter and nephew doing so well. Her worry over Colleen's return was shattered by what she had seen last night before they were brought home. *I'm glad she has that Cliff boy. He seems sweet,'* Jenny thought to herself as she made a plate of eggs, bacon and hash browns for Laurie. *'I hope they're all happy.'*

James Johnson appeared outside the sliding glass door. He had been up early as usual and went for a walk back to the clearing where he had told Mike about his family legacy a few short months ago. It seemed like a lifetime. The strain of the day before was nearly gone from his body as his restored powers quickly ratcheted back up to full strength. He had not realized how much the oath had cost him.

His musings of the morning had much more to do with the progress his nephew had made. It was clear Mike was the one foretold in their family book. James was anxious to see what his nephew would accomplish next. Having already turned the world James knew existed on its head, he couldn't fathom what else might be in store for Mike and his family. James smiled at Laurie, who was eating breakfast as he came in. At least everything was working out the way he had hoped.

A few minutes later Mike shuffled in, still looking a little worse for wear. Laurie extended her hand and Mike lightly ran his fingers from knuckles to forearm before leaning down to kiss her on the top of her head. Aunt Jenny had heard the shower turn off and had a plate of breakfast prepared. She laid it in the spot closest to Laurie but before she could retreat back to the kitchen, Mike hugged her. "Thank you, Aunt Jenny," he said before letting go.

"For breakfast? You forget I know your appetite now after you have been out playing. There's more if you want it," she patted his cheek and turned to go. Before she got too far, Mike spoke again.

"Not for breakfast," he began. "Or not only breakfast. For everything this summer, Aunt Jenny. And for sticking with Uncle Jim for all these years even in the face of the world we are forced to deal with." This elicited a grin from Uncle Jim who had always said he would be lost without his wife. "Also, for introducing me to Laurie. I couldn't have made it through this without her. I have never been more sure of anything in my life. I could not have gotten through this without both of you being so supportive." He sat down to his breakfast, both females sharing a look as they wiped back tears at the sincerity and fervor in his voice.

Uncle Jim leaned over to clap his nephew on the shoulder, "Well said Mike." The older man had settled down with the morning paper and his coffee. He took a sip and went back to the article he had been reading.

"Uncle Jim," Mike said after he tackled a few mouthfuls of his breakfast. "Damien, Cliff, and I have worked out a preliminary distribution of the assets from the families who forfeited yesterday. It was why I was so late. There is a sizable estate marked for you as a new member of the Council." Uncle Jim looked ready to protest so Mike continued, "As the High Triad, we aren't taking no for an answer. You are a businessman, Uncle Jim. You will understand all of this better than most. And besides, you deserve it for the years taken from you."

Uncle Jim merely nodded when the phone started ringing. Aunt Jenny grabbed it first, and after a brief hello, handed the phone to Mike. "It's your mom."

"Hey Mom," Mike said around the mouthful of scrambled eggs he had managed to take before the phone was put in his hand. "How are you and Connie? I trust everything went well with you two getting home? Sorry I didn't call but I only got up a half hour ago. It was a late night."

"I'm sure it was," Sally replied. She still wasn't sure what to make of everything she witnessed. "I needed to hear your voice and know everything was ok. Your sister and I are fine. I don't know if I will ever understand what happened. I'm so happy to hear your voice and know you're OK."

"I am great mom. Love you, give Connie my best," Mike said. "I'm going to eat breakfast now but maybe Laurie and I can visit after we talk to her parents."

"That would be nice, dear," Sally said. "Give your Aunt a hug for me. I will see you later." Then the connection ended and Mike laid the phone on the table.

# Epilogue

The next few weeks flew by between Council meetings and preparations for Homecoming. Though a newcomer to the school, Mike had earned himself a spot on the ballot for Homecoming King amongst the usual jocks and popular kids. The feeling was bittersweet in comparison to the Prom events six months earlier. Colleen had integrated into the group well, especially with her and Cliff becoming an item. Mike had been pleased to see Cliff really come into his confidence once he wasn't holding himself back gift wise.

Colleen, Laurie, Anne, Liz, and Deb formed a powerful friendship over the next couple weeks. Liz and Damien grew closer after his revelation. It was decided to at least clue Deb and Chad in, so the others didn't have to tiptoe around them. Chad had been even more impressed with Mike after the new information regarding the accident at Laurie's church not really being an accident. They both handled the revelations about their friends well. Deb had made Mike do the coin trick he had performed for Laurie many times after being told. There had been a bit of worry about revealing their world to those not a part of it in a direct way, as in Liz's relationship with Damien. Mike was glad to include Deb and Chad. No one had to guard their actions as much when it was the friends together.

The excitement built over the course of the week and by Friday afternoon there was a palpable air of anxiousness in the school. The football team had been doing very well and the weekend's Saturday matchup against their cross town rivals was looking to be a good one. Mike wrapped up the reports for the next Monday Council meeting and was starting on his homework when Laurie called. Her and the other girls, along with the rest of the homecoming committee were decorating for the dance after the game. Mike had begged off from helping due to the mounting paperwork. It seemed everyone wanted his seal of approval on every project. Well, his along with Cliff and Damien's. All three were realizing how much bureaucracy there was in being the High Triad.

Mike began using the study in the old Gohr mansion, merely as a better place to work than his Aunt and Uncle's dining room table. He rarely slept in the house though and therefore had not had the staff come off of light rotation. The knock at the study door spooked him. Damien or Cliff would have contacted him telepathically before appearing in the room, so for there to be a knock was an oddity itself. "Who is it?" Mike called, closing his biology textbook.

"Pardon my intrusion, Mr. Keller," said an accented voice as a pale face poked into the room. "I was hoping we might have the opportunity to formally meet." Mike recognized the face in an instant. He had no name to go with it, but it was the same pale face he had seen in the halls of his old high school.

"I thought you were a figment of my imagination," Mike tensed, ready to defend himself. "Who are you? How can you appear and disappear so quickly? You're not gifted or I would feel it."

"You have the right of it, Mr. Keller," the man said as he came the rest of the way into the room. "I am Lord Marcus Selencius. Regent of North America for the Blood. I believe the term of reference you will be searching for is... vampire."

Mike sat stunned. Had Marcus wanted to kill him he would have been unable to act on any of his defenses. Mike had read a few references to the Blood in his research into the Council, but it was always vague and seemed more like a powerful family, mostly in Europe who had little dealings with the Council. Mike felt stupid for having never made the connection to vampires. "So, you are telling me vampires are real and you're their leader?" Mike asked slowly.

A grin split the face of the vampire, showing his fangs. "You would be mostly correct," Marcus began. "Six months ago you didn't really think your kind existed, or about you being a part of it all. You would be amazed at all the layers in this planet we all inhabit. As for being their leader, I am what you would call more akin to a King, President, and top law on the continent. I answer only to my sire, the leader of the Blood for the whole of Earth."

"If I haven't encountered you or your kind before, I assume there is a no contact clause?" Mike said, his training in Council ways and laws asserting itself. His mind was still reeling from the truth of the existence of vampires, *What else is out there?'* he wondered briefly before focusing on the person before him.

"Something of the kind," Marcus said calmly. He was well aware of Mike's temper and did not want to spark a war. He needed the human before him like he needed blood to sustain himself. "Typically, unless a matter of importance crosses jurisdiction, we have nothing to discuss. Rarely do my kin have any reason to seek out anyone of your kind. Usually it is minor disputes over territory or if kin of mine accidently feeds on one of yours. The effects are not pleasant, for either party."

Marcus's matter of fact tone when he talked of feeding on people sent Mike scrambling to control his Darkness within. It had been mostly dormant the last few weeks since the battle with Blake Kosgrove and his supporters. It reared up ready to attack as Marcus stepped forward, pointing to the chairs arranged in front of Mike's desk. Mike nodded and the vampire sat down smoothly. "So, to what do I owe the pleasure of your visit this evening? I warn you, I am not at liberty to speak for the Council at large without at least the input of Cliff and Damien."

"I hope it won't be necessary," Marcus said, suddenly showing nervousness as he picked at a piece of lint on his suit jacket. "I am merely hoping to enlist your aid in a growing matter. Something which could cause both of our kind a bit of trouble. It is delicate and will require as much discretion as you can manage."

"If any of the myths about vampires and their immortality are true, then I understand your stretching this out. I don't know if I can help you or if I will, but let's get to the bottom of why you are here and go from there," Mike pushed. He was tired and in no mood for games. He still wanted to meet up with Laurie later. Now he was going to have to brief Damien and Cliff on this impromptu meeting.

"Forgive me, I am accustomed to dealing with the old men of the Council who relish the dance in these negotiations," Marcus smiled. "I will cut to it then, but it requires a little background. A vampire is beholden to their maker, or sire as we typically refer to them. Any command issued by a vampire's sire must be complied with, even to the point of walking into the sun without protection. As you can imagine, this would result in the vampire's death. Any newly risen vampire is made to give oaths to the leaders of the Blood. This allows for law and order."

"Sounds like the taking of a person's right to choose how to live their life," Mike retorted. The Darkness was struggling to take control and blast the vampire.

"Please, let me explain," Marcus said quickly. He had noticed how Mike was gripping the arms of the chair he was seated in. "We have had our own rebellions in centuries past. There were those of my kind who felt we also should rise up and rule the world, with disastrous results. Our confinement to the shadows and night time hinders us more than you would think. These oaths were put in place to prevent any vampire from feeding on an unwilling donor, from forcing another to become a vampire, and to alleviate the rising death toll amongst our kind."

Seeing the nobility in Marcus's claims, Mike calmed visibly. "So you have a new rebellion brewing do you?"

"Correct," Marcus replied, glad to see Mike relax his grip on the arms of the chair. "There is a, sad to say, growing faction of young vampires who seek to break their bonds and do as they wish. I say young, but most of these are a few hundred years old. Their leader is unknown, but they seem to have found a way around some of the restrictions of their oath. There have been fresh, newly risen vampires found roaming several major cities the last few weeks."

"And a newly risen vampire wandering around is bad for your business," Mike stated, watching the nod from the vampire across from him. "I think I better call Damien and Cliff so we can decide what to do here." At a nod from Marcus, Mike quickly dialed his friends on their cellphone, which was easier than telepathy when you didn't know exactly where the person was.

# About the Author

Andrew M. Ferrell lives in NE Wisconsin with his wife and three children. When not enjoying the day to day life of fatherhood, he explores other worlds through writing or reading fantasy and science fiction. He also runs a small indie press he founded in 2017.

He occasionally blogs about it on his website, http://www.andrewmferrell.com

Facebook: http://www.facebook.com/authorAMF

Twitter: http://www.twitter.com/andrewmferrell

Instagram: http://www.instagram.com/andrewmferrell

www.ingramcontent.com/pod-product-compliance
Lightning Source LLC
Chambersburg PA
CBHW020019030726
47499CB00007B/2175